SURVIVAL
INSTINCTS

ALSO BY JEN WAITE

A Beautiful, Terrible Thing

SURVIVAL INSTINCTS

A NOVEL

JEN WAITE

DUTTON

DUTTON

An imprint of Penguin Random House LLC
penguinrandomhouse.com

LIBRARY OF CONGRESS CATALOGING-IN-PUBLICATION DATA

Names: Waite, Jen, author.
Title: Survival instincts : a novel / Jen Waite.
Identifiers: LCCN 2019043751 | ISBN 9781524745837 (hardcover) |
ISBN 9781524745851 (ebook)
Subjects: GSAFD: Suspense fiction.
Classification: LCC PS3623.A356557 S87 2020 | DDC 813/.6—dc23
LC record available at https://lccn.loc.gov/2019043751

Printed in the United States of America
1 3 5 7 9 10 8 6 4 2

BOOK DESIGN BY ALISON CNOCKAERT

To Vivienne,
I love you infinity.

SURVIVAL INSTINCTS

THE CABIN

ANNE

You look at me and ask without speaking. Protect me, *your eyes say. But this is the cold truth. From the moment you were born, the only thing I knew for sure was that I couldn't protect you. Not really. Not completely. Even before you were born, I couldn't stop a man from hurting you. Imagine for a moment that I was able to keep you safe and sound, wrapped up in the warmth of the womb for those long nine months, and then safe beyond that, beyond my body. At some point I would have still had to set you free and wait for the world to unleash itself on you. All parents understand this on some level, especially those of little girls. Right now, though, I hope you believe that I can save you. Because when I tell you to run, when I open my mouth and command you, softly and firmly, you can't know what I know. That in the end, I can't protect you; no one can.*

FOUR DAYS
BEFORE THE CABIN

ANNE

The day Anne decided to go to the cabin was also the day she took Thea clothes shopping at the mall. Her daughter's pants didn't fit; the size 12s, the ones she had just bought because Thea had grown out of her size 11s, rode up around her ankles. Thea, long and lean and all arms and legs, like a colt, was growing so quickly these days that her age no longer correlated with her size.

"Do you like these?" Anne asked, holding up a pair of bright yellow stretch pants. Sometimes she could lead her daughter with the tone she used. Lilting up at the end—"Do you like *these*?"—and a touch of excitement in her voice. Thea barely glanced before responding, "Ew," and shifting her eyes toward a gumball machine near the entrance of the store. It didn't always work, the lilt.

They wandered around the store, a coffee in Anne's hand, a smoothie in Thea's, with the leisurely, aimless gait reserved for a half-empty American shopping mall. It was Tuesday afternoon, and Anne had scheduled her last client for the 1:00–1:50 p.m. slot. Afterward, she picked up Thea from school early and they'd gone straight to the mall, a move she'd hoped would spare them from the after-work crowd—the crowd that Anne was usually lumped in with—parents hell-bent on accomplishing last-minute shopping, dragging their kids from store to store, tinged with frantic desperation. The move had worked; the mall was nearly empty when they arrived.

"Ok, well, let's hurry up and find some stuff you like." Anne switched to her best authoritative mom voice. "School is letting out soon; it's going to get crowded in here." *And turn into the tenth circle of hell*, she thought, scanning the entrance as teenagers started to ooze in; high school kids skipping last class or the entire school day. She watched a girl and a boy, who couldn't be older than fourteen, dart their tongues in and out of each other's mouths and caress each other's facial piercings. Anne let out an audible grunt of disgust. *Do your parents know where you are?* The teenage girl was wearing a shirt that looked like a bra and the boy wore pants that sagged down almost to his knees, revealing yellowed boxer shorts. Anne swiveled her eyes down her own body: white button-up shirt, gray trousers, sensible black flats. She touched the edge of her head, tucking stray brown hairs into the bun at the nape of her neck. She looked back to the girl and boy laughing into each other's mouths. *What a curmudgeon you've become.* "Hey, sweets, off your phone." She plucked Thea's twelfth birthday present, an older generation iPhone, out of her daughter's fingers and dropped it into her purse. So much for being less curmudgeon-ey.

"Mom!" Thea glared as if she'd just been sentenced to a week of collecting litter on the highway.

Anne smiled back. "Focus, Thee."

Anne ran her fingers along a rack of embroidered blouses and her thoughts shot forward to tonight; after dinner was made, homework was done, and Thea was tucked into bed with her night-light and a Nancy Drew Mystery (Anne's old set that Thea had looked at skeptically, eyeing the wilted pages and dusty spines, but she now was on the fifth book in the series), she would put on comfy pj's and thick socks, pour herself a glass of wine, build a fire in the living room, and sink into the sofa. They'd been moved into the new house for six months now—an old white farmhouse set on six acres of land—but she hadn't had time to throw a housewarming or even veg out with a glass of wine. She was still getting used to the vastness of the new house, all the open space, creaking wood floors, and bare walls. There was so much still to furnish and decorate; tonight, she told herself, she would just *enjoy it*. This was what she had been working toward, after all, for the past eight years.

She had opened her private therapy practice five years ago, after completing a three-year master's program, in Charlotte, Vermont, a quiet town that bordered Lake Champlain. When she opened her doors, she didn't have a single client, only a handful of friends who promised to pass the word and the hope that there were others who were looking for a light in the dark. The first few years she steadily built her clientele, eventually moving from a sparse white office off a dirt road into a beautiful brick building in the center of town, which housed the services of other mental health professionals. And she found that she had guessed correctly—there was no shortage of people seeking help in disengaging and healing from abusive relationships, even in a little Vermont town. Six months ago, to coincide with Thea starting sixth grade, Anne had made another leap—moving herself, her practice, and her daughter to Burlington, where she could charge twice the amount per hour and (she hoped) begin a new chapter. At $120.00 per fifty-minute session, and her client list steadily growing, Anne was doing well, very well; the new house with four bedrooms, hardwood floors throughout, and three fireplaces was physical proof of how far she'd come. It would be even more satisfying if her daughter hadn't changed so drastically in the past few weeks, from a kind, inquisitive, horse-obsessed kid into an angsty, volatile preteen. At first, Thea seemed genuinely happy and excited to start fresh; she loved Burlington, she raved about her school and the small group of friends she'd made (three other nerdy, kind, wonderfully weird girls), and she talked incessantly about how much cooler the teachers were at her new school. But about a month ago, something changed. Anne still saw glimpses of the Thea she knew, but her daughter's under-the-breath comments and disdain for everything, especially Anne, seemed to be increasing daily. Anne tried to remember what age she'd gone through this phase and could have sworn it was much, much later than twelve years old.

Pulling her own phone from her purse, Anne watched Thea sort through a pile of jeans. The idea of going away for the weekend had started to sprout that morning when she and Thea had fought, once again, about the no-social-media-until-you're-eighteen rule. Her daughter had said that she was worse than Voldemort, to which Anne had replied, "I believe you mean He Who Must Not Be Named." Thea had not thought that was funny.

Anne was aware of the irony that she felt completely at ease, even masterful sometimes, empowering her clients to form healthy boundaries and to break free from toxic relationships, but when confronted with the fact that her twelve-year-old daughter seemed to be developing a hatred for everything Anne said and did, she reacted like a teenager herself, awkward and insecure. She had done some quick research at work in between clients and an idea had begun to blossom: a girls' getaway.

She scrolled through the Airbnb listings now, looking for the one that had caught her eye earlier. The main picture showed a log cabin nestled in snow, smoke billowing out the top. A deck protruded off the back with sparkling white Christmas lights lining the railing. The title proclaimed "Your White Mountain Getaway!" She clicked to a picture of the interior—a roaring woodstove on a brick hearth surrounded by big, plush couches (if Thea happened to see the massive flat-screen TV mounted to the wall behind the woodstove, so be it). Anne was about to ask Thea what she thought about a trip to the cabin in a few weeks when she had a thought.

She brought up her messages and texted Rose: Thinking of weekend getaway to White Mountains with T . . . It's been a few weeks since we've seen you. Would you want to come? She threw in a couple of smiley faces and one kiss face. If Anne's close relationship with Thea had become strained recently, Thea's relationship with Rose, Anne's mother, had only continued to blossom. It had been hard on Thea, at first, not being able to see Rose daily, but Rose visited once a month and called Thea every Tuesday night; tonight Anne would hear Thea's giggles echoing down the hallway from her bedroom. Rose spoke in soft, soothing tones and had a different baked good for every one of life's problems. Literally. Her mother owned a bakery in town called Rose's Sweets. Rose and Thea used to have tea parties with baked bread that Rose would bring home fresh from the bakery oven. If Rose weren't Anne's own mother, Anne would resent how naturally motherhood came to her, especially with Thea.

Anne imagined Rose padding around the kitchen of her parents' house, grabbing her favorite blue fired-clay mug (her fingers brushing briefly against her dad's favorite whiskey glass, collecting dust) from the open shelves, and standing in the soft sunlight as she poured her third cup of coffee of the afternoon. She'd have been up since three a.m.—even on her days off, her body was stuck on bakery time. Rose's reply came almost instantly: Wow! When are you thinking?! Sounds like fun! Count me in! I can't wait!

Anne wrote back: That's a lot of exclamation points! Maybe in a few weeks when it gets warmer? Mid-April? and then backtracked the message, clicking Delete with her thumb while balancing the two shirts and pair of leggings that Thea was loading into her arms.

She looked at the listing again. From the looks of the booking calendar, late March was off-season in the small ski village of Loon, New Hampshire. She watched Thea, weaving through a rack of shirts, laughing with her whole face when a shirt fell off its hanger onto her head; for a second Thea was two years old, draping a blanket over her head in plain view, *You can't find me, Mama.*

She wrote: What about this weekend?

THREE DAYS
BEFORE THE CABIN

THEA

It was raining as Thea wrote in her diary, a small white journal with an actual lock that clasped over the front and a tiny key that she kept in a jar on her bedside table. Big, fat drops of rain splattered against her windows, making her feel even more melancholy, but in a good way, as if the weather had decided to validate her pain. She glanced around her new room, pausing in her scribbling to bring the pen up to her mouth. She nibbled absentmindedly on the end of the pen, already chewed down to a shriveled stump, and watched the rain fall harder outside. A few seconds ago, there had been a deep rumbling of thunder and the big, fat drops had given way to a torrential stream of water that cascaded past her windows. Thea shivered even though the windows were shut, sealed tight against the rain and wind. Although she hated her mother, she liked the new house, and she especially loved her new room. After a moment of staring at the soft blue walls and listening to the rain, she continued to write: *I used to love three people with all my heart. And now I have only Mimi and him. How could my own mother do this to me?*

Thea put the pen down, satisfied with the end of her journal entry, and stretched out in bed, laying her head against a cool, fluffy white pillow. She closed her eyes, listening to the rain hit the windows like a firehose and feeling hot tears roll down her cheeks, down her chin, and pool on her neck. Her mother would be calling her down for breakfast soon and Thea couldn't decide if she wanted her mother to finally see her anger, her sadness, or if she wanted to keep it hidden, so that it could burn and grow. The longer she kept it a secret, the more impossible it felt to confront her mom. And what could her mother even say to make it better at this point anyway? Thea inhaled shakily and, to keep from crying, tried to focus on the blue wall across from her, but her throat ached and her mouth trembled downward. She finally put her face into her pillow and screamed. When she lifted her head, she took a deep, shaky breath and sat up.

"Thee," she heard her mom's voice drifting up from the bottom of the stairs. "Honey, breakfast is almost ready." A pause and then: "I don't hear the shower yet. It's been a couple of days, baby. Please wash your hair. Come on, let's go, let's go, let's go."

Thea snorted. Her mother was always doing that. Preempting. Like she knew Thea was going to lag. Like she couldn't even give her a chance before annoyance and impatience crept into her voice. *Well, fine*, Thea thought and crossed her arms. *I'll take my time*. She laid her head back against the pillow and closed her eyes until she heard "THEA. Let's GO! We're going to be late for school again. In the shower." And then, as if she just couldn't help herself, "Now!"

Thea groaned and slowly moved her limbs out of bed and quickly stripped off her fleece pajama bottoms and a gray long-sleeve top, almost threadbare from the frequency with which she wore it. She shivered as the cold air pricked her skin, tiptoeing on the balls of her feet into the small bathroom off her bedroom, touching as little surface of the cold tile floor as possible. She pulled the glass door open and turned the silver knob all the way to the left, toward the H, and then waited for the telltale steam to fog the shower door. While she waited, she leaned her elbows on the marble countertop and glanced into the mirror hanging directly opposite, suddenly shocked by her own reflection, by the sameness of it; her physical appearance hadn't changed at all—the same light blue eyes and straight blond hair reflected back at her—and yet everything inside her was different. She stared for another moment and then stepped into the stream of water, gasping with a painful pleasure as the water seared her skin. Thea swung the shower door shut and stood in the burning stream of water with her eyes closed for several seconds. When she opened her eyes, she saw only fog at first. Little by little, her eyes adjusted, and the glass door came back into view, now completely opaque. Without thinking, she traced a shape into the condensation with her pointer finger. And then, this time purposefully, traced her initials and his initials, above and below the heart. She watched as another layer of fog slowly formed, creeping over her drawing, whitewashing it away. It was fitting, she thought, like the relationship itself, invisible to the naked eye, etched just below the surface. Her initials faded first, *TT*, and then his, *TR*.

Ted Redmond.

It felt impossible that prior to this school year, she didn't even know him—that he had existed elsewhere before her, and she, too, had had a whole life before him, before she walked into Spanish class a few months ago. He wasn't even supposed to be at her new school—it was only due to a chain of fortuitous events that he had stepped foot inside Frederick H. Tuttle Middle School in South Burlington and into her Spanish class—and that thought, of them never knowing each other at all, caused Thea physical pain. She was in the midst of playing out this horrific scenario in her head when her mother's voice burst into her consciousness, making her jump.

"Out of the shower. Let's go!"

"Mom!" Thea projected her voice over the pounding water. "Don't sneak up on me, I almost slipped in the shower. You could have *killed* me."

"You have two more minutes to rinse," came her mother's reply from just outside the bathroom door. "The whole bathroom is completely fogged up, you know. Are you sure the water's hot enough? Geez, Thea." She heard her mom's feet padding out of her bedroom.

Thea closed her eyes again as her mother's voice trailed off. *Leave me alone.* The shower provided a temporary solace from her mother's nagging. Instead of spinning the knob to off, she inched it farther and farther the other way, letting the water scald her skin until she could no longer stand it. She felt for the knob again and braced herself for the halt of hot water. Once the water stopped, she stood enveloped in thick, hot air for a moment and then opened the glass door to a burst of cold air. She inhaled the fresh air into her lungs and toweled herself off quickly, glancing at the comb on the counter before passing it by, continuing into her bedroom, where she pulled on jeans and a blue top. She was about to cross the threshold of her bedroom into the hallway when she circled back and ran into the bathroom. She brushed her teeth vigorously, spitting into the sink loudly at the end for her mother's benefit, and then plodded very slowly to the staircase and made her way down the stairs, hanging on to the bannister and taking each step thoughtfully, much to her mother's annoyance, she assumed. She stopped on the landing and looked up at the skylight.

The rain was still coming down in thick streams and the water whisked over the glass, like river rapids. Thea closed her eyes and imagined the water cascading over her face and body; in her mind's eye, she saw his initials, *TR*, a secret kept in her shower door.

When she first started at her new middle school that fall, she walked the strange halls with a knot in her stomach, hoping with equal amounts of fervor that no one or anyone would talk to her. It took forever, at least five days, but she eventually made a friend, a petite brunette named Olivia, in study hall. Livi introduced Thea to two other girls, Zoe and Gretchen. ("We formed a book club last year," Livi had whispered. "You can be our fourth member. Just don't tell anyone at school. Obviously.") So by the second week of school, Thea had a thin shield of armor against the strangeness of the new place. But still, she dreaded the classes where she didn't have a friend, particularly Spanish class, which was filled with glossy-haired girls and loud boys—the "popular kids" who somehow took up the whole room with their bodies, leaving nothing for Thea. She did her best to make herself invisible in Spanish class, which usually wasn't difficult, considering no one noticed her anyway. Thea's mom once told her that she had the kind of beauty that people would appreciate later in life. Thea had not responded to this obvious lie. She was content to be invisible, to blend in, to take up as little space as possible. That all changed, though, when she met Ted.

She opened her eyes when she heard her mother laughing.

"What are you doing, water bug?"

Thea glared. Her mother hadn't called her *water bug* in years and, instead of the term feeling nostalgic and warm, it made the pit in her stomach clench even harder for everything she had lost. Her childhood was all ruined, and it was her mother's fault. A month ago, everything had changed—her entire life, everything she knew, had unraveled in twenty-four hours—and her mother was blissfully, infuriatingly ignorant.

Now, her mother's impatient voice cut into her thoughts again, "Breakfast is on the table." Thea slumped toward the dining room, marveling again at how vastly different this house was from the place where she grew up.

As Thea spooned yogurt and muesli into her mouth, she felt her mom preparing to speak; across the table, her mother's body shifted and she looked at Thea in a hopeful way before opening her mouth. "So, Thee. I was thinking, this weekend we could go away together. A little adventure!"

Shit. Panic rose up. The absolute last thing she wanted to do was spend time with her mother, especially just the two of them alone. Though, she realized with a tiny bit of relief, she wouldn't have any chance to see him on the weekend anyway.

"Come on, it'll be so much fun." She heard a note of desperation creep into her mother's voice. For one second, Thea's throat closed up as she remembered their trip to Disney over her winter break. Sleeping side by side in a king-size bed, even though their suite had two bedrooms. And the sharpest memory from that trip was not seeing the magnificent castle for the first time, but waiting an hour in line for the Tower of Terror and then the panic Thea had felt when they finally approached the elevator. "Mom," she had whispered, "I can't. I can't—" Her mom had grabbed her hand and laughed. "Oh, I'm *so* glad you said something! Come on, let's get out of here." And they'd spent the next ten minutes giggling with relief as they made their way through the dark hallways, hand in hand, weaving around the crowds of people waiting to drop through the air. Her mom turned to her when they reached fresh air. "Hey, Thee." Her mom dropped to eye level with her. "Any time you don't want to do anything, just tell me and we'll leave. No questions asked. K?" Thea had nodded and enveloped herself in her mom's warm body, completely safe, cocooned in her mom's arms.

"What do you say, Thee?" Her mom was looking at her expectantly. "You and me and a cabin in the White Mountains. Look, this is the place." Thea glanced at the iPhone her mom held out across the table; the cabin did look cozy and there was a huge flat-screen TV in the picture. As much as she dreaded spending an entire two days with her mother, she could imagine sprawling out on the comfy-looking sofa and watching a movie. Her favorite right now was *Pride and Prejudice* and she could bring the DVD—even though DVDs were probably going to be obsolete soon, she had asked her mom for it when they were checking out at Best Buy a few months ago because it was on sale for $4.99. She kept it in the top drawer of her dresser, like a prized possession, and watched it once a week.

"Mimi's coming, too." Her mom was still looking at her expectantly and smiling. "I thought we'd pick you up from school on Friday and head straight out. We could be there by dinner. I know you have book club on Fridays, but I'm sure Livi and the girls will understand." Thea took in her mother's pleading voice and the slightly wild look in her eyes; she could make any demands she wanted. Thea snatched the iPhone from her mom's hand and zoomed in on the picture. "Do you think there's Wi-Fi? Can I bring my phone?" Thea knew the answers would be *yes* and *yes*. And maybe this weekend she could talk to Mimi, ask her the questions she so desperately needed answered. She realized that Mimi had, by omission, lied to her as well, but she blamed her mom for this. She was sure that her grandmother would tell her the truth if she asked her directly.

Thea took another bite of yogurt, still looking at the living room of the cabin. Her heart sped up as she thought about Mr. Redmond and her warming their hands over the fireplace together, popping *Pride and Prejudice* into the DVD player. No. She shook her head to physically reset. Her and *Ted*. He had told her that she could call him Ted, at least when they were alone together. She repeated his first name in her head several times as she pinched the screen and the fire came closer and closer.

TWO DAYS
BEFORE THE CABIN

———

THE MAN

The man had been driving for a long time. He hadn't stopped since he got out except when he needed to fuel up, piss, shit, or eat. He hadn't dawdled. He'd gotten right back into his truck. A couple of hours ago he pulled into a dusty gas station that was set right off the highway. He filled up his tank and stretched his legs. It still felt odd to be allowed so much space. He stuck to walking in straight lines whenever possible. From his car to the gas pump. From the pump to the cashier. From the cashier back to his car. And then the straight line of the highway. This time, though, he could feel someone watching him as he unscrewed the gas cap and lifted the nozzle into the throat of the gas tank. His hand shook slightly and he concentrated on keeping his eyes downward, to his black cowboy boots. The tips were scuffed; they needed a good shine, though it had been ten years since he'd last worn them, so, all things considered, they looked pretty damn good. The abrupt release of the latch under his fingers signaled a full tank. He made his way to the small shop, keeping his eyes trained on his reflection in the double glass doors. His reflection always startled

him. He looked ordinary, and for that he was grateful. In his last sessions, he had told them that the hunger was still there, would always
be there, but they hadn't listened. Fucking shrinks. What was the
point if they didn't *listen*. So far, though, he hadn't gotten sidetracked.
He was doing well. Only a few more hours and he'd have her.

The cashier was male and the man smiled to himself. Easy peasy.
He asked for a pack of Marlboro Lights and a Bic. He threw a few
crumpled bills onto the counter and waited for change. "Actually," he
said to the cashier, "keep the change." He was feeling cocky; he could
do this. He strode back to his car, eyes straight ahead. He didn't look
to the right even though he felt her there.

"Sir." Her voice sounded like a song. "Excuse me, sir."

Out of the corner of his eye, he could see the woman jogging
toward him, the one who had been watching him while she pumped
gas at the station behind him.

"Your thingy is open," she said. Then with a laugh, "I mean your
gas thingy."

"Oh." His tongue felt thick. He managed to say, "Thanks," and
screw his mouth up in what he hoped looked like a smile. He walked
around to the other side of his car and screwed the lid on until he
heard the *click*. For the first time since he'd pulled into the gas station, he let his eyes wander. He watched the woman with the song-
voice climb into her front seat. She raked her fingers through long
dark hair and adjusted the rearview mirror. No one else in the car.
Fucking bitch. He was doing so well and here she was, practically
begging him. He slowed his breathing and closed his eyes. No. Not
dark hair. The last one had dark hair. He pressed on the fleshy web
between his thumb and pointer finger. The place where her teeth had

left a crescent moon scar. He started his car and peeled out of the gas station, back onto the highway.

The man looked at himself in the rearview mirror. "You passed," he said and grinned. The signs whizzed by; sixty-eight more miles until he was home.

ONE DAY
BEFORE THE CABIN

ROSE

Rose sipped her steaming mug of coffee and surveyed the mounds of snow from behind the glass door that led to her patio. Even with the outdoor lights on, she had to strain her eyes against the dark. She ran her eyes over what was visible of her backyard—her hydrangeas, rhododendrons, and rosebushes all covered in snow—and clucked, "How are you all holding up out there?" In a month, maybe less, she would start her morning routine by pulling on jeans and a sweatshirt, lacing up her Bean boots, and taking her coffee outside. Early spring was a time for communing with her garden, cleaning up leaves, picking up sticks, talking to her plants, checking to see how everyone had weathered the winter. But for now, she could only sip in silence and wait for the snow to melt. It had poured a couple of days ago, the rain melting through most of the snow, and Rose had let herself hope that this was it—the true beginning of spring. But last night six inches of snow had been dumped from the sky; a mocking wink from Mother Nature, *Gotcha!*

These were her favorite hours, the hours between when she awoke, at three a.m., and when she left for the bakery, at five a.m. When she first started Rose's Sweets, she struggled for months to adjust to the early rise schedule, but she insisted on always being the first one in the shop, always arriving at least a half hour before the first-shift bakers. When Sam grumbled and reached for her hand, trying to slide it into the warm crook of his arm, convincing her with grunts to stay in bed a few minutes longer, she would gently explain that she had to set a good example. "It's the trickle-down effect, hun. If I'm late, even once, then the bar gets lowered, and before you know it—"

"Ok. Ok," he'd mumble. "I'm so proud of you. I love you."

"I love you, too," and by the time she'd creaked off the bed, his breathing would be back to the deep exhalations and inhalations of the unconscious.

Even though she'd eventually entrusted her manager and staff with opening the bakery, her internal clock still woke her at 3:02 a.m. every morning. Usually, she shuffled around the house, picking up whatever she'd left about the night before, making coffee, tending to her garden (or staring at it wistfully depending on the season). But this morning she had things to do. Rose gazed through the glass for another minute and took one more swig of coffee, savoring the heat in her mouth, before striding to the oven. She pressed Bake and set the temperature to 350 degrees. She gathered the sugar and the butter she'd left on the counter overnight and tossed them into the KitchenAid. Cracking the eggs, stirring in the flour, and whisking baking soda into hot water (her signature move—well, that and the cornstarch) were all second nature; within minutes, she was spooning big chunks of chocolate chip cookie dough onto two large sheets.

She smiled to herself and hummed as she taste-tested the dough. Perfect. These were Thea's favorite, and she couldn't wait to watch her granddaughter's face light up tomorrow in the car on the way to the cabin. She missed her granddaughter fiercely. She was still getting used to only seeing Thea and Anne every few weeks since they'd moved from Charlotte to Burlington. Two days at this cabin in the mountains sounded wonderful. And she hoped it would perhaps help to patch things up between her two loves. "A girls' getaway," Anne had said. How fun.

Rose spent the rest of the morning writing out a letter for her next-door neighbor, who would be looking after Sal. The border collie wouldn't be awake for another couple of hours. He used to be up with her every morning, bounding around the house with a stuffed bear in his mouth, ready to expend massive amounts of energy at three a.m., only to be disappointed, every single morning, when Rose would rub him between the ears and whisper, "Bye, love. Daddy will be awake soon to take you out," as she closed the door on his hopeful face. Now, Sal was going on fourteen and took his time getting up in the morning. Something, she knew, that Anne wished Rose would do a bit more of as well.

"Well," Rose said aloud to her daughter's chiding in her head, "I can relax when I'm dead." She swept her eyes over the kitchen and living room, satisfied that everything was in place before she set off to the bakery. The genuine warmth and lightness in her body surprised her as she poured the last of the steaming coffee into a to-go mug. *Isn't it interesting*, she thought, *how many different people you can be in one lifetime.*

THE MAN

The man opened his eyes and peered up at the ceiling. He stretched out his legs. In the twin bed they reached past the bottom of the bed frame. His ankles scraped against the footboard. It felt strange but good to be back in his childhood home. Normally at this time of day on a Friday afternoon his mother would be puttering around downstairs, starting to take out ingredients for dinner that night, and, when he was younger, hollering for him and his brother to get outside into the fresh air.

He pulled the thick flannel sheets up around his chin, transferring the warmth from his lower half to his chest. The sheets were red and green striped. He knew without looking at the tags that they were discount imitation L.L.Bean sheets purchased at Sears by his mother. He remembered her face that day on the way home from the store. The way she'd smiled too much at nothing and spoken too loudly to him in the passenger seat. And then the way afterward she had peeked glances at him, narrowing her eyes, when she thought he wasn't paying attention. They had gone out on a mother-son shopping trip, which was rare—usually his mom took him and his brother; it was more efficient, she said, to shop for both of them at once. This time, though, it was just the two of them.

"In the car. Right now. Nope, just you." She'd nodded at him as he and his little brother both stood up from the couch, where they were watching cartoons on their TV with its bunny ears antenna. "I got a letter from the school that your first school dance is in a week, right before Christmas break. You didn't tell me," she said, looking up from rummaging in her purse. "You need slacks and a button-down. Where are my god darn keys." She paused again, straightening her body. "Shoes. Coat. Car. Now."

Hot air blew into their faces as they shuffled through the front doors of the department store. Twinkling white lights and colorful glass balls hung from the ceiling and lined the walls. The boy thumped his boots against the black welcome mats, and chunks of ice melted quickly into the fabric. His mother took his hand but he shook it away, shooting her a look. "Mom."

"Fine. But stay close."

They weaved their way around groups of shoppers, his mother's blunt heels clicking against the shiny linoleum floor. The boy kept his eyes on her heels, watching the nude pantyhose crinkle and stretch with each step.

"Here we are." She stopped in front of the boys' dress apparel, her eyes already wandering to the adjacent section. "Pick out a few pairs of slacks to try on. I'm going to pop over to the bedding area. It's right there." She pointed to the sheets and down comforters folded neatly into rectangles a few yards away. "Are you listening?" She squeezed his arm. "I'll be just over there. I want to get winter sheets for you and your brother. Back in a flash." She was already walking away, moving determinedly.

The boy was only going to look at tan pants and dress shirts; he was only going to wander through the racks, grabbing random items, knowing when it came down to it, his mother would do the picking anyway. But then he saw her. She was around his age, sixth grade he would guess, but she didn't go to his school; he would have noticed her before. Her shiny brown hair was pulled into a ponytail and she was wearing a pink raincoat and pink rain boots. He wondered if she was from out of town, somewhere where they didn't have thick, sturdy snow boots that were hauled out of the basement in late November. Before he realized it, he was following her, slipping out from amongst the dress pants and into the center aisle. He glanced quickly toward the bedding area and saw his mother in profile, bringing a sheet set up to her nose. The girl walked slowly, pausing at a perfume counter to smell a strip of scented paper, running her hands over a pair of dangly earrings, stopping to look in a full-length mirror. The boy wondered where her parents were. He trailed her closely, so close that he could have reached out and pulled her ponytail, jerking her toward him, catching her completely unaware. He saw where she was going before she got there and his pulse sped up. He stepped carefully onto the escalator step as it changed from a flat surface to a mound and then took two more steps up so that he stood on the step behind her.

"Do you want to go around me?" The girl spun, her face screwed up with irritation.

"No." His heart beat hard and fast.

"You're crowding me." She sighed loudly and turned away from him, standing her ground, crossing her arms over her raincoat.

"Sorry." They were almost to the top now. The girl gripped the rubber railing in anticipation and took one step forward. The boy took a step at the same time, pushing into her back, sending her down on to the metal grate where the steps sucked into the machine. He watched as she twisted her body, landing hard on her wrists and knees. The machine moved her body forward and she flailed, trying to right herself as the ground moved beneath her. The boy stepped carefully around her.

"Help!" The girl's voice was shrill and tears slid down her face. The boy watched as the bottom of her rain jacket caught in the metal grate.

Two adults appeared out of nowhere, one frantic, one calm. The calm one quickly jerked each of the girl's arms out of the jacket as the frantic one pulled the girl up.

"She's ok," the calm adult said. "She's ok."

The frantic one, the girl's mom, the boy decided, from the way she was holding the girl close and rubbing her wrists, said, "What happened, Susan?" over and over.

"He pushed me," Susan said, pointing to the boy. Her face looked like a quilt, patched with bright pink and stark white streaks. She began to sob in earnest. The boy watched her throat convulse.

"No. It was an accident," he said, and then noticed his own mother, running up the escalator, taking two steps at a time, looking uncharacteristically out of sorts. "It was an accident," he said again, to his mother this time. "I bumped into her and she fell."

"I'm sure it was an accident," Susan's mother said. "I'm sure he didn't mean to push you. Of course he didn't mean to push you." Her voice shook.

The boy watched Susan for as long as he could as his mother pulled him away.

Now, lying in his childhood bed, in his childhood house, he enjoyed the silence for a moment. He pulled on khaki pants from his duffel bag and the gray sweater he had been wearing since he got out. He crept down the stairs, realizing only when he came to the spot that always let out a loud creak that he didn't need to be quiet. His eyes slid over the family portraits lining the walls. A series of pictures from the same September afternoon when he was ten and his brother was eight. His mother and father hovered over him and his younger brother, bright fall colors burst from the frames. "Beautiful family," he murmured as he descended. Even he knew it was an odd thing to say, given the circumstances, and that thought kept a smirk on his face as he took the last stairs down to the first floor. On his way to the kitchen, he paused at the family computer, shook the mouse, and watched as the screen came alive. It took him a few moments to re-member his way around the desktop, but he eventually found the In-ternet icon and clicked. He typed in the letters with his pointer finger, scanned the results. The fifth link he clicked on took him to a page filled with a grid of pictures. He remembered this social site, but barely—it'd just come out when he was fifteen. The man stopped breathing for a moment and then carefully brought up the first pic-ture, the most recent, according to its time stamp, and looked at the location tag. The caption read: ON OUR WAY! #FIREPLACE #WEEKEND #FROSTYRIDGECABINS. It was hard to believe that this wasn't a trap.

How could it be so easy? Did people really show their lives like this on a minute-by-minute basis? But the longer he stared at the picture, the more he realized his eyes weren't playing tricks on him; it was easy because it was meant to be.

He walked into the kitchen and stopped. He turned his face away. He didn't like blood. He stepped carefully around the pooling liquid, making sure to grab his father's gun from the kitchen counter. He turned off the lights and did a quick visual check that everything looked tidy before closing the door behind him. He cracked the door back open and grabbed his father's car key off the front hook. He climbed behind the wheel of the blue Saab and typed the location from the picture into the GPS: Frosty Ridge Cabins, Loon, New Hampshire.

ONE DAY
BEFORE THE CABIN

ANNE

"Amon-oo-sock?" Anne tried out the letters on the small green sign pointing to the winding road through the mountains.

"Amo-nu-sux." Rose squinted at the sign through the passenger-side window as the bulky SUV slowed and turned off Rum Hill Road of Bath, New Hampshire, onto the mountain road. "Try saying that ten times fast." Rose laughed and reached her hand into the back seat. Thea reached for Rose's outstretched fingers with the hand that wasn't playing Fruit Ninja, or whatever other game from the list of "acceptable apps" Anne had compiled, on her phone.

"What, Mimi?" Thea asked, and then looked at the sign. "Oh, Ammonoosuc."

"However you say it, this is the road we take to the cabin." Anne smiled in the rearview mirror at her daughter.

Anne watched from the corner of her eye as her mother dug into a paper bag at her feet and pulled out three chocolate chip cookies. "I think it's time for these," Rose declared, handing a cookie to Thea.

"Yesss! Thank you, Mimi." Thea grabbed the cookie and tossed her phone onto the empty seat beside her.

Anne kept her eyes on the road. "Can you just break me off a small piece, Mom? I need both my hands on the wheel right now." The road twisted higher and snow swirled lightly against the windshield. Rose broke off a small chunk and placed it in Anne's palm. "This is pretty neat, huh?" She popped the cookie into her mouth and glanced back at Thea again.

"Yeah. How much farther?" Thea asked, through a bite.

"It's about thirty minutes on this road, Thee." She heard a groan and added, "Oh, come on, it'll go quick and it's beautiful."

It was beautiful. Anne tried to take in the snowcapped mountain peaks looming ahead while keeping her eyes peeled for other cars zooming around the switchbacks in the road at sixty miles per hour.

The last time she had been to a cabin, she realized suddenly, was with Thea's father before Thea was born. The memory of sitting around a fire, her head against a soft flannel shoulder, flashed into Anne's mind. She pushed out the image just as quickly. She had always believed in being truthful, especially with Thea, about difficult subjects. She'd always trusted her daughter's intelligence, intuition, and perceptiveness, even when Thea was a small child. But she had never told Thea the whole truth about her father. She was going to—she told herself she was waiting for the right moment, for Thea to be an appropriate age, and then they would sit down and Anne would tell her everything. Two years ago, though, instead of telling Thea her biological father's name, Anne had blurted out another name. She had panicked; it had just happened—but afterward she felt immense relief. It was done. She was safe inside her lie. If Thea ever googled the name Anne had given her, a million generic results would pop up.

She would never have to break Thea's heart and she would never have to talk about *him* again. The last time Thea asked about him, Anne told her daughter, yet again, that there really wasn't anything to tell—he vanished shortly after she was born and then they moved, just the two of them, from New York to Vermont, and it had been the two of them ever since. "Not everyone who has a baby is actually ready to be a parent," Anne had explained again. But that last time, instead of asking more questions, Thea had snorted and walked away. Anne had heard the expression, about how silence can be a lie, but whoever came up with that didn't comprehend there are some stories that don't need to be told.

Eyes on the road, Anne commanded herself, *and thoughts away from him.* The road really was becoming a bit treacherous. Anne's too-big SUV hugged the outside of the mountain as they climbed higher and higher and the road itself was covered in a light sheen of ice.

"Anne, the next overlook we pass, should we stop in? These views are stunning." Rose had her phone out, snapping wobbly pictures of the mountain in the distance.

"Sure, I could use a stretch, too. Sound good, Thee?" She looked into the rearview mirror to see Thea's lips moving and head bouncing to whatever song pelted through her earbuds, fingers flying across the screen. "Who are you texting, Thee?" Anne rolled her eyes at Rose. "Great, perfect, glad you're enjoying this family time," she said at the girl in the mirror. She smiled and shook her head. "I have a preteen," she whispered to Rose.

"How are things going on that front?" Rose asked quietly. "Still . . . tense?"

"I mean, at the end of the day we're best friends, obviously." She cringed at how desperate she sounded, but when she stole a glance at

Rose, her mother was nodding along genuinely. "But, everything I do annoys her and we're just having some . . . boundary issues," she finished.

"Growing pains," Rose responded. She was quiet for a moment and then, "She's idolized you since she was a baby. You have always been her world. Do you remember how she used to cling to your leg every waking moment when she was a toddler?" Rose laughed. "Even a few months ago, you guys walked arm in arm everywhere. She needs to find out who she is beyond your relationship. It's natural. You did the same thing." Anne felt her mother's glance. "You know," Rose lifted her arms, "the whole spreading of the wings thing."

"*Idolize* is a strong word." She laughed, but tucked Rose's words away for later. The spreading of the wings had caught Anne totally by surprise. Their Friday morning dates (Thea's new school started late every Friday) had come to an abrupt halt a few weeks ago when Thea refused to get out of bed, and their weekend movie nights had been replaced by Thea asking to spend the night at Livi's. Anne wondered secretly if Thea's recent moodiness was correlated to the end of Anne's "friendship" with Lyndon, the Canadian man she'd been seeing for the past few months. She'd introduced him as a friend and he'd only come over for dinner twice, but still . . . Thea had liked him. It was possible that she had secret pinings for a father figure and perhaps she had been hopeful Lyndon would fill that role. That would be completely understandable and normal. As a therapist, Anne understood that children, especially in the ten- to eighteen-year-old age range, constructed much of their own identities out of that of their parents, even absent parents. It was healthy for Thea to be interested in a father figure, and, of course, for her to wonder about her biological father, but at some point, Anne was certain, she would bloom into a young adult and begin to shape her identity based on her own beliefs and experiences. Thea would distance herself from Anne, as puberty set in, and begin to learn about the world for herself. In fact, that phase seemed to be already well under way. They'd had numerous discussions by now about different types of families, and Anne had always kept her dating life, or lack thereof, not secret per se but . . . private; there was no point in introducing Thea to someone unless it looked like it was getting serious, and that had only happened once, with the Canadian, who was now safely across the border. He'd told her, quite suddenly, that he no longer felt safe in the States, and that he had a flight home in a week. "The work relocation was always just a trial. I asked to go back to our home office and my bosses had no problem with it. So. Back I go. You know . . . you could come." He'd said it cheerfully, casually. She couldn't begrudge him his decision (it was the sixth mass shooting that had made national headlines since he'd arrived), but she was also taken completely by surprise. She thought, for an instant, about taking Thea and leaving the country, starting over up north; instead, she hid her shock by agreeing and demurring, also cheerfully, "Of course. That makes total sense. But I can't yank Thea out of school again, so . . . good luck!" That was that. The friendly, short exchange felt bizarre yet mature. Anne cried that night after Thea went to bed, but it was for the best. She saw that now; much better to cut things off before they got any more serious. Now Anne was free to go back to the "good-timers" as she called them—the string of short-term yet somewhat sexually fulfilling occurrences. There was no shame, she thought, in calling up the lawyer with better-than-average foreplay skills (of course, she'd have to make it absolutely clear that she was not going to be calling him "Daddy" as he'd requested the last time).

"Oh, here we go!" Anne turned to Rose and slowed the car,

nodding at a sign: SCENIC OVERLOOK—¼ MILE. The snow fell steadily as they pulled into the parking lot, a layer of white dust covered the ground.

Thea pulled her earbuds out of her ears at the sudden stop of the car. "Where are we?"

"Just stopping to stretch our legs and look at the view." Anne unbuckled and swiveled around. "You can take some pictures on your phone."

"I'll stay in the car."

"Thea," she snapped. "What are you— Did you re-download Instagram?" She took a breath, reeled herself back in. "Thea, please get off your phone. We're here to enjoy ourselves, ok? Let's just get out and take a look around. We're not far," she added.

Thea sighed and unbuckled, pocketed her phone, and slid out of the back of the car. She walked toward some big boulders and picnic benches at the edge of the parking lot. Anne watched her go, all skinny limbs, like a stick figure come to life. Beyond the boulders the earth dropped off, giving way to vast sky and hulking White Mountains in the distance.

"It looks like a huge painting by that painter. Oh, what's his name? Do you know who I'm talking about?" Rose held a pretend paintbrush with one hand to the sky. "You know, with the easel and the smock and the hair? The guy Dad used to watch to relax at night."

"Bob Ross!" Anne shrieked as the name popped into her head.

"Yes!" Rose pumped her fist in the air and her face lit up in a smile showing a small gap between her two front teeth. "Bob Ross! Oh. Oh." The change in her mother's face and tone was so dramatic that Anne immediately snapped her head around. Thea stood on a boulder, her back to them, straining forward to capture the view with her phone's camera. One sneaker slipped forward, and then she was hopping on one shoe, swaying backward and then forward again. Even though Anne had already started running, she was too far away.

"Thea!" she screamed as her daughter lost the little equilibrium she had and gravity and momentum sent her over the front of the boulder into the abyss. Before Anne reached the rock, Thea's head popped up.

"Oh my god." Thea laughed. "I can't believe I—" She stopped talking when she saw her mother's face. "Mom?"

"Don't ever do that again," Anne panted, hugging her daughter tightly.

"Do what? I was just trying to take a picture." Thea squirmed out of her mother's arms as Anne wiped her eyes. "Mom, there's a ledge. See?" She pointed to the ground jutting out, visible only from right beyond the boulders.

"Yes. I see that now." Anne put her head between her knees. "Holy shit, Thea."

"Mom!"

"I'm sorry. Don't say shit. Jesus Christ." She poked Thea's arms and legs. "After everything you've been through, I want to make sure you're ok. That nothing—is—broken." Anne tugged and squeezed and tapped on each word. "How is your head? Does your head feel ok?"

"Mom, I fell like an inch," Thea said, pulling away.

Rose joined them, running to Thea and embracing her tightly. "Ok, girls, back in the car. Let's get going while we're all in one piece." Rose steered them both back to the SUV.

Anne settled into the front seat and waited to hear the clicks of the safety belts. She took a deep breath and placed her still trembling hands on the steering wheel and eased her foot onto the gas. "Okay! Let's go to the cabin."

ONE DAY
BEFORE THE CABIN

ROSE

They pulled into the cabin's gravel driveway around six p.m., the sun long gone from the sky. Rose peered out the passenger-side window, eyes straining, as they crunched through the parking lot. It was more of a condo, really, located in a complex of other identical cabin-condo hybrids called Frosty Ridge Cabins. There were ten or so dark brown cabins scattered in a semicircle. Each with a huge window lining the front and a brick chimney peeking out of an A-line roof. Her daughter parked the car in front of Cabin #3, set toward the back of the semicircle. Rose climbed down from the car slowly, stretched, and stood for a second, taking in the cabins and the deep wooded area beyond. Most of the cabins looked uninhabited; only one cabin, right next door to theirs, had a puff of smoke billowing out of the chimney. They lugged their suitcases and canvas totes up two sets of stairs covered in packed snow. Anne tinkered with the lockbox as Rose and Thea shivered behind her. "Got it," her daughter exclaimed, revealing a small silver key. Rose prodded her granddaughter ahead of her and then walked through the front door herself to find an immaculate yet cozy interior. Right off the entryway was the kitchen, with light brown cabinets and a large white island that opened to the living room, in the center of which sat the woodstove from the Airbnb posting Anne had sent; woodland-themed decorations (complete with two old-fashioned wooden cross-country skis nailed to the wall in an *X*) were sprinkled tastefully throughout the space; each bedroom housed a queen-size bed cloaked in a fluffy down comforter and a bottle of Pellegrino waited in the fridge. Rose unpacked her tote bag of goodies into the fridge and cabinets (dark chocolate, mac and cheese, cookies, Ruffles potato chips, wine, and bourbon), while Anne started a fire.

"This place is so well stocked, Anne." Rose plucked two wineglasses from a cabinet and a handful of ice from the freezer, impressed.

"Isn't it great? What do you think, Thee?" Anne called from the hearth.

"It's awesome, Mom." Thea had already zeroed in on the game shelf and was carefully removing a board game from the middle of the stack.

"That's a good one." Anne pointed to the box in Thea's arms. "I used to play Trouble when I was your age." Rose noticed her daughter's effort to keep her tone level, but she could detect Anne's pleasure in Thea's small nod of warmth.

"Really?" Thea poured out the contents on to the floor, eyeing the bubble dome with dubious interest. "Do you know the rules?"

The three of them ate mac and cheese and played Trouble by the fire. Behind Thea's head light flurries of snow fell outside the big window. Rose took in Anne's smiles—not the tight, quick ones she'd gotten used to—genuine warmth lit up her daughter's eyes. Maybe this was just what her daughter and granddaughter needed.

Afterward, Thea asked Rose to tuck her into bed. Rose glanced at Anne, hesitating for a second, but Anne smiled. "Great, I'll catch up on some work."

When Rose emerged from Thea's bedroom a few minutes later, Anne was in a recliner by the fire, sipping wine and looking at her laptop, brow furrowed. Rose sank down on the couch and they sat in comfortable quiet, the crackling of the fire and clinking of a glass hitting the table the only noises.

"How did it go?" Anne asked without looking up.

"She's a doll." Rose smiled and pulled a blanket over her body. She remembered when six-year-old Anne would lay her head on Rose's stomach, giggling at the gurgling from within. "You're my soft pillow, Mom," she used to say. Now that Anne was an adult, Rose knew that her daughter worried about her ever-expanding middle and her health in general, and she couldn't blame her really—Rose still worked ten-hour shifts at the bakery and took cholesterol pills to combat years of indulging on Rose's Sweets. She always listened to her daughter's attempts to get her to modify her diet (kale, no thank you), go part-time at the bakery, and do some light exercise, but she had no desire to make any changes.

"Are you working?" Rose asked, taking in a large mouthful of wine.

"Just responding to some e-mails. Actually"—Anne flashed her screen at Rose—"I was thinking we could go here tomorrow and then do a hike nearby."

"A hike?" Rose laughed and stretched her feet toward the fire,

"That's ambitious." She peered at the picture on Anne's laptop. "That ice castle place looks beautiful, though. Very cool, honey."

"It's not really a hike. There's a nature reserve with all kinds of trails about five minutes from here. More of a walk really."

"Sounds good to me. A walk is more my style."

"Mom, I've been thinking." Anne paused, closing her computer screen. Rose sighed. She knew what was coming. "Do you think it might be time for you to go part-time at the bakery again?"

"Hmm. I don't see why I would." Every few months, her daughter brought it up and, in thinly veiled tones of frustration, they both pretended as if Rose might be considering it.

Anne's voice softened. "I just think it would be nice for you to relax a bit. You could come to Burlington more and see us, work outside in your garden . . . Remember when you semiretired before Dad died? It seemed really good for you. I think Dad would want you to enjoy life."

"I do enjoy life!" Rose set her glass down on the table, in preparation for reciting this part of the conversation. "I like working at the bakery. I get to get out of the house and see people. Dad understood that, and he supported me. But"—she smiled, taking the edge out of her voice—"I will think about it. Happy?"

Her daughter smiled back and sighed, not convinced. "Yes."

They sat in silence for a few more minutes, Anne's face buried in her laptop, Rose's in the magazine she'd picked up from the coffee table. The woodstove spit out a crackle every few seconds and the snow continued to fall lightly outside.

Rose shifted on the couch and said, "Remind me to talk to you about something tomorrow night—when you're not working." She kept her tone light, casual.

Anne looked up from her typing briefly; the air changed for a split second. Rose kept her eyes down, studying the magazine, until her daughter said, "Sure, Mom," and went back to her laptop. Rose flipped the page on her lap, counting to thirty in her head before stealing a glance at her daughter.

THE MAN

The man looked at the GPS. Three hours down, three and a half more to go. This leg of the trip was a lonely country road scattered with large, isolated houses with long, twisting driveways. He imagined gray walls, fireplaces, long wood tables where families sat and ate breakfast. He thought about stopping at one of the houses and taking a look around—they were all set far back from the main road. The perfect distance. It might be to his advantage to get it out of his system, so that he could go into tomorrow relaxed. But he tapped the gas and drove steadily, letting his mind wander back to the day of the shopping trip when he had met Susan. That same night, hours later, he'd almost drifted to sleep when his mom tiptoed in and sat at the end of his bed. She had cupped both hands around his feet and squeezed him awake.

"It was an accident, right?" she whispered. "The girl tripped?"

He took a moment to think about the question. "I don't know."

"Sometimes, when we have a lot on our mind, like schoolwork and chores and . . . I know you've really been trying to be better with your brother . . ." Her voice got low and all he could hear was deep, insistent breathing. "Sometimes we do things that we don't mean to do. This will be our secret. There's nothing wrong with you, ok?"

"Ok."

He felt her waiting, still pressing his feet like the answer was somewhere between his toes. The bed lightened; it was silent again. He couldn't be sure she was even still in the room.

"Mom."

"Yes." Her voice came from across the room.

"It was an accident."

"Good boy."

The man turned this memory over in his head as he drove; he'd learned how to be with his thoughts for hours, with no need for external interaction. Up ahead, a car braked suddenly and the man brought his mind back to the present. He could not afford to get into an accident right now. He watched as a large raccoon and five baby raccoons skittered across the road, lit up by headlights flooding them from both directions. People had stopped their vehicles for these six rodents.

For the rest of the drive, he kept his thoughts focused only on what was coming. By the time he reached the cluster of fancy cabins, he'd been driving for almost seven hours, and it was late, the pitch black punctured only by his headlights. He turned slowly into the parking lot and drove past the wooden sign shaped like a mountain range that announced: FROSTY RIDGE CABINS. It was too dark to see much of anything, but he pointed his lights toward the two cars in the lot—a large black Lexus SUV and a blue RAV4—and memorized the licenses plates before he made his way back out to the main road. He pulled off into a small clearing and reclined his seat, the engine still running. His eyes burned. He strained to keep them open, but eventually he gave in to the heaviness. He would sleep for a few hours, wake up refreshed and ready for the day.

When he woke, the sun streamed through the windshield like it was trying to crack the glass, and the gas meter sat just above empty. The clock read nine a.m. He made a U-turn and drove back to the Frosty Ridge complex, this time slowly easing his way around the empty parking lot. He'd fucked up; she was gone.

ANNE

It was clear as soon as they pulled into the parking lot that this was a bad idea. Anne had hyped it up over breakfast as a "cool surprise" but she could see from Thea's embarrassed expression that she had miscalculated. Shrieking toddlers raced through the parking lot, pointing at the massive ice structure. Disney character mascots roamed around, posing for pictures and giving hugs to fanatic three- and four-year-olds.

The ice castles themselves were magnificent, just like in the pictures she had clicked through online last night after they arrived at their cabin. Now, Anne watched her daughter drag her feet through the ice castle. Thea kept her distance from the character mascots, especially the plushy moose (or was it a reindeer?) asking for a high five, but as she wandered through the maze of ice, she perked up a little, skimming her fingers against the ice walls and watching water spurt out of a hole in the ground with some other kids. Thea loved water when she was little. Anne had called her water bug because no matter what the season, Thea wanted to be in water, even before she knew how to swim. She would beg to wear her swimsuit every day and some days Anne would relent, letting her wear a pink flamingo bathing suit underneath her school clothes.

"Mommy! I can't wait to grow up!" Thea yelled when she was three years old, an age where everything that came out of her mouth was a burst of magic; Anne never knew what she would say next and found herself almost constantly amused by the workings of her daughter's mind.

"Why do you want to grow up?" Anne had nudged.

"So that I can swim with horses. I am so excited to swim with horses!" Thea jumped up and down, gleeful in this sudden realization that growing up might involve swimming with horses.

Anne laughed out loud at this memory, grateful that such a small moment had found its way back into her head nine years later. Rose looked at her and smiled. "What?"

"I was just remembering something Thea said when she was a toddler." Anne paused. "Do you remember how Dad taught Thea to swim in one day when she was . . . what? Three and a half?"

"Of course I do. He took her to the community center pool and she came home saying she'd jumped off the diving board. I just about had a heart attack." Rose laughed. "Ah, the toddler years. They were the best of times, they were the worst—" Rose stopped. "I'm sorry. I didn't mean to bring up . . ."

"Mom"—she forced a smile—"it's fine. Those years were rough for all of us." She glanced at her mother. "But look." She pointed to Thea. "We're fine now." Anne squeezed Rose's hand and smiled again, this time genuinely. Because it was true. They were fine, better than fine.

"What did you want to ask me about, by the way? Or talk to me about?" Last night, when her mother had said she had something she wanted to talk about, Anne had been in the midst of responding to work e-mails. Sara, a newish client, had canceled her appointment for the second week in a row. Anne had flagged the e-mail and wrote a reminder note to check in with her on Monday. During their last appointment, Sara had finally started to open up about why she was coming to therapy. She had described her relationship with her husband as "really good," but revealed last week that there were times, "not all the time; it's honestly pretty rare," during sex when he would turn from loving to violent.

"It's not rape," she had said quickly, answering a question Anne hadn't asked, after describing an incident where he suddenly grabbed her by the ponytail and brought her head down roughly to his penis.

"When it happens, I just shut down. Like . . . my body goes numb. It's hard to describe." She rubbed her hands together and sat up straighter. "It's not rape," she repeated. "I haven't really said no or told him to stop . . . but . . . it scares me."

"I think that sometimes we decide that labeling something gives it power. Makes it real," Anne said gently. "And that if we don't call it out by name, then we can kind of put it into a box and hide it away. But whether or not you label it, whether or not you say 'this is rape' or simply say 'this behavior scares me,' it's still happening and affecting you in the same way."

This was a scenario that fell into a gray zone, like many scenarios that she dealt with in her practice. Technically, from what Sara had described so far, there was nothing that obligated her to break client confidentiality—reporting Sara's husband to the police for rough sex would not only likely result in no charges but could jeopardize the woman's safety further. And yet, Anne was certain from Sara's body language and carefully selected words that she had only disclosed the very tip of the iceberg. Anne knew she had to tread carefully; she wanted to continue to develop Sara's trust while at the same time reevaluating her patient's safety with each piece of new information she received.

Now, Anne nudged her mother. "Remember? You said you had something to tell me." In the past few years, Anne had started paying attention to any lapses in Rose's memory. So far, she hadn't noticed anything too concerning, but sometimes she couldn't tell if her mom was developing memory problems or if her mind was just . . . elsewhere.

"Oh, we can talk tonight," her mother responded. "It's not a big thing. After Thea goes to bed." Rose crossed her arms over her chest and made a loud *Brr* sound. "Should we get going?"

"Ok, Thee," Anne called out. "Ready to grab lunch?"

"And then the hike, right?" Rose murmured beside her.

"Yep! Well, more of a walk."

THEA

Thea stared at the cheeseburger in front of her. She had taken a single bite out of it and the inside glistened with fat and gelatinous cheese that hung over the edge like a wilted flower. It was suddenly the most disgusting food Thea had ever seen and she had trouble fathoming how it had been her favorite meal prior to this bite.

"Thea?" Her mom spoke through her own bite of fried haddock. The oily white fish and crusty breading, almost as repulsive as the burger on Thea's plate, peeked out from behind her lips as she asked, "Why aren't you eating? What's wrong? Are you feeling ok?"

"Nothing is wrong," Thea answered quickly. "I'm fine. I'm just not hungry." Thea took a long drink of lemonade through a straw, to demonstrate that, while her appetite for solids was nil, her body was still functioning. Her mother sighed in her usual way, but seemed, if not pleased, somewhat abated by Thea's intake of liquid glucose. As her mom and Mimi chatted about dinner (they were always planning their next meal even if they were literally just sitting down to the one in front of them), Thea let her thoughts wander, as they often wandered these days, to Mr. Redmond, Ted. Her new middle school offered an elective foreign language starting in sixth grade and Thea had chosen Spanish over French (the only two choices), against her mother's wishes. Spanish made a lot more sense than French, practically speaking. Thea's mom conceded that point, though it didn't stop her from retelling a story from her year abroad in Paris, about her uptight French roommate, Marianne, who, on principle, refused to speak to *l'Américaine*, wore all black, and communicated mostly in expletives. Why her mother presumed these tales would tempt Thea to take French, she did not know. In any case, after the first two weeks of Spanish class, Thea had come to the very disappointing conclusion that her mother may have been correct; she hated the class. Her teacher, Señora Pilas, was a squat, mean woman with short black hair and a large mole on her top lip. She used a ruler, not to actually hit the kids (though Thea was certain she would if the school would allow it), but to smack their desks if they got an answer wrong or talked out of turn. The class environment was stressful and hostile and Thea felt her stomach twist every time she stepped foot inside Señora Pilas's sterile classroom. The afternoon she met Mr. Redmond for the first time, she had made up her mind—she would go to the principal's office and ask to drop the course; it was an elective, after all, a bonus class. Besides, Livi, Zoe, and Gretchen were all taking French. She walked into the classroom feeling as if a weight had lifted off her shoulders, knowing it was one of the last times she would have to be in the same room as Señora Pilas. As soon as she stepped foot over the threshold, though, she could feel something was different. The energy was excitable, frenetic almost, with kids chatting and laughing, hanging out of their seats and standing in clumps, and Señora Pilas, usually perched at the chalkboard in front of twenty silent, rigid students, was nowhere to be seen.

Thea took her place in her usual seat next to Ronan, a quiet, lanky boy, almost as skinny as her, with glasses and sandy-colored hair; she pulled her name card out of her desk console and set it atop her tan, smooth desk, facing outward. They each had a Spanish name—if the English name could be translated fairly logically into Spanish, that was the name they went by in class, if not, they got to pick an entirely new name in Spanish. Thea's card read *Téa*. Boring. She looked at Ronan beside her, a bit enviously, as he adjusted his own name card, which read *Javier*.

"Where's Señora Pilas?" Thea whispered, though she didn't need to whisper; the other students were only getting louder and more ani- mated. By way of replying, Ronan nodded his head toward the chalk- board, grinned, and started drawing in his notebook. Thea looked up. Big cursive letters filled the chalkboard.

Your substitute teacher's name is Mr. Redmond.

Thea had never seen anything more beautiful. She glanced at the clock above the door of the classroom. 2:45 p.m. It was already five minutes past the start of class and there was no sign of the sub. No wonder the room felt like an amusement park—the only thing better than a substitute teacher was no teacher at all. Thea turned to Ronan/ Javier and said in a normal voice this time, "Nice." Then she reached into her book bag and pulled out *Stargirl*, the novel she'd started the night before for book club. She tuned out the jabberings and squawks of her classmates and immersed herself in the world of the strange girl who captures the boy's heart. Thea wished, for the hundredth time, that the book had been written from Stargirl's point of view, instead of the boy who loves her, but she understood by now that oftentimes girls' stories were written by men.

"Hi, guys, sorry I'm late. Got a bit turned around in the hallways." Thea looked up from her book. The voice was young and smooth and she half expected to see a boy her age striding up to the front of the classroom. The voice came from a man, in fact, though one on the younger side, at least compared to Mr. Jeffries, her math teacher, and Mr. Connor, her English teacher, who had frizzy white hair and halitosis, respectively. He stood with his back to them for a moment, looking at the chalkboard; Thea could only see the side of his face, but he looked just as surprised and out of sorts as her classmates to see his name written in authoritatively looping cursive letters.

"Well, I'm Mr. Redmond," he said, nodding at the board for confirmation and turning, finally, to face them. He was young. Probably just out of college. He had straight light brown hair, an oval face, and a patrician nose. He looked like royalty, Thea thought; his face was made up of fine, delicate lines.

"I'll be your substitute teacher today." He looked again at the board. "Ms. Pilas is. Ms. Pilas has been having—" He stopped. Blood ran into his cheeks and Thea leaned forward in her desk, rapt. "Well, she'll be out for a while. Indefinitely. I'll let Principal Teaman fill you in on the details." He looked down at his shoes. "If she sees fit. In any case," Mr. Redmond continued, "my name is Mr. Redmond. I mean Señor Redmond." He smiled here, as if making an inside joke. Thea caught his eye and smiled back, encouraging him: *You can do this.* "I guess I'll start by telling you a little bit about myself." Mr. Redmond leaned back against the chalkboard and then quickly righted himself, brushing white dust from his back awkwardly. "Whoops, I messed up my name. What was I saying? Oh, right, I graduated from the University of

Vermont. I worked for Teach for America straight out of school and now . . ." He lifted his hands, palms to the ceiling. "I'm here. So— Oh yes, you, uh, sorry, I don't know names yet, but, go ahead—"

"Rachel," a girl in the back row with jet-black hair and blunt bangs said, keeping her hand in the air as she spoke her name. *Of course Rachel is the first to ask a question,* Thea thought with a silent groan. Rachel looked like a young Cleopatra and had the confidence, and a slightly haughty demeanor, to match, which was apparently very appealing to boys in the sixth grade. Thea, on the other hand, appealed to exactly zero boys at school, and as she slunk lower in her chair, she wondered what it would feel like to have that kind of natural magnetism.

"Rachel. Go ahead, Rachel," Mr. Redmond said with a smile.

"I have two questions. One. How old are you?" Snickers wafted through the room like wind blowing through leaves. "And two. Are you from Spain? You don't look Latino." More snickers. Thea rolled her eyes at Ronan.

Mr. Redmond laughed. "I am twenty-four years old. And no, I'm not from Spain, which is a European country, by the way, but I spent my junior year abroad in Bogotá, which is where I learned Spanish. I also tutored kids, during my senior year and the past two years, to keep my language skills sharp."

"Do you still give private lessons?" Rachel whispered just loud enough and cupped her hand over her mouth at her own audacity, and the other girls in class tittered and the boys groaned and someone said, "Gross."

The rest of class passed quickly. They went around and said their names and three things about themselves, at Mr. Redmond's request. Mr. Redmond seemed genuinely interested in each student's revelations, nodding vigorously and asking follow-up questions. When it was Thea's turn, she stated her three personal facts quickly and without emotion, hoping to pass the spotlight to Ronan as soon as possible. "One. I was born in New York City. Two. I am an only child. Three. My mother is a therapist." She followed the formula of several of the other students and sat still, willing her heart to slow.

"All right, a New Yorker!" Mr. Redmond put his hand up and leaned toward Thea's desk. Thea felt a surge of blood rush into her face and reached her hand toward his, clumsily, managing to only half connect with his open palm. "Where in the city did you live? I grew up about an hour outside the city, so I made the trip in all the time when I was a teenager." He leaned back on the chalkboard and smiled at Thea.

"I didn't really live there," Thea replied quickly. "I was born there, but my mom and I moved to Vermont right after I was born." Her hand went to her scalp automatically, a nervous tick, searching for the stitches that had been long healed. She realized that no one in this new school knew about her "episodes" or her surgeries or all her time spent in the hospital. She pulled her hand through her hair in what she hoped looked like a confident, cool girl gesture.

"Ah, gotcha, ok. Well, hey, if you ever decide to visit your hometown, make sure to let me know. I'll give you a list of places to see." His mouth spread into a big grin and Thea nodded.

"Ok. I will." She bent her head over her desk and pretended to write something in her notebook. Her heart beat in her ears. He moved on to Ronan. She missed the rest of her classmates' answers, replaying in her head their exchange, the way he lit up when she said she was born in New York.

"Thee, you're pink. Do you feel hot?"

Thea looked up from her burger. "No! Mom, I'm fine. Leave me alone." It came out angrier than she intended, but why was her mother always looking at her, trying to get inside her head? Couldn't she just worry about her own life instead of constantly invading Thea's? Thea flushed harder as she took in her mom's hurt expression. Her mother was so sensitive. Jesus. "I'm sorry, Mom. I'm fine. I'm just thinking about all the homework I have to do tonight, and it put me in a bad mood."

"Don't worry about that now, honey. We're on vacation. Well, a mini vacation at least. Let's have fun today and I'll help you to-night, ok?"

Thea smiled back and nodded, but she had to break away from her mother's face after a few seconds. Her eyes were so genuine, and yet Thea knew the truth. Her mom had lied to her for years. A month ago, Thea had called her best friend, Maddie. Maddie still lived in Charlotte, and though they had promised to stay best friends forever, Thea could feel that they'd grown apart even in the few months since she'd moved. Maddie had asked, again, about Thea's father: "Oh my god, what if he's in Burlington? What if you, like, bump into him on the street but you don't even know it's him!" Maddie, along with the rest of her Charlotte friends with their perfect cookie-cutter families, found it fascinating that Thea had never met her father—and seemed to think it was some kind of game to figure out his identity.

"Maddie, oh my god," Thea began, haughtily, reciting the speech she had given many times before. "I don't have a dad. I just have a mom. It's not a big deal. Not all families are comprised of the tradi-tional nuclear unit." She felt so wise and mature compared to her old friends in Charlotte. By growing up without a father, especially in a small, homogenous town, she just understood life truths that the other kids had yet to learn. And now, of course, she was a city kid. Thea continued, "And, honestly, if you had lived anywhere but Charlotte your entire life, you wouldn't think it was a big deal, either." There was silence on the other end of the line, and Thea pictured her friend's face flushing a deep crimson. *Good*, Thea thought. Maddie was a snob. Thea couldn't even remember why they were best friends, except that they had always been friends, since they were four years old.

"Yeah, but you have to have a dad. Like"—Maddie giggled—"your mom didn't just get pregnant on her own."

Thea rolled her eyes and shifted the phone on her shoulder. "Maddie, I've told you this literally a thousand times. My biological father could not handle the responsibility of being a parent. So he left. Not everyone that *has* babies is meant to actually *raise* babies," Thea said, emphasizing the same words her mother did. But Maddie's words had gotten under her skin this time, and the next time she asked her mother about her biological father, her mother's response had seemed false and hollow. Maddie was right, Thea realized, her dad existed somewhere in the world, and it was bizarre that she knew *nothing* about him. She had always just accepted her mother's explanation; she never thought to question the fundamental rules that made up her life. And yet . . . What if her mom was wrong? The thought felt jarring, illicit—simply because it had never occurred to her before. What if her dad had actually been searching for her for years? Maybe he just didn't know how to get in touch with her; maybe he'd lost track of her after they had moved from New York to Vermont. Maybe he lived overseas or maybe he was some kind of famous musician or actor. There were so many possibilities that she had never thought of before and, after years of never second-guessing the fact that it was just her and her mom, it suddenly seemed urgent that she find her other parent, the one she knew nothing about but had created half of her DNA. And so she had googled his name on a computer at the school library. Her mother had spit out his full name two years ago, with the caveat, "Now you know everything I do. I know this isn't what you want to hear, but I didn't know him well. I'm sorry. Please just leave it, Thee." Once she decided to ask the Internet, she couldn't believe that she hadn't thought of doing so before. "Joseph Graham"— she typed in the letters one at a time, holding her breath as she clicked Enter. She looked at the top results, a dozen or so Facebook listings and Instagram accounts, a lawyer from Texas with his own practice, an actor in L.A., a football player from Minneapolis. Even narrowing by age and race, she would be left with too many prospective men to make an accurate identification. Her study period ended before she could dig any further, and she spent the rest of the day pondering how she could make progress with her search. The only information she had about her biological father, other than his name, was that he lived in New York, or at least he did at one point, when her mom met him. She could try adding "New York" to her search but doubted that would narrow the results much more. Then she realized with a jolt that shot her up in bed, she could search for her mom. She knew plenty about her mother, Anne Claire Thompson, and it was possible that her mom and dad were listed together somewhere on the Internet.

The next afternoon, she broke away from her small group of friends and rushed to the library again during her study period. She sat down at the computer, excited to test her theory, and typed in "Anne Claire Thompson, New York, NY." Google spit out the results instantaneously and Thea scanned the page until her eyes landed on a wedding registry. Thea clicked, confused and excited—her parents got married? Why would her mom leave that out? She didn't realize until after she was on the page that her father's name was wrong. It took her another few minutes, of reading and rereading the wedding website, and then the baby shower registry website and then the *New York Times* article, to understand that everything her mother had told her about her father had been a lie. She sat at the school computer past the start of her next class, heart pounding in her ears, trying to hide her face with her hands so that the librarian wouldn't see the mix of sweat and tears. The words from the article flashed across the screen. *Homicide. No arrests made. Survived by his daughter, Thea Thompson.* She was shaking so badly by the time she walked into English class that the teacher immediately sent her to the nurse, without even reprimanding her for being twenty minutes late. She sat in the nurse's office, across from Ms. Kim, the school nurse for the elementary and middle schools, and answered in a whisper, "I'm fine," when Ms. Kim asked her what hurt. When the nurse took her temperature, though, it was 101 and so her mother was called. Thea sat in a shivering ball on the cot reserved for the sickest kid in the nurse's office at a given time, waiting for her mom to pick her up. While she waited, she thought about what she had seen and what she now knew about her father. If she asked her mom about what she had discovered, her mother would lie again, Thea was certain of it. She needed more time to think. When her mom finally arrived, kneeling down by the cot and scooping her into a hug, Thea's arms hung limply at her sides. "I'm fine," she repeated. She hadn't said a substantial word to her mom since that day.

Thea couldn't reconcile the two truths she knew about her mother in her mind: one, she was her best friend, the person she loved the most in the world; and two, she had been actively deceiving Thea her entire life. She had asked Mimi last night, when she was tucking her in at the cabin, about her father. Thea decided not to reveal what she had seen on the school computer; even though she trusted Mimi, she might tell her mom and Thea didn't know how her mom would use that information, what other lies she might come up with to skew the truth. For now, Thea would keep it to herself.

"Why won't my mom tell me anything about my dad?" she asked. She could tell by her grandmother's face that Mimi understood this time was different from the other times Thea had asked.

Mimi took a breath. She seemed to be working something out in her mind. The silence lengthened. Finally, "I know it's not fair," Mimi began slowly, carefully. "I have always believed your mother should have told you the truth from the very beginning, but . . ." She took another breath, her eyebrows arched and filled her forehead with deep creases; she was thinking again. Thea held her breath. "She's not ready, Thea. She's human, too, you know, and flawed. What I will tell you is that she loves you very much. From the moment you were born, every choice she's made has been to protect you. Even though I disagree with her about some of those choices, she's always tried to do what's best for you. Your grandad said to me once, 'Anne is the strongest person I know.' And coming from an ex-marine, that's saying something." Rose smoothed Thea's hair behind her ear. "At times, though, I think your mom has mistaken strength with closing herself off from life. I'll talk to your mom this weekend, see what I can do, but this is a conversation for the two of you." Thea was not expecting this answer, which only opened up more questions. When would someone finally tell her the truth? Why would her mom have lied about her parents being married? None of it made any sense. She opened her mouth to get her questions out, but her grandmother cut her off before she could speak. "Thea. It's time for bed." It was a command. She had never heard a hard edge to her grandmother's voice before.

"Fine." Thea felt tears prick her eyes. She turned into her pillow to hide her face.

"I love you." Thea felt Mimi's warm lips press against the back of her head and then she walked out of the room.

Sitting in the restaurant booth now, a white, hot rage bubbled up inside Thea and she took a bite of hamburger to keep herself from crying.

"There you go, love," Mimi said, clapping her hand on Thea's back. "Good that you eat. You're going to need energy for this afternoon. We don't want to have to carry you on the trail," she said with a chuckle. Mimi kept her hand on Thea's back and made small, circular motions as she chewed and swallowed. The movement filled Thea's face with blood again as she remembered Mr. Redmond's hand on her back.

"Mimi, that tickles," Thea said, shrugging away. "So, wait, what are we doing next?"

ONE HOUR
BEFORE THE CABIN

THE MAN

It was nearly one p.m. The man had waited all morning and afternoon for her to come back to the condo parking lot. Finally, he screamed into his steering wheel and decided he just wanted it to be over. At least he could be in control of how it ended. The man drove around aimlessly, looking for a good spot to do it. The gun sat next to him in the passenger seat. There weren't many other cars on the road—just the last vacation stragglers, looking to break up the bleak winter with a ski weekend. No sign of the black SUV or the blue RAV4.

He drummed his fingers against his father's steering wheel and looked down at the gun on the seat beside him. He slowed the car, scanning side streets, looking for a quiet spot, somewhere he might not be found for a while. The man pictured his body slumped in the front seat, peaceful for once, and smiled. He saw the street sign out of the corner of his eye and stepped on the brakes hard, turning the wheel, no time for the blinker. Julia Street. His stomach tightened into knots of longing; the feeling was almost unbearable. When he was a child, he'd thought this longing feeling must be some relation to what other people described as "love," but when he got older, that same feeling led him to Julia. So, he reasoned, it couldn't be like love at all. The road was dotted with small houses, close together, not ideal, but it had to be this street, he felt it in his bones. He drove to the very end of the long, windy road and then circled around slowly in the small cul-de-sac at the end of the street. The man pulled his car to the side of the street, edging up on neutral lawn, halfway between two brown houses. He peered into the house across the street. The blinds were drawn and smoke billowed from the chimney. Light filtered through the thin blinds and he could make out the outline of someone bustling around inside. He shut his eyes. Imagined the mother, chopping an onion and throwing a handful into a sizzling pan on the stove. The father reading a book in the living room, feet propped up on an ottoman. And the daughter. Her face filled his mind, bangs and pink cheeks. She lay in bed, listening to music through her headphones, writing in her journal about her crush at school. He opened his eyes and looked at the house again. It was still now; he couldn't make out any shadows flitting across the rooms anymore. Empty. He thought he heard laughter and spun his head around, looking for the person mocking him. There was only the silent street and the dull houses. He felt for the gun near his waist, stroked the top of it. What was he waiting for? *Coward*, said a clear voice. "Shut up," the man said aloud. *I am calm. I feel nothing.* He pulled out the gun and held it in his lap, dropped the magazine between his legs and checked—eight bullets left. He jammed the magazine back into the hollow end of the gun and brought it up quickly under his chin. He closed his eyes again. Pointer finger on the trigger. His eyes fluttered open to the sound of a high-pitched creak. The front door of the house across from him had opened halfway and a figure stood in the doorway, back to him. He put the gun down slowly, wedging it in between his legs, almost invisible. He watched as a girl slammed the heavy wooden door behind her and then pushed it all the way closed with her backside. She wore a puffy white coat and purple hat with two braided tassels trailing down past her ears. A black dog heaved down the front steps, pulling her along, its tail slapping her legs as she followed closely behind. The dog looked like his own childhood dog, a lab, old and fat.

"Excuse me." He rolled down his window. The girl snapped her head up, startled. "I'm sorry, do you know if I'm close to 16 Julia Street?"

The girl walked slowly toward him, tugging the old lab, when she got close enough that he could reach out and touch her, he said, "I've just driven up and down the street and I can't seem to find number 16." He laughed. The girl smiled, showing big white teeth covered in braces.

"Well, my house is one thirty-two, so you want to go down almost all way to the main street for sixteen." Her voice was high and sweet. The man kept his eyes on her eyes but in his peripheral vision saw a single strand of hair coming out of her hat and resting against the white collar of her coat. Red. The man's hands began to tremble and he placed them against the wheel.

"Do you think you could possibly show me? It's just that I've been down and back a couple of times and somehow I keep missing it." He worked to keep his voice warm and open. This was how it was supposed to happen. One last taste before nothingness.

"Um." The girl's cheeks flushed. "I think if you just, if you just—" She stumbled and laughed. "I'm sorry, I don't think I'm supposed to—" Her eyes fell to the dog and then her head craned around toward her house. The man could feel time pressing down, closing in. He leaned all the way toward the passenger-side door until his head was out the window, inches away from her.

"I'll drop you right back at your house. You can bring your dog. Hey there." He gave a low whistle and the dog's ears perked up. "I've already tried twice to find the house. I could really use your help."

"Ok . . ." The girl sounded defeated and the man felt a surge of blood rush through his body. He knew he had won.

"Here, come on in. You can let the dog in the back." He smiled again. He thought about the eight bullets left; the dog wouldn't be a problem. "You're doing me such a huge favor. It will only take a couple minutes."

The sound of a wail pierced the air. "JO." A sharp voice. The man looked up to see a woman, holding a shrieking red-faced baby, in the door frame of the girl's house. "It's dinnertime!" she yelled. The man couldn't see her face clearly, but her voice was hard. The baby's cries filled the air in short metallic bursts. "Inside. Right now."

"Oh," the girl breathed out. "I'm sorry, I have to go!" He felt the relief come off her in waves as she backed away, pulling the dog with her. She turned and ran toward her yard, up the front steps and into the house. The mother waited for a second, staring, and then slammed the door shut.

The man pulled his car into drive, eased off the edge of the grass, and back onto Julia Street. He turned onto the main road again, cursing himself, the girl, and the mother. He drove for a few miles like this, until his rage bubbled down to a simmer and then he drove in silence. A sign pointing to a mostly empty parking lot caught his eye and he put on his blinker. He pulled into a space on the far right-hand side of the lot. There were only a few other cars parked. He sat thinking for a few minutes, and then he picked up the gun and put it in his mouth. His thumb found the trigger; he started to squeeze. He released the trigger. A black SUV rumbled through the lot, coming to a stop right in front of the welcome lodge. At this distance, if he squinted, he could make out the last three numbers of the back license plate. The air in the Saab hummed. He moved his eyes up. Two people in the front. A driver and passenger. Both female. He slid the gun out of his mouth and placed it in his lap. *If they have dark hair, I'll let them go*, he said to himself. The driver got out. She stood for a moment, took a deep breath and exhaled. Dark hair. The female passenger followed, older than the driver. Dark hair. The man checked the license plate again. The older one buttoned up her coat and circled around to the back of the car, opened the trunk, and began pulling hats and gloves out; a red scarf dangled from the edge and then fell, pooling around her feet on the ground. He picked up the gun. Put it back in his mouth. Thumb on the trigger. Two women. He was wrong. The back door of the SUV opened. A third passenger got out.

ANNE

As soon as they stepped out of the SUV into the cool stillness of the nature reserve, Anne could feel everyone's mood improve. They left the lurking disappointment from this morning in the car and took in the peaceful quiet surrounding them. Anne felt her body relax and took a few deep breaths of fresh air into her lungs. The parking lot was empty save a few abandoned cars scattered around—other hikers (or walkers, in their case), she assumed. They parked right in front of a small log cabin that must have also served as a welcome center during peak season but seemed to be closed today. Posted on the door and walls of the cabin were maps of the reserve showing all the different trails: Beginner trails dotted the maps in green, intermediate in blue, and advanced in red with the warning "these trails may contain severe and/or extreme conditions." Anne made a mental note to follow the green dots.

"Ooh look, it's snowing!" Thea exclaimed and stuck out her tongue to intercept fat snowflakes as they fell to the ground. "It's so pretty here."

Anne grinned, basking in her daughter's good mood. "It's beautiful," she agreed.

"Mom, don't be cheesy, though," Thea said. But she linked one arm in Anne's and the other in Rose's and pulled them toward the entrance to the trails marked by a wooden arch.

"Should we figure out which trail we want to do?" Rose asked, looking over her shoulder toward the log cabin plastered with maps.

"Mimi, we can just follow the green. Look." Thea pointed with her nose to a green arrow painted on a tree. "Right, Mom?"

"Sounds good to me." Anne clocked the next green arrow a few trees down. "It looks like this trail is well marked, Mom," she said over Thea's head to Rose. "I don't think we'll have any problems."

Rose smiled and shrugged, taking one last squint at the welcome cabin. "All right, girls. I'm following you two."

The path, encompassed by trees thick with snow, ran along a wide, gushing river. Anne watched the water rush forward, moving furiously through jutting rocks toward . . . the ocean? She did a mental check. Yes, all rivers lead to a larger body of water. She gave herself a pat on the back just as Thea asked, "Where does the river go?"

"The Atlantic, honey," Anne said. It had started in earnest a few weeks ago—her daughter questioning and critiquing everything Anne said and did—but there were still instances when Thea accepted Anne's words as fact, merely because she fit squarely in the category of "adult." More and more, though, Anne felt her authoritative façade crumbling. She tried not to dwell too much on how little she actually knew about life, about the world, about raising another human. She wondered if other so-called adults felt this way—that life, and especially parenthood, was a guessing game. Guessing which answer, which punishment, which reward would lead to the least fucked-up young adult. Considering her daughter had spent the majority of her life in and out of hospitals, Anne felt she had quite a bit of catching up to do in the game.

"Brr." Rose shivered and placed her free hand over Thea's glove. "Don't get too close. Look at those rapids!"

Thea sighed. "Mimi, I'm not going to jump in. I would get hypothermia like . . . immediately, right?" Before they could answer in the affirmative, two hikers were almost on top of them. The noise of the river and the bend in the path had masked their arrival from the opposite direction almost completely.

"Whoa!" the woman called out, giving the leash in her hand a hard tug before a huge dog licked Thea's face. "So sorry about that!" She laughed as the man yelled, "Riley, down!"

"Look at you. You're beautiful." Thea was bent over the dog, stroking his huge furry ears before Anne could say, "Thea, you have to ask before you pet." She turned to the couple and smiled. "It looks like it's ok." The husky sat quietly thumping his tail as Thea whispered sweet nothings in his ears.

"He's humongous," the woman said, adjusting her sunglasses up to rest on silver hair. "But he's a big teddy bear, don't worry."

"He loves kids." The man crossed his arms over a bulky ski jacket. "Big teddy bear," he repeated.

"Beautiful dog," Rose said, and they all stood admiring the majestic white-and-gray-furred animal before the man whistled.

"Come on, Riley." He gave a wave as they moved away. "Enjoy the hike, ladies. It's a great day for it."

"Mom, what kind of dog was that?" Thea asked as they continued around the bend to see a straight path of white sprawled ahead as far as the eye could see.

"I think a husky, Thee. Kind of like a well-trained wolf that likes people." Anne dug into her backpack and pulled out a furry white hat. "Put this on, please."

"Mom, I'm fine."

"Not arguing about this. It's negative five degrees out here. The hat goes on."

Thea rolled her eyes (Anne didn't see this, but a mother knows) and pulled the hat snug over her head. "Is it really negative five degrees, Mimi?"

"Not quite." Anne shot Rose a glance. "But it will be soon," her mother finished.

For the next twenty minutes they trudged on; the sound of the gushing water punctuated by Thea kicking a rock and a discussion of dinner plans. Thea wanted to go out to a pizza place in town, and they all agreed that they would go straight from the trails to the restaurant, followed by roasting marshmallows in the wood fire at the cabin.

Anne heard the crunching behind them first. She turned her head over her shoulder to see a man, closer than she would have expected, walking toward them briskly, head down, body hunched forward. Rose's head followed next, glancing behind them and then at her daughter, noticing that Anne had noticed, too. Later, Anne could pretend that she felt a chill, that she immediately, instinctually *knew*—but truth be told, her heart did not accelerate and her hands did not shake. Perhaps because the dog couple had surprised them at first but turned out to be lovely, or perhaps, more likely, she felt insulated, protected, much like the nature reserve itself. She should have known that one is never really, truly safe. She knew it was no way to live, expecting at any given moment that something could happen, travesty could strike, and life could be irrevocably altered. But there were too many moments in her past, moments that had sliced her life into "befores" and "afters," for Anne to shake the feeling. In any case, when Anne first saw the man, she wasn't frightened. He wore a thin gray sweater and dark khaki pants. His hair was thinning on top but he had a thick beard. Within thirty seconds, the purposeful crunching was right behind them, and then he was passing them with a "Hi" that came out more like an exhale than a word. Anne's "Hi" and Rose's "Hello" chimed together and they shared a glance.

"He's in a hurry," Anne remarked.

"He should really be wearing a jacket," her mother said and shivered, as if absorbing some of the cold for the man.

"Let's turn back in a few minutes, 'k?" She glanced up to the sky. The sun was starting to set and she could feel the air turning from thirty degrees laced with sun to just thirty degrees.

"Ok, let's race to the next tree with green and then turn around!" Thea took off without waiting for confirmation. Anne groaned, "Jesus Christ," to Rose before taking off after her daughter. She started slow, testing her arms and legs, letting her body warm up. She dug her boots into the snow, pumping her arms and widening her strides. It felt good to run. Faster and faster. Her mouth broke into a smile and she whooped into the air to let Thea know she was close. She watched Thea's gangly arms pumping wildly, her daughter's head bent in determination. "I'm gaining on you," Anne yelled and she heard Thea's excited scream over the roar of the river. It felt so good to play with her daughter again, and she was so intent on catching up to her that at first she didn't even notice the man. She had almost closed the distance between herself and Thea when, for some reason, her eyes moved beyond Thea. Her first thought was one of confusion. *Why is he running, too?* The man ran in a straight line, his hands formed sharp points, his mouth tightly sealed. And then: *Oh god, what is he running from?* Anne stretched her eyes beyond the man, scanning the path, waiting for an animal to come barreling out of the woods, her breath now coming in ragged spurts. Her eyes darted from the man to Thea, who was still running wildly a few yards ahead, head still bent, completely unaware of the man and whatever danger surrounded them all. It only took a few more seconds, maybe even just one more second, for Anne to realize that the man was not running away; he was running toward. It was his eyes; in the seconds before they all collided, she saw that there was no fear in his eyes, only a glint of excitement. And then, finally, the last coherent thought that shot through her head, though even while she was thinking it, she knew it didn't make sense: *Why is he running at Thea?* Because he was, without a doubt, running directly toward her child.

In those last few seconds before impact, she knew only that she had to put her body between the man and Thea. "Thea," Anne choked out. Thea screamed again with glee, at her mother's voice so close. A couple of minutes ago, at about the halfway point of the race, Anne had felt her body maxing out, and she knew she had reached her top speed. She now found that she could go faster. She pushed in front of Thea right as the man angled himself at his target, opening his arms from sharp points into what looked like a hug. Anne let out a guttural "No" and lunged from behind Thea into the inside corner of the man's body. For a moment they kept moving, Anne and the man, their bodies tangled together, her chin mashed into his chest, his arms circling her in a rough embrace, and then her head snapped back and she was airborne.

She landed flat on her back, the air knocked out of her. She tried to yell to Thea from where her daughter lay startled and dazed on the ground after glancing off Anne's back, but all she could do was open and close her mouth like a fish. The last time she had the air fully knocked out of her was in high school. She went to catch a pop-up— "It's mine," she called to center field, claiming the white ball blotting out the sun in the sky. The ball whizzed up, up, up and then down, down . . . except she underestimated how far she would have to move to meet the ball with her glove, and at the last second, she dove, glove outstretched, salt and sweat blurring her vision. *Smack*, she felt the ball in her glove right as she landed hard on her side. As the crowd cheered, Anne had the very clear thought, *I can't breathe. I am going to die*, and then a command as if from outside her head, *Keep your glove closed*. Of course, eventually her lungs opened back up and she gulped in air and stood up shakily, opening her glove to reveal the white orb tucked inside.

How long did it take for her lungs to expand back out? As Anne laid on the ground, watching Thea struggle to stand on her skinny legs and then, once her daughter found her balance, run toward her, she realized that it had taken too long because she couldn't call out to Thea to run in the other direction.

The man had been temporarily stunned—either by the surprise of a body being hurled at him or perhaps some damage to his ribs after contact with the hard point of Anne's chin. He sat on the ground, breathing hard, his knees up, his bare hands flat against the icy snow. Then he stood up and began to move fluidly toward them. Anne felt a trickle of air seep into her lungs and her body spasmed slightly. She looked from Thea to the man approaching her daughter from behind and back to Thea. She managed to croak out a pathetic, "Thea," before Thea was flying away from her, the force of his hand into the back of her daughter's head sending her sideways like a paper bag catching the wind. Thea's head hit the ground with a dull *thud* and then she was still. "No," again a weak croak. Anne got up on her hands and knees and started to crawl toward Thea, tunnel vision blurring out the man so that for a moment it was almost as if he had disappeared, his form melding in with the trees.

"I would advise you to stop moving." His voice came out flat and dull.

Anne heard him but she didn't hear him because there was her daughter, lying on her side on the cold, hard ground, not moving, her face turned away. The white furry hat had landed halfway between where Anne was and where Thea lay. She kept her eyes focused on the hat as she dragged her body forward. She had to see her child's face. Her breaths came ragged but steady now. Somewhere in the depths of her mind, she recognized this state of calm, the numbness in her body, the blood going frozen in her veins, that occurred right before her brain understood that everything was about to change.

"I didn't want to do this," the man was saying from far away. No, not far away, right above her. But she had to see Thea's face; she needed to see Thea's face and then she would know what to do next.

"I didn't want to do this. Goddammit," the man said again. He sounded angry, like he wanted a response, so she said, "Ok," as she inched forward. Now she was by the hat, halfway there. Thea's hair, fine and stick-straight (the opposite of hers and Rose's dark curly hair, so thick the stylist used a straight razor), pooled out of the collar of her jacket. Snow, falling steadily now, landed on the strands and melted. A scream of rage bubbled into Anne's throat and she shoved it back down into the hollow of her stomach.

A metallic sound came from right above her as Rose's voice, loud and cheery, sailed through the air, "Anne, what are you guys doing?" Her mother's tone, as if she was joining a big group dinner on a cruise ship, disoriented Anne and she stopped, perched on her elbows. The man must have been startled as well because she heard him mutter, "Fuck."

The four of them remained still for a moment—Anne hunched on the ground near Thea, Rose a few yards away, smiling, and the man standing, Anne assumed, right over her.

Thea was almost within reach now. Anne sucked air into her body and started moving toward her daughter again. She needed to make sure Thea was breathing. Her fingernails dug into ice, snowy slush soaked through the knees of her jeans as she continued forward.

"Anne!" Rose's voice, this time straining just a bit, overlapped with the man's command.

"Stop. Fucking. Moving."

Anne could see the side of Thea's face now—her daughter's mouth gaped open slightly and Anne thought she could see her body moving ever so slightly with inhalations. She tore her eyes from Thea, suddenly aware of the closeness of the man and the sharpness of his tone. As her eyes lifted from Thea to the man, she realized what the metallic sound was from before. He pointed the gun straight at her head. "Oh," she said. She was suddenly aware of the gushing river, the snow falling in big clumps, the glints of sun peeking through the trees, and the man with a gun who had knocked out her daughter during a hike. No. Not a hike. A walk. She thought, *This is real. This is happening.*

The man walked around Anne and bent over Thea. He scooped

her small body into his arms and placed the gun against the side of her head. The scream bubbled up again, but this time Anne swallowed it down quickly and carefully.

"Follow me," the man said. He turned and walked deeper into the reserve.

FIFTEEN MINUTES
BEFORE THE CABIN

ROSE

Rose knew before Anne did. She watched her daughter and her grand-daughter race down the white straightaway toward the man, toward danger. She tried to scream and warn them, for she realized right away, as soon as she saw the blur of the man up ahead, that he was trouble, but her voice melted into the air. Rose knew, in fact, or had a feeling at the very least, as soon as the man passed them on the trail. Anne would call that paranoia (and Rose *had* been wrong on occasion about people, but mostly she'd been right), and so she had shut her mouth into a thin line and swallowed down the bad feeling.

Now, she watched her daughter collide with the man in slow motion. She sucked in a breath as Anne flew through the air and landed in a heap on the ground. Her eyes flicked from her daughter to Thea, who had landed a few feet away. The man, Anne, and Thea formed a triangle. The man at the top, Anne to the right, and Thea to the left. *Get up, girls*, Rose willed her daughter and granddaughter. What had she read recently? That in a kidnapping, you were much more likely to stay alive if you kicked up a fuss. Scream, punch, run. None of these things were happening.

Rose felt in her coat pocket for her phone. Had she left it in the car? She dug into her left pocket, nothing. Right pocket, nothing except for chalky unwrapped gum. And then she remembered. She had placed it in an inside pocket of her jacket, one that zippered from top to bottom instead of side to side. She fumbled with her coat snaps, keeping her eyes glued up ahead, and once her coat was open, she pulled the zipper down, yanked the phone out. No service. It didn't even read EXTENDED at the top like it did in the basement of the bakery. She dialed 9-1-1 and waited. Nothing. She was expecting this, as about halfway through the walk she had snapped a picture of Anne and Thea walking up ahead, heads bent together in conversation (*Frame worthy*, Rose had thought) and noticed that the one bar from the parking lot had disappeared.

Rose watched Thea stagger over to Anne and then. No. She tried to scream again but this time she couldn't even be sure she made a sound. The man had walked over and stood behind Thea for a moment, watching. For a split second, Rose had thought that maybe it had been an accident, them running into each other. Maybe she *was* being paranoid and the man was going to pull Anne up from the ground and apologize. And then, as if an afterthought, he reached back his hand and whacked Thea's head so hard that Rose saw her entire body lift off the ground and then collapse onto itself on the snow. A memory flashed into Rose's mind, an image really: the metro in Paris, the scuffed floor of the subway car, a door sliding shut, an automated voice speaking words she couldn't understand, and a businessman burying his head into the newspaper. She had visited Anne during her junior year abroad in Paris. Anne had called home in tears a few weeks into her stay—she was homesick, she couldn't under-stand anybody, and maybe she shouldn't have broken up with her college boyfriend after all. Rose believed that a good dose of tough love was sometimes necessary, but her daughter had sounded truly . . . alone. Rose wanted to visit Paris anyway; she'd never been to Eu-rope, never been outside of the Northeast, and the bakery was doing well enough. Sam stayed home to look after the dogs, and also to, as he said, "Give you two a little mother-daughter bonding time." Rose knew her husband was secretly relieved to have the dogs as a reason to stay behind. Sam recognized his strengths as a parent and, the older Anne got, the more he left the emotional counseling to Rose.

It was October, Anne had been there over a month and by that time her daughter knew her way around the 7th arrondissement, where she lived with her host family. Anne was ecstatic to see Rose, and it seemed that the security of having her mother there clicked everything into place. Her daughter introduced Rose to the local shopkeepers, they bought croissants and baguettes from the *boulange-rie* around the corner and walked thirty minutes to the Place des Vosges park, where they drank wine and ate cheese in the glint of the afternoon sun. Her daughter suddenly seemed extremely confident in her decision to break up with Chris, the college boyfriend: "He's suuuuuch a good guy, you know? But this is my time to be free, you know?"

The week was magic—Rose quickly understood why, as she walked along the cobblestone sidewalks arm in arm with her daugh-ter, Paris was nicknamed the "City of Love." On her last day, they decided to go to the famous antique market located at the top of Paris, about a half-hour metro ride from Rose's small hotel. Les Puces, it was called: the Fleas, the largest flea market in the world, where, according to Rose's guidebook to Paris, thousands of antique dealers set up shop selling everything from vintage clothing to dressers from the nineteenth century. On the train to the north of Paris, that afternoon, Rose spotted a man walking toward them from the opposite end of the subway car—Rose was positioned facing the man, whereas Anne had her back to him, gabbing to Rose about her French friend Marianne who was "So, so chic." He was homeless, that much was evident from his tattered clothing and the stench that immediately permeated the air as he approached them. As he drew nearer, Rose could hear that he was muttering under his breath in French, something that sounded like "salad" (later, she'd asked around and come to the conclusion that he had been murmuring *salope*—slut. A nasty-sounding word, Rose thought, in both languages). Rose kept her attention on Anne, but that familiar mixture of pity and uneasiness churned in her stomach. As he moved closer and closer in her peripheral vision, she made eye contact with the businessman across from them. Suddenly, the vagrant was standing right in front of them, unbuckling his pants.

"Mom?" Her nineteen-year-old daughter's question was half confusion, half fear, and to Rose she sounded ten years old again.

Rose looked again to the businessman, but he had the newspaper he'd been reading pulled up from his lap to his head, blocking his view completely of what was happening three feet away. Rose looked up at the homeless man and then slowly moved her eyes down to his hand holding his flaccid penis. He licked his lips and said the salad word once more and lurched toward Anne. Rose stood, before her brain registered what was happening, and put herself between Anne and the homeless man and screamed, "No!" She stepped toward him, inches from his member, and growled, "If you come any closer to my daughter, I will rip it off." Whatever was lost in translation was made up for in Rose's tone, stance, and expression. He pulled his pants up and ambled back the way he'd come. Later, she'd come to realize two truths from that incident: 1) she would do anything, *anything*, for her daughter, and 2) she could not count on others for help.

That memory flashed into Rose's mind as Thea's body hit the icy ground. Rose would also do anything to keep her granddaughter safe. Though she'd never said this aloud, the moment Thea entered the world, Rose felt a love coursing through her body that was different from what she felt for her own child. A love without her own ego in the mix, a love stripped to its purest form. She had already done the unthinkable once to protect this love, and she was prepared to do it again, if need be.

Rose stood very still. Although she understood it was the body's natural predisposition to panic, to launch into fight or flight, she believed more in her own self-discipline and she told herself very sternly *not* to panic. She quickly came up with the most viable solution to this problem. She was at a good distance from her girls and the man. Enough of a distance that if she ran back toward the parking lot, he would either let her go, allowing her to reach the parking lot and call for help, or he would chase her, thus giving the girls enough of a head start to disappear into the woods, though she wasn't sure how far Anne would make it carrying Thea . . . The plan wasn't perfect but it would have to do. Maybe she would run into another hiker on the way back, someone who could get back to the parking lot faster or get to Anne and Thea before the man . . . Her brain spun on this thought.

Focus, Rose, she told herself. She was about to turn on her heels when the man took out the gun and pointed it at the back of Anne's head and the plan changed.

Now she was running as fast as she could, which was a slow jog, toward the man and Anne and Thea. No one seemed to notice her, at least not Anne nor the man, until her voice broke the charged silence. Her lungs burned and she wanted to gasp for air but her tone had to be right.

"Anne, what are you guys doing?" It worked. Rose kept her eyes on Anne, but she felt the man snap his head toward her, disoriented, knocked out of his rage by the casual cheer in her voice. Rose moved her eyes to Thea. Her granddaughter had the appearance of someone in a deep sleep; not the stillness that happened almost immediately when life left a body. She felt a rush of relief so strong that her knees almost buckled, but she forced herself to stay upright. She tried to communicate to Anne with her eyes. *Thea will be ok. But we need to be smart.* Rose's eyes burned into Anne. The message was not received. Her daughter seemed to be in shock; Rose had seen Anne like this only once before. Rose wished she could shake Anne's mind back into her body: *We need all hands on deck right now, sweetheart.* Anne began to creep toward Thea again, and again the man's face filled with rage. He was going to do it, his finger was on the trigger. *What would Sam do right now?* Rose needed more time.

"Anne!"

"Stop. Fucking. Moving."

The urgency in her voice and the hollow calm in the man's seemed to shake her daughter back to the present. Anne raised her face first to Rose and then to the man. Rose saw the recognition register on her daughter's face when she saw the gun. She was no longer in control of this situation, not even a little bit. The man scooped Thea up as if she weighed nothing and placed the barrel of the gun against her granddaughter's pink cheek.

As they followed the man down the path, Rose began to plan.

ANNE

They walked for only a short distance. The man held Thea, Anne walked right behind, her eyes glued to Thea's legs and shoes, bouncing at each stride, and Rose rounded out the procession. The man took a sharp right off the main path, away from the river. At first she thought they were veering off into the middle of the woods, but a red arrow caught her eye and Anne realized they were still on a marked trail at least, though a "dangerous" one according to the maps. This trail was barely one person wide. Tree roots sprouted up out from the ground and branches snapped against their jackets. *How will he hike an advanced trail carrying Thea?* She pushed the thought out of her mind and focused on Thea's feet. She had to get her daughter to a hospital. Most likely she had a concussion, but there could be internal bleeding. A brain bleed. The words popped into her head before she could stop them. Memories from the NICU and Boston Children's Hospital flew through Anne's head. Oh god. She didn't notice that the man had stopped and she had to hitch herself back on her heels to avoid stepping on his boots. He turned his head to the left and then slowly to the right, as if he were looking for something. She tried to catch a glimpse of Thea's face, but her daughter's head was turned up to the sky and she could see only her chin. He wasn't supporting Thea's neck properly. She imagined lunging at him, knocking the gun from his hand and . . . then what? Before the sequence could go any further, the man started to move again. This time off the trail, into the woods. He walked quickly, weaving through the trees. Suddenly, Anne saw where he was going. At first just the dark roof and red clay chimney came into view through the trees. And then, as they crunched their way closer, the whole structure appeared. A small, squat log cabin, sitting peacefully in the woods.

THE MAN

The girl was lighter than he expected. Even bundled in her oversize winter coat and lace-up boots, he carried her easily on the short walk. The women trudged behind him, the mother right behind him, close on his heels, and the older one farther behind, struggling to keep up. The man had made a calculation to bring the women along and he was pleased with his decision. Shooting the gun could have attracted stray hikers or the couple with the dog he'd seen in the parking lot. But more than that, he thought they might be useful, especially considering the girl was unconscious. He hoped she wasn't hurt badly. As he led them into the woods, he glanced at the body in his arms every few minutes—he needed to reassure himself by checking the tiny spurts of white air coming out of her nose. Every time he saw her breath, his pulse slowed and a warm feeling grew in his stomach; she was alive. He had been alone his entire life and now he had her and everything would be different.

He kept his eyes on the trail markings. The map plastered on the side of the welcome center had shown the hut, marked by a brown triangle sitting on a brown square, about a quarter mile after the start of the first red trail, set back a few hundred feet into the woods. The man grew agitated the longer they walked. They should have found it by now or at least seen signs. He wondered if the map was wrong—if the building had been torn down years ago or maybe he'd missed it somehow, maybe while he was looking at the girl. He cursed under his breath; this wouldn't work without the cabin. He heard muffled whispers over the wind whipping his face. Someone was taunting him, telling him that he should have used the gun in the parking lot. He stopped abruptly and listened. He shut his eyes closed for one second, disgusted with himself. He had failed; he'd been given a gift and he had squandered it. *I am calm. I feel nothing.* The gun burned his hand. The man opened his eyes and they fell on a small square sign, posted to a tree only a few feet ahead. The sign showed a crudely drawn house and an arrow pointing to the right. Painted blue letters on the arrow spelled out WARMING HUT.

The man didn't believe in a higher power, but he couldn't help but feel this was preordained. He turned to the right and began walking, his step light, his mind clear. He felt the girl's stringy hair brush against his hand and he checked, once again, to be sure she was breathing. The man had restrained himself for so long, had buried his nature for ten years because he had no choice, and now he was being given one last chance.

THE CABIN

ANNE

They approached the cabin and the man put Thea down in a heap on the small deck that wrapped around the front. Anne burned to reach out and touch her daughter's forehead, to wrap her arms around her daughter's body, and to listen to her chest as it rose up and down, but she ground her teeth and stayed where she was, a few feet behind the man. Anne watched him test the front door—first pressing against it firmly with one hand and then heaving his body against it. Once, twice, he slammed his body into the door. On the third smash something gave way with a *pop* and the door flung open. He motioned with the gun, still in his right hand, for her and Rose to enter first.

Anne walked into the small one-room cabin first, with Rose right behind, and took in the space before turning her eyes back to the man and Thea still on the porch. The floors were covered in a layer of dirt and grit, the windows so dirty they were almost opaque. There were two wooden chairs, barely still pieced together, the bottom slats sagging to the ground. It must have been a warming cabin, at one point, for hikers and campers, but judging from the condition, no one had been in charge of its upkeep for years. Anne watched her breath form a ring of smoke in the air. She couldn't be sure, time had morphed from a straight line into loops and spikes, but she calculated that it must have been between three and four p.m., judging from the dim glint of light in the trees. The man's gray sweater had ridden up from carrying Thea, exposing white skin burned red from the cold, and Anne had a sudden thought that maybe he would catch hypothermia and then realized that, though her daughter was bundled in a winter coat and mittens (thank god those had stayed on), her small body was the least likely to survive the cold.

Anne and her mother waited in the middle of the one-room cabin. The man bent over and scooped Thea back up. Anne wanted to hurl herself at him and claw at his face until he released her daughter. Instead, she clenched her jaw. He crossed the threshold and looked from Rose to Anne, as if suddenly aware of their existence. "Sit," he commanded, nodding to the back of the cabin. Anne lifted her eyes to his face quickly. Dark hair, forming a peak at the top of his head, and a thick beard masked most of his face. She and Rose backed up and sat against the wall farthest from the door. The man seemed to be considering where to put Thea. He walked to the right of the door and then paused.

"She needs body heat." Anne opened her arms and felt Rose stiffen beside her. She was desperate to hold her daughter; she had no thoughts beyond that—as if her touch alone would transport them to some other reality.

"Don't talk." He hesitated but then moved toward them. Anne held her breath as he lowered Thea's body into her arms. She kept her eyes on her daughter and tried not to flinch as his hands brushed

94

her arms. Thea was warmer than she was expecting, and her chest rose and fell steadily. She noticed something in the man's face before she dropped her eyes. She felt a spark of hope.

The man paced the opposite side of the cabin, muttering. Anne could make out "I told them. I fucking told them not to . . ." She closed her eyes. The man didn't look familiar, but . . . Was this her worst nightmare coming true? An ex-husband or boyfriend of one of her patients? She glanced at him again quickly, this time searching the parts of his face not covered in beard. His eyes revealed his youth; she guessed he was early to mid-twenties. She ran through her current list of clients in her head. No, all the women she was seeing were in their thirties or older. And this young man struck her as wild, manic, and unkempt to the point of being squalid—not the ex-partner of a well-to-do Burlington woman. So, this was random—a random act of violence. She exhaled. She could do this. She had counseled dozens of women, and several men, in abusive relationships. Though she rarely made face-to-face contact with their partners (her practice specialized in extricating oneself from a toxic relationship, not saving it), she was versed in the personality traits that often accompanied mentally and physically abusive partners. Each client's circumstances and backgrounds differed substantially, but there were common threads that seemed to be woven into every relationship. The thickest, brightest thread being that the abuser, no matter how horrific his actions, believed himself to be a victim. And she had had her own personal experience with abuse, but this man was not Ethan. She glanced at the man again quickly—he paced near the door, his movements manic, and shook his head back and forth, muttering under his breath. No, this man was not Ethan. She held on to that thought and opened her eyes. She could do this.

"Where are you from?" Anne asked softly. The man was still pacing and talking to himself. At the sound of her voice, he spun around. "Shut the fuck up shut the fuck up shut the fuck up," the words came out rapid-fire.

Tears stung her eyes. She looked down at Thea and watched her breath come out into the room in a tiny cloud. A thought passed clearly through Anne's mind: *You are useless and weak.* She had never been able to protect her daughter; in fact, she had put Thea in danger even before she was born. How could she have thought she could save her daughter from this man when she couldn't save Thea from Ethan? She gave in to the tears that had been building and put her head to her knees. All these years later and she was going to fail again.

FOURTEEN YEARS
BEFORE THE CABIN

ANNE

Anne met Thea's father when she was twenty-five. She had moved to New York straight from college—not because New York was the place where all her dreams would come true, like so many other young people in the city, but because she was able to jump on the train from SUNY New Paltz to the city for job interviews her senior year; she wanted to have a job at a law firm lined up right after graduation. It was the compromise she had made with herself—she hadn't taken the LSATs or started applying to law school during senior year, but she would work as a paralegal for a year or two, get some hands-on experience, and then apply. In hindsight, perhaps not so much a compromise as tapping the brakes, unsure that she really wanted to be an attorney. Anne only knew that she wanted to make a lot of money—though the bakery was booming now, she had watched Rose struggle for years and witnessed Sam grapple to secure carpentry jobs each month for as long as she could remember. That would never be her. She would be able to pay her mortgage with money tucked away for future vacations. Her kids would be able to pick any college they wanted, not base their decisions on the financial aid package. And so, lawyer it was—at least, that's what Anne told herself as she filled out paperwork, scanned documents, and ate dinner at her computer each night (it was free if she stayed past eight p.m.). Three years later, she still worked as a paralegal at a boutique law firm that specialized in financial transactions, supporting a team of four attorneys, three men and one woman, all in their late thirties, all making close to half a million dollars a year, and all completely and utterly miserable.

"Run, Anne," Paul whispered, early on, at the end of a meeting. "There's still hope for you."

"I would do literally anything else," Stephanie echoed two years later, pouring herself a cup of lukewarm coffee in the kitchen at three p.m. "Anything. It wouldn't even have to pay." She dumped four creams into her mug and swirled the liquid around thoughtfully. "Well, that's actually not true. I have a million-dollar mortgage on my apartment, so I guess it would have to pay."

When Anne was sent to Ethan's firm to drop off signature pages three years into the job at the law firm, panic about her chosen career had set in fully. She'd told her parents that she'd been studying hard for the LSATs, when in reality, the fat, red book remained shiny and untouched on her coffee table.

"Hi, I'm here from Thatcher and Reed. Just dropping off some paperwork for . . ." She looked down at the envelope. "Rob Yoon." The receptionist, an older man with white hair, asked for her license, told her to "Look into the camera," printed out a sticker with her face on it, and sent her to the elevator bank. "You want the twenty-sixth floor," he called out as she wavered. She turned right and dashed into the box just as the door was sliding closed.

"You know these doors don't have motion sensors," the man already in the elevator said. "Could have lost an arm . . . or more."

"Are you serious?" Anne reflexively rubbed her upper arm. "That seems like a serious safety violation."

"I'm kidding," he said, then broke out laughing. "By the way, which floor?"

She spun around to look at him and gave a short laugh. As soon as she saw the man standing behind her, she flushed, turned back around, and stared straight ahead. "Twenty-six, please."

"Perfect, you're on the express." He had thick, dark hair, a slight dimple in his chin, and clear blue eyes.

Anne looked at the wall of numbers. Twenty-six glowed bright yellow. "Thanks." She glanced back at him over her shoulder and tried to give a casual smile. Her heart thudded in her chest.

When the doors opened, she stepped out tentatively; they were in a hallway that led to giant glass doors in both directions. The man stepped around Anne and strode to the left. At the glass door, he turned. "Where are you going?"

"I'm dropping something off for Rob Yoon?" It came out as a question.

"Ah, other way then." He walked toward her.

Her brain went static and she overcorrected her nerves by responding with a sharp, "Got it," and turned on her heels toward the other set of doors.

On the way out, while Anne was waiting for the elevator to take her back to the lobby, one of the glass doors opened and the same man was striding toward her again.

"I saw you leaving and wanted to give you my card." He looked nervous now. His nervousness gave her confidence. She smiled. "Oh, that won't be necessary. I think I have everything I need from Mr. Yoon." His face fell and then righted itself quickly into a small smile.

"Right. Ok. I actually meant—"

"I'm kidding." She grinned and took his card, touching his fingers lightly. A tingle traveled up her body.

"I suppose I deserved that," he said with a wink. And then, "I'm Ethan. I really hope you get in touch."

THE CABIN

ROSE

Rose shut her eyes, willing her daughter to be quiet. "Shut the fuck up shut the fuck up," the man spat the words out. Rose moved her eyes to Anne: *Don't*. But Anne had her face down, staring intently at Thea. Rose had been developing a plan and it didn't involve her daughter psychoanalyzing the man. She needed the man to leave the room so that she could communicate with Anne. By the looks of him pacing the room in small circles, like a caged animal, it seemed possible that he would leave them for a few minutes eventually. Rose didn't know exactly what he wanted with them, but she didn't need to know—she knew enough about what people were capable of, and she needed to get her daughter and granddaughter out of the cabin before his intentions clarified. She remembered back to the Facebook article she had clicked on: "Women—read this, your life may depend on it," one of those clickbait titles meant to terrorize you into reading, but it had worked. The article hadn't been revolutionary, but it had reinforced what she already understood—action, you must act—in a situation like this, the worst thing you could do was nothing. Of course, easier said than done when a twelve-year-old has been knocked unconscious by a gun-wielding maniac.

Rose pictured Sam sitting next to her on the cabin floor, stroking her arm calmly with strong, calloused fingers. Her husband would know what to do and she tried to still her mind, hoping for some divine inspiration. Sam's character was a blend of integrity, intelligence, and action—he meant what he said and he acted with care and precision. So few men had these qualities nowadays, or at least the blend of all three. *Shame*, Rose thought. Her neighbors, a lovely family of four, let their lawn grow out until the kids could practically get lost in the tallest weeds. The husband worked from home, some sort of tech job, and yet he couldn't seem to work a lawn mower on a consistent basis. Sam, on the other hand, had always kept their house and lawn pristine. It was who he was: thorough, foresighted. Rose squeezed her eyes shut. *Sam, are there holes in my plan?*

Rose was deep in her thoughts when the man turned toward them. "Do not move." He cracked the front door of the cabin open, peered outside, and then pulled it open wider. "Do not fucking move," he repeated, and then slipped into the dark. Rose's heart thudded, adrenaline rushed through her body. Now. They had to act now.

"Anne, when he comes back, I'm going to surprise him—throw my body at him when he walks in the front door." Her words came out in a rush and sounded silly even to her own ears, like an amateur actor on stage rehearsing a fight sequence out loud.

"Mom, no." Anne said the words like they were final. "We don't even know what he wants," she whispered. "Before, when he brought Thea to me, I swear to god he looked like he thought he'd made a mistake. I think I can talk to him . . . get him to let us go . . ." Her voice trailed off.

"That is not how these situations work," Rose whispered back. "Why do you think he brought us here?" She let the question hang in the air. "We have to *do* something. Something he doesn't expect."

Anne nodded toward Thea. "And how are we supposed to do that with Thea unconscious?" She took a breath and they both listened. Footsteps crunched toward the front door. "Just, please. I can do this, Mom."

The door opened. They fell quiet. Rose watched their breaths travel up toward the ceiling and disappear. It had only been a few minutes since they were forced off the trail and the temperature had already plummeted. They were going to freeze to death. Rose closed her eyes again. She prayed that Anne was right—that the man was rethinking his decision to bring two women and an unconscious child to an abandoned cabin. Perhaps he really would let them go, or run himself right out of the mess he had created. But with Ethan, no amount of waiting, or reasoning, had made any difference.

ROSE

She had met Ethan for the first time when Anne brought him home for Thanksgiving. Anne had only been dating this new boy for a handful of months and Rose had said jokingly, in an effort to dissuade Anne from bringing a stranger to Thanksgiving, "Don't you think you should let him get to know you a little bit better before he meets the whole family?" They both knew she was referring to Sam, who could be a scathing judge of character, in his quiet, reserved way. Anne had sighed over the phone. "Mom. I really like him and you guys will, too. I promise. I'm bringing him."

And she had been right, for the most part. Ethan was handsome and charming and helpful. Setting the table and running to the oven.

"I got it, Mrs. Thompson." He had smiled, whisking the oven mitt out of her hand and removing the turkey carefully from the oven, a bead of sweat forming on his brow.

She had smiled back and said, "Why, thank you!" and hoped that it sounded genuine. Because he was a lovely boy, or man, she should say (thirty-five years old, ten years older than Anne; though, according to

Anne, that was nothing at all, especially for New York City), but there was something about him that made her uneasy. He clearly adored Anne, he had made partner at his investment bank just this past month, almost unheard of for someone his age, and his manners were impeccable. But. Rose couldn't put her finger on it, and so she swallowed it down and laughed and chatted over Thanksgiving dinner and tried to convince herself that this was "the one," as Anne had confided to her earlier that day. "I know it's soon to say that," Anne had said sheepishly, "but I just *feel* it."

Her daughter had "just known" once before, with the boyfriend before Ethan. Three years ago, Rose and Sam had visited their daughter in her first apartment in New York. Anne had gushed over the phone about the new guy she was seeing and how excited she was for her parents to meet him, but when Rose and Sam showed up to the restaurant that evening, on the Upper West Side where they were all meeting for dinner, Anne arrived alone, eyes puffy and red.

"We're done," Anne had said over dinner, voice wavering, betraying the confidence of her words. "I honestly want nothing to do with him. Ever. Again." She swabbed a piece of bread into the pool of olive oil on her plate. "He's so messed up."

"What happened, honey?" Rose had asked, glancing at Sam with a raised brow.

Sam had added, "Sorry to hear that, Anne. Seemed like you liked the guy."

At this, Anne's eyes welled with tears again. "I did. I really did. But then today, we were hanging out and he was like, 'I think I'm too young to be in a monogamous relationship.'" Anne rolled her eyes. "We're twenty-two, not nineteen."

Rose and Sam shared a discreet look of amusement before Rose responded, "Well, that's too bad. It sounds like he's confused about what he wants. But there are plenty of guys in the city. And you know what? You should enjoy being single right now! You're so young. I mean"—she kept a straight face—"you're not nineteen, but you're still young."

"Your mom is absolutely right. Live it up, Anne," Sam talked while poring over the wine list.

"Yeah, you guys are right," Anne said forcefully. "I just hope Drew gets a venereal disease."

"Anne!" Sam's baritone layered over Rose's exclamation. But they were both relieved—their daughter tended to put all her energy into whatever passion project she was working on at the moment—and now that energy could be funneled into her paralegal job and exploring a new city.

The next morning, Rose and Sam met Anne for breakfast at a touristy place near their hotel. When they walked into the restaurant, Rose saw her daughter sitting at a table in the middle of the room, glowing.

"Hi, honey, you look wonderful!" Rose hugged her daughter and settled into her seat at the table.

"Drew came over last night." Anne beamed.

"The guy with the venereal disease?" Sam asked as Rose said, "Oh. Wow."

"Dad." Anne laughed. "He begged for me to give him another chance. And he said"—Anne paused here and took a breath—"he got scared because he has such strong feelings for me."

"Oh boy," Sam said as Rose responded, "You seem really happy. Just take things slow and see what happens."

"I am. I am so happy. I think this could really be something . . ." Anne picked up her menu, still smiling with all her teeth.

That relationship followed an up-and-down, off-and-on, emotional roller-coaster progression for two years, until Anne had walked in on her boyfriend in bed with two other women and finally realized that Drew hadn't been lying when he'd said he thought he was too young to be monogamous.

Ethan seemed a large step up from Drew, and Rose could see why her daughter was so taken with him, especially after her prior relationship. Ethan knew himself and he seemed to know he wanted Anne. It must have felt wonderful, after Drew, to meet someone so self-assured, so confident, and so *sure* of what he wanted. And then, that night as she was reading her novel, a thriller about a woman who witnessed a terrible crime, it occurred to Rose: Ethan reminded her of Peter. His easy smile, his loud laugh, the way he tried so hard to please everyone. He reminded her of the man she had loved before Sam. They had met outside of a Pizza Hut restaurant. It was winter and it was one of those winters in Vermont, less and less typical these days, when snowstorm after snowstorm dumped more than six feet of snow onto the ground. Snowplows and shovels pushed and heaved the snow into piles lining the sidewalks and into mounds in the middle of parking lots. Rose was driving the car her parents had sold her when she turned eighteen, with the stipulation that she paid its bluebook's worth, plus a small amount of interest each month. The night she met Peter, she left class, climbed into the old car she thought of as new, and went directly to Pizza Hut. Every Friday night she stopped and picked up one cheese (for herself and two younger sisters) and one pepperoni, mushroom, and green pepper pizza (for her parents). It had snowed heavily in the morning and tapered off by the afternoon, and, that Friday night, even though the three young male staff had arrived early for their shifts to shovel snow from the parking lot, revealing faint white parking lines for cars to tuck into, there was still a solid foot of snow that covered the entry of the restaurant from the road. Rose waited at the light for the arrow to turn green; the blinker made a sharp clicking sound in her ears as she surveyed the mound of snow that her car would have to clear. The light changed and she swung the steering wheel to the left, tapping the gas as her tires rolled over the small snowbank. She felt a hard metal crunch and the steering wheel jerked in the opposite direction. Rose calmly steered the car into a parking space at the far end of the parking lot and exited the car. She looked at the slash in the back tire and then looked toward the snowbank. The curb peeked out from where her tires had cut through the snow. Rose sighed and crossed her arms. She walked, arms still crossed, into the restaurant.

"Excuse me. I seem to have driven my car right over the curb. The snow was covering it completely." She looked accusingly at the young man behind the counter. "My back tire has a large gash in it." She led the man, boy really—he looked to be about her age when she glanced at him out of the side of her eye—outside to her car. He looked at her tire and laughed. "You're not going anywhere with that, huh?" Rose glared at him and shivered. It was starting to snow again in big, fat flakes. By the time he had fiddled around in the trunk of the car, plucking out a tire that looked like a toy, and some tools she didn't even know were stored in a secret compartment, he had apologized a dozen times. By the time he had unscrewed the gashed tire and fastened the spare in place, the knees of his gray slacks were soaked through and his hands were red and stiff from the cold.

"Thank you, I'm sorry I was . . . irritated before. It's just that my parents have only just sold me this car and I panicked." Rose looked down at the boy tightening the bolts a final time, and noticed for the first time since she approached him at the Pizza Hut counter that he had perfectly shaped dark eyebrows, a square jaw, and curly brown hair that fell just past his eyes. She smiled. "I'm Rose, by the way."

"Hi, Rose. I'm Peter." He sprung himself up off the ground and reached out a frozen hand, grinning with his teeth; his smile lit up his whole face and shone right through his eyes. "Your pizza is on me tonight."

Peter had grown up in St. George, one of the smallest towns in Vermont. When he wasn't working at Pizza Hut, he was on his way to becoming a journalist, taking on local culture assignments for the hometown paper. He was the smartest boy Rose had ever met; when they talked, lying with their faces inches apart on his bed, she felt she was learning something new, seeing the world in a different way. He used words that she'd only read in thick books, and he listened intently when she spoke, as if her words held some universal wisdom that even she couldn't quite grasp. Peter felt like her destiny, like everything that had happened before him was not actually made up of meaningful moments or experiences after all but only a dull period of waiting for him to appear.

Peter swept her off her feet so completely that when she found out she was pregnant, just three months into the relationship and one year into nursing school, she was thrilled. He was too, or at least he said he was, wrapping her in his arms and whispering, "I'm going to do this right."

She hadn't thought that was an odd thing to say. Or that Peter must already have been terrified he was going to screw things up. He never told her much about his past but he alluded to "difficult things" in his childhood that had made prior relationships impossible. "But not this time. This time is different," he had said. And she had believed him.

They moved into a small apartment, close to Rose's school, and the heady infatuation they had both felt for the past three months seemed to morph overnight into a sort of slow-moving dread until, by the time she miscarried a month later, she felt for sure that the baby had felt her mounting panic and decided to dislodge itself, rather than come into their world. She knew that wasn't medically possible, but she had never quite been able to shake the belief. She recognized all the symptoms she had learned about earlier that year (heavy bleeding, severe cramping, nausea). She called Peter from the toilet and left a shaky message: "Meet me at the hospital. I'm losing the baby."

The first time she told the nurse that her boyfriend would be coming soon, the nurse believed her. "I'll keep an eye out," she had said, giving Rose's hand a squeeze. By the fourth "He's coming," the nurse looked at her sadly and nodded, wiping the cold sweat from her forehead. "Just try to rest, sweetie."

The months that followed were a dark blur. She never saw Peter again. He had left town by the time she got home. His belongings removed from the apartment so precisely that she wondered if she had imagined the whole relationship, though she had an ache in her gut that proved otherwise. She thought of Peter, and of Claire (she had decided the baby was a girl), constantly for months. And then when she started to fail her nursing exams and had to drop out of school, she decided that that was enough. Every time Peter or Claire popped into her head she picked them up and placed them into a box (in her mind the box was blue with a white bow), until eventually they stayed there, in that box, and she could choose when to take them out, which was almost never.

She met Sam two years later at the bakery where she worked, first as a cashier and then as one of the morning bakers. Sam came in to get coffee every morning. He was quiet and slow-moving, his energy so different from that of the frenetic buzzing that had vibrated out of Peter. She found out by asking around that he was in his late twenties and an ex-marine, a scout sniper (which didn't mean anything to Rose until she saw the reactions of other servicemen and -women when Sam would reluctantly reveal his designation); Rose found out later that he'd been medically discharged after losing sight in one eye. After he left the marines, he moved to Charlotte because "it seemed like a town where not much happens." He took his attention to exacting detail and applied it to carpentry. Instead of spending hours crouched on the ground, measuring how many millimeters a light wind to the east would skew his bullet, he spent hours in his shop, carving and sawing and sanding wood into exquisite pieces of furniture.

It took Sam sixteen coffees and a combined hour and a half worth of small talk to gather the courage to ask Rose out on a date. They took things slow. Rose liked slow; slow felt safe. She wasn't sure that this man would stand the test of time, but selfishly, Rose decided that Sam was exactly what she needed after Peter. She didn't feel butterflies and her stomach didn't do loops when he reached for her hand during the movies, but she felt her insides relax when they were together, as if her body knew something her mind had yet to acknowledge. And then one night in bed, a year into their courtship, they cracked each other open. She told him about the baby she had lost and he told her about the friend he had lost, not even in a fight, but by stepping on a land mine, just a few feet from where Sam stood. Sam had only lost sight in one eye from flying debris; his friend had been cut in half. After that she stopped being afraid he would leave, like Peter did, because they had shown each other their hidden parts, and they had both decided there was more beauty in those parts than fear. She understood then that magic could come in many forms.

Lying in bed that Thanksgiving night, she took Peter out of the box for a moment and spun him around in her head, looking at him from all angles. Yes, it was uncanny, the similarities between Peter and Ethan, and once she saw them, she couldn't unsee them. She had forgiven Peter long ago—they were both so young and he had tried, she knew he had really tried, but in the end, he couldn't overcome whatever demons he had kept hidden from her. Still, she didn't want the same kind of man for Anne—a brightly burning spark of a man that fizzles out just as fast as he catches. She tossed and turned all night, fretting about whether to say anything to Anne. But what would she say? *Your boyfriend reminds me of my ex that I've never told you about who abandoned me while I bled out our child in the hospital?*

By the time she woke up, she felt a vague panic but was no closer to deciding what to do about Ethan. She walked into the kitchen. The concentrated, early morning sun shone a beam of light straight through the room and illuminated Ethan drinking a cup of coffee at the table, still extended with the leaf Sam had brought up from the basement. He looked small sitting at the long table all alone, and the picture she had drawn of him last night in her head suddenly seemed silly and dramatic compared to this human man in front of her. His face lit up when he saw her. "Good morning, Rose. I made coffee."

She never said a word to Anne. Two years later, when she got the call from the hospital, she realized she'd been wrong about her son-in-law. Yes, she could admit that to herself. Ethan wasn't anything like Peter. He was something else entirely.

FOURTEEN YEARS
BEFORE THE CABIN

ANNE

They went to brunch on their first date. She had e-mailed him the same night they met; she waited six hours and then couldn't wait any longer, her stomach flipping as she sent off her number with a quick note, It's the elevator girl. He texted ten minutes later. What are you doing tomorrow morning? She would have recoiled at the suggestion of brunch for a first date from any other guy. It seemed so intimate, so exposed. But as soon as she slid into the booth of the diner Ethan suggested, Anne felt at ease, like she was home. They laughed over eggs and coffee, not talking about anything at all, nothing she could remember anyway. Afterward they walked around the city for hours. It was a perfect spring day—winter had finally given way to consistently warm days and the oppressive heat of the summer was still months away. They talked about their childhoods (she grew up in a farmhouse in Vermont, he on an actual farm in Indiana), what they missed most about their hometowns (her: the smell of the air, him: his dog), and what they loved about living in New York (this they agreed on: that the city, though it could feel harsh and cold and overwhelming, was the most exhilarating place either of them had ever been).

At one point Ethan stopped in the middle of the street and turned to her. "Ok, Anne, I want to hear your deepest, darkest secret. You tell me yours and I'll tell you mine. Let's just get it out of the way."

"Wow. Deepest, darkest secret. Great first-date question." She laughed. "Hmm. Ok, my deepest, darkest secret." She took a breath. She hadn't said this out loud yet. "I don't think I want to be a lawyer." It had been weighing on her, eating away at her thoughts, and in that moment, at the age of twenty-five, it felt like her whole world was hinging on the decision about law school.

Ethan put his arm around her and pulled her close. "Annie, if that's your deepest, darkest secret, I think you're going to be ok."

She felt her body relax. He was right. She suddenly knew without a doubt that if she was with Ethan, it would be ok.

"Your turn."

"I have no soul," he deadpanned.

"Ah! So that's why your eyes are completely black?"

"Exactly." He broke his blank stare with a chuckle and then fell quiet for a moment. "I haven't told anyone this, but I know it destroyed my parents when I left home. I think that's my darkest secret." He glanced at the ground. "And because of that, I don't really visit. I feel too guilty. I mean, I send money and we talk on the phone sometimes, but . . ." He shook his head. "They don't understand me. No one in my family does—no one in my family has ever left the Midwest. I don't know . . ." His voice trailed off. "I'm sorry, was that too much?"

"Of course not. I want to know everything about you." It was out of her mouth before she could stop it, and she felt color seep into her cheeks. "Sorry, now I'm saying too much."

Ethan laughed. "Not at all. This doesn't feel like a first date, does it? I feel like we've known each other much longer."

Anne smiled shyly. "Me, too."

A month later, she was spending almost every night at his apartment. A year later they were engaged.

They were married in a park overlooking Lake Champlain. It was early summer. Anne would be pregnant with Thea in six months' time. The night before the wedding, Anne stayed at an inn attached to an old red barn where the reception would be held; her six bridesmaids—she still had close friends at that point—arrived the morning of with their lavender strapless dresses in garment bags and pouches of makeup tucked under their armpits. The six of them crammed into the small yellow inn room and avoided each other's elbows as they changed from jeans and T-shirts into gowns. Anne stood still, holding her breath, as a couple of them wove the lace ribbon along the back of the corset bodice of her dress, yanking it tight at the bottom and tying it into a knotted bow. Two more fussed with the veil, securing it onto stiff strands of hair and then dusting the sides of her head once more with hairspray. One of Anne's bridesmaids, a friend since elementary school named Whitney, set up shop in the bathroom as the in-house makeup artist.

"I'm sorry to make you work on my wedding day, Whit. Here, chug this," Anne said, shoving a glass of champagne into her friend's left hand, which was momentarily void of brushes and creams and glitter. Whitney set the glass down on the bathroom counter. "I'll drink after. And stop, I offered. This is my wedding present to you. Just relax and enjoy yourself." Whitney said all this with a furrowed brow, not looking at Anne but at the face in front of her. She finally clucked in disapproval. "Can I pluck your eyebrows?" she said to Lana, a college friend with dark brown eyes and a long, thick black braid running down her back. "I'm going to say no to that," Lana replied dryly.

"Ok, then you're done. NEXT!" Whit scooted her off the chair and motioned to the next in line.

Lana sidled up next to Anne and rolled her eyes. "Just FYI, the full-brow look is in right now."

Anne laughed. "Whit is just very no bullshit. She wasn't trying to insult you. I think she just wants everyone to have the same look, you know?" She felt her heart flutter nervously. She had been taking constant stock of all the different personalities coming together today and playing peacemaker amongst her friends from home and college.

Lana smiled. "I'm not offended, Anne. I'm amused. It's incredible that she offered to do makeup for everyone." Whitney had spent an hour and a half on the bride's hair and makeup, leaving her an hour to do everyone else. Anne and Lana looked at the four bridesmaids still waiting to have their makeup done as Whitney worked slowly and meticulously on Theresa, who sat with her eyes closed in a state of bliss as Whitney softly brushed foundation on her cheeks.

"I think Theresa's gonna need a cigarette after this. Look at her face. I think she's climaxing," Lana whispered.

"I heard that," Theresa said from the chair. "And, yes, this feels fucking gooooood," she sang. "Please, don't ever stop," she groaned with her eyes closed.

"Ok, I'm glad you're enjoying yourself, but we have"—Anne picked up her phone and turned it over—"an hour before we have to leave for the ceremony. So. Whit. You're doing so amazing, but—"

"Yeah, yeah, ok, I'll speed it up." She stepped back and peered at Theresa's face. "Goddammit I'm good." She whistled to herself.

"Are you excited? How are you feeling?" Lana asked in the dry monotone that Anne had finally gotten used to after rooming together their freshman year. Lana hovered closer and Anne inhaled her slightly musky scent. It reminded her of twin beds and deep purple sheets and listening to soft guitar playing into the wee hours of the morning.

"I *am* excited. I feel a bit nervous, but mostly excited," she said. "I'm meeting Ethan's parents for the first time today." She looked across the room to the full-length mirror on the bathroom door, swung open against the wall. She saw a woman in white, serene and radiant.

"What? You're meeting them today? On your wedding day?" Lana's tone changed almost imperceptibly at the end of her questions, deepening an octave. By now Anne knew that the slight variation in her monotone signified shock. Lana had met Ethan several times, along with her other bridesmaids, either in the city or at home in Vermont. The first time Anne introduced Lana to Ethan, at a dim, crowded bar on the Lower East Side, Anne had been nervous—usually she had a sense of what the dynamic would be like amongst her friends, but in this case, she had no idea what to expect. Lana's taste in people was discerning and, Anne had noticed over the years, her directness made people uncomfortable, sometimes even combative. As Anne had chatted with Lana's boyfriend, Steve, she'd strained over the din of the bar to hear Ethan and Lana's conversation, but could only see glimpses of Ethan's face, serious and intense, behind Steve's head. At the end of the night, Anne hugged Lana goodbye and heard in her ear her friend's raspy voice: "Interesting guy. I think you should keep him."

But Anne hadn't told Lana or any of her friends that she had yet to meet Ethan's parents. It happened all the time, she told herself; couples didn't meet each other's family for various reasons—maybe they lived in another country or were too sick to travel. Some halves of a couple would never meet their significant others' parents. They were lucky that both sets of their parents were alive and healthy. But that was the thing—Ethan's parents were alive and well, and yet she knew almost nothing about them, other than what Ethan had told her on their first date. She asked Ethan occasionally, at the beginning of their relationship, about his parents: What do they do for work? What are their personalities like? When are they going to visit? Ethan responded vaguely that his dad ran the family farm, his mom had been a stay-at-home parent, and both of them, but particularly his mom, had a fear of flying. After Anne pushed for more details, Ethan responded quietly, "I just don't fit into their world anymore. They think I've sold my soul to the devil . . . or Wall Street." He sighed. "We've never understood one another. I'm sorry, it puts me in a bad mood to talk about it." He looked down at the floor, and she felt a sharp pang of guilt for needling him about a topic that clearly caused him pain. "But you know what puts me in a great mood?" He paused for dramatic effect and then tackled her on the couch. "You."

She never brought up his family again.

Now, she struggled to explain to Lana why it wasn't odd at all that she'd never met her fiancé's family. "They live in the Midwest and don't like to travel so they haven't visited us in New York yet. They were supposed to fly in last night but their flight got delayed and then canceled." She jammed her words together without taking a breath. "But they got an early morning flight from O'Hare so they should be landing just about now."

"Huh. Interesting." Lana was back to monotone.

Anne picked up her phone off the bedside table and texted Ethan, Have your parents landed? She glanced down occasionally as Lana rambled on about the food co-op she and her boyfriend, Steve, had joined in Brooklyn. Anne nodded and asked about the gardening lessons they were taking together to grow organic vegetables. She hadn't heard from Ethan since yesterday morning when they kissed goodbye before going to their separate hotels. She picked up her phone again. No response from Ethan. Then again, he was probably busy getting ready himself, with his three groomsmen (all of them colleagues from the bank), at the hotel where the four of them stayed last night. She couldn't explain why she felt so anxious. *Everything is fine.* Right as she was about to place her phone back on the table, she saw the dots of Ethan typing. She waited for his response, staring at the screen, barely listening to Lana's description of the best type of soil for a vegetable garden.

Just then, Rose popped her head into the room. "Ten-minute warning, girls." Rose gasped when she saw Anne. "Oh my goodness. You look beautiful. You all look so beautiful."

"Mrs. Thompson, don't cry yet." Theresa rushed to Rose and squeezed her tight. "You gotta save those tears for the vows."

Anne looked at her phone—no dots, no text—and strode toward

the bathroom, calling out, "Five-minute warning, guys" and then back to the bedside table, peering down at her phone. She was being silly, paranoid. Everything was fine. She ran through a list of reasons in her head why everything was fine and tried to shake the sick feeling from her stomach. Just then, a text from Ethan flashed across screen.

They're here. See you soon, Mrs. Mills ☺

A burst of air escaped her body. She wasn't even annoyed this time that Ethan seemingly refused to acknowledge that she was keeping her last name: Thompson. "Ok, everyone, time to go!"

"Let's fucking do this thing!" Whitney yelled as all six bridesmaids tumbled out of the room and into the hallway. "Oh my gosh, I'm so sorry, Mrs. Thompson." Whitney slapped her hand over her mouth, blushing deeply.

Rose grabbed Whitney's hand and swung it in the air. "You're not the first person to drop the f-bomb in front of me. I'm married to an ex-marine, you know."

They exited the inn and walked down a gray stone pathway to the last bus, waiting on the circular driveway in front of the barn. The morning had been overcast, the sky coated in gray, a slight chill in the air, but now Anne shielded her eyes as the sun suddenly broke through.

"Congratulations!" the bus driver hollered as Anne boarded. She beamed, the nerves starting to leave and her body filling with excitement.

Rose and Sam sat at the front of the bus chatting with the driver, and the bridesmaids and bride filled the last rows. Anne looked out of the back window as they rumbled toward the park and watched the weathered red barn fade into the distance in a cloud of chalky smoke. Whit grinned from across the aisle. "Ready?"

"Yes!" she shouted back.

Hours later, at the reception, Anne put her arm through Ethan's. "Where are your parents?" She had glimpsed them at the ceremony, sitting in the front row, across the aisle from Rose and Sam, in their marked seats. "Should we go find them?" Ethan opened his lips and tipped a brown bottle back, draining the contents. He stood silent for a moment, looking around at the crowd, and then grabbed her hand. "All right, let's go."

They wove through the guests, over the empty portable wooden dance floor, past the bar area, and came out at a quiet expanse, filled with white-clothed round tables. Most of the guests were milling around, talking and laughing, but Ethan's parents sat at their empty dinner table, chatting. She studied them as they approached. Ethan's mom threw her head back and laughed at something Ethan's dad said and gave him a whack on the arm. Ethan's dad still sat stiffly but his face broke into a wide smile, pleased with whatever had just come out of his mouth. His smile opened up his face and he rubbed his shoulder dramatically where his wife had hit him. "Anne!" he cried, noticing them. "Look, Lynette, it's the happy couple. And they've come just in time to witness some elder abuse." At this Lynette roared with laughter, a unique high-pitched cackle that made Anne laugh, too.

"Tom," Lynette finally said. "Stop that. She'll think you're being serious."

Both of their words were tinged with a Midwest accent. Anne

wasn't sure what she had been expecting but it was not this warm, lovely couple in front of her. Ethan's mom jumped out of her chair and ran over, enveloping her in a tight hug. "Oh, honey, it's so nice to finally meet you. I kept asking Ethan, 'When are you going to let us meet your beautiful girlfriend?' You know, for months I said to Tom, 'Is she even real? Maybe Ethan has a blow-up doll in his apartment.'" At this Lynette burst into laughter again. She was a small woman, and her buoyancy and energy seemed to overflow out of her physical form in waves. Tom looked at her and shook his head, clearly amused but resigned to let Lynette take charge of this situation, and every situation, Anne assumed with a smile. "Well, I guess better late than never." Lynette held both of Anne's arms and then hugged her again.

"It's so nice to finally meet you as well." Anne squeezed Lynette back and then moved toward Tom; he tried to stand as she approached, but she quickly closed the gap between them and leaned down to him.

"Great to meet you, Anne. Welcome to the family." Tom smiled again and she saw neat, square teeth up close. "And, heck, not a bad place you grew up in, eh?"

"How was the flight?" Anne asked, twisting her face into a sympathetic expression. "I'm so sorry that you couldn't drive. I know you—"

"Anne." Ethan grabbed her arm. "Can you come with me? It's an emergency. Sorry, Mom, Dad, I'll bring her back, I promise."

"Do we get a hug from our son?" Lynette was still smiling, but her voice, for the first time since they'd met her, sounded uncertain. Anne looked from Ethan to his mother. Ethan broke into a grin and scooped his mother off the ground. "You get more than a hug." Ethan whirled Lynette around as she let out one of her high-pitched laughs and hollered, "Put me down. Crazy boy." Anne grinned. Ethan's parents were lovely.

"It's good to see you, son." Tom strained against his chair and pushed himself to a standing position. Ethan shook his father's outstretched hand and Tom pulled him into a hug, clasping him around the back. When they separated, Tom sat back down. "Well, go on, put out whatever fire you started."

"We'll be back soon," Ethan called over his shoulder, pulling Anne beside him.

"What is the emergency?" she asked, bewildered. "We barely said hi. I absolutely love your parents. They're so great," she rambled on as they cut back through the crowd. "Ethan? Are you going to tell me?" She stopped midsentence. They were standing on the dance floor. In front of them a full band was setting up, a woman tapped a microphone as three men carried speakers and instruments from a white van to the stage.

"What?" she began, staring at the stage and spinning her head around looking for Rose and Sam. "What's going on? We hired a DJ. Ethan." She looked up at him. "What is this?"

Ethan's face broke into a huge smile. "I canceled the DJ. I knew having a band was important to you, baby, so I got you a band." He gestured to the group setting up. "They came all the way from New York. They're supposed to be the best." Ethan looked at her and his face dropped. "I wanted to surprise you. I thought you'd be happy."

"I am," she said. "I am. I'm just shocked. I'm sorry, this is amazing." She tore her eyes from the stage and looked at Ethan. She smiled as she took in his face. "This is amazing," she repeated. "Do my mom and dad know?"

"I wanted it to be a surprise for everyone." Ethan waved at Rose and Sam as they approached the dance floor. Anne fought the tightness in her chest and smiled at her parents. She knew how much it meant to her mom and dad to pay for the wedding. Well, mostly Rose—she'd been the one who had planned every detail with Anne in the preceding months, from the bridesmaids' bouquets to the DJ. But Ethan just wanted to do something nice for everyone; her mom would understand, might even be thrilled. *Everything is fine.* Anne kept the smile plastered on her face.

"Wow." Sam clapped Ethan on the back. "Holy smokes. Did you do this?" Sam asked, pointing the beer in his other hand toward the stage.

"Yes, sir." Ethan tapped his own beer against Sam's. "I wanted it to be a token of my appreciation for everything you guys have done for us. I mean, welcoming me into the family and the wedding and—"

"We were happy to give you this wedding," Rose cut Ethan off. "But, of course, we wish we could have afforded a band. Thank you, Ethan, what a wonderful surprise." Rose gave Ethan a hug.

"It's amazing."

"Annie, you've said that three times." Ethan laughed, looking from Sam to Rose. "Well, I just hope I get a dance with the mother of the bride before the night is over."

Rose chuckled. "Oh, I'll make sure you do."

Later that night, after the band had packed up and left and one of Ethan's groomsmen had puked into a bush beside the barn, Anne tugged Ethan's arm for the third time. "Are you ready? I'm exhausted." As if on cue, she yawned into her hand. Her parents and the bridesmaids had all left more than an hour ago. Hugging both of them goodbye, Rose had whispered in her ear, "That was a great party." And it was. The band had been a huge hit—people danced for hours (with Uncle Bob freestyling in the middle of the dance floor to every-one's surprise) and sang along to "99 Luftballons." Anne felt silly, and a bit guilty, for her annoyance with Ethan earlier. He'd only been trying to surprise her with something she had wanted since they'd first started planning their wedding. She watched her new husband laughing with the last guests standing, his three groomsmen and some New York friends who were accustomed to staying out until four a.m. She was so lucky to have him, and she made a mental note to show her appreciation more often. "Ethan, are you ready?" Anne asked again, suddenly exhausted.

"Ok, ok. We're going. We're going. Let me just say goodbye to everyone." She watched as Ethan stumbled over to his groomsmen, hugging each of them in a way that told her he was about six to eight beers in. She laughed as he made his way back over. "What's so funny?" His speech was slightly slurred but not too bad—the "What's so" came out as one word, but his movements were mostly fluid.

"You're just cute when you get all touchy-feely with your friends." She stood up and stretched her arms over her head. "I'm so tired."

"I hope you're not too tired," Ethan said as he circled her waist roughly with his arm and fell into clunky step beside her.

"What do you have planned?" She tried to sound coy and flirty; she tightened her jaw muscles against another yawn.

"Oh, I'm planning to keep you up all night tonight," Ethan whis-pered into her ear.

"Yeah, good luck with that," she said, nudging her hip into his side playfully.

As soon as they got into their room at the inn, Ethan pressed against her from behind, pinning her to the wall. "Do you like that?" His voice hoarse in her ear. She suppressed a giggle at his porno persona and nodded her head, the textured wall scratching her cheek. She felt his weight grow heavier on her; she flinched and waited for him to pull back.

"You're hurting me," the words came out muffled under his chin. His skull dug into the side of her head. The wall grated against her cheek. She shut her eyes and tried to breathe. The dress was already too tight against her rib cage and Ethan's chest pressed harder into her back, squeezing the little air left in her lungs out of her body. She coughed, choking on her breath. "Stop," she wheezed at Ethan. She felt his hand move into her hair and her neck jerked backward. She used all the air in her lungs to yell, "Ethan, stop." Pressure came off her body and she gulped in more air.

"Annie," Ethan's voice filled the silence left after the yelp had dissolved. "I'm so sorry. I don't know what happened. I think I blacked out or something."

Anne turned to face her husband. His eyes were glistening. He stepped toward her, reached for her hand. "I'm so sorry," he said again, as she placed her hand in his tentatively and he drew her in. "Did I hurt you?"

"No," she replied slowly. "Not really. I just couldn't get you to stop."

"I'll never get this drunk again, baby." Ethan stroked her hair gently, kissing the top of her head. "I will never hurt you, I promise." She felt his shoulders begin to shake. "I'm so sorry, baby, I'm so sorry."

"It's ok." She wiped the tears from his face. "Everything is fine."

THE MAN

The man watched the child from across the room. She looked peaceful, pushing air out of small, white lips. He suddenly felt calm. This was inevitable. His heart slowed, his fingers steadied; he readied himself.

The last time he felt this way was nearly ten years ago, before he went away. He remembered his last night in his childhood home. Staying up, waiting for his parents to fall asleep before sneaking downstairs and out the front door. He had already decided at that age, the age of sixteen, that if the hunger wasn't going to go away, then he had to go away. He knew what he needed to do and he didn't want to do it with his parents nearby. He already had the spare key to his father's car in his pocket and he slipped into the old white Saab, holding his breath as the engine turned over and came to life. He backed out of the driveway of the long, tan ranch-style house he'd lived in since he was a baby and drove toward 95 South. The whole thing was too easy. Anticlimactic. If his parents had woken up and run out of the house, hollering in their bathrobes, he would have tapped the brakes, put the car into reverse, and resigned himself to another day of gray. If he had had neighbors who kept an eye out for that troublesome teenage boy, then he might have scrapped the whole plan, but like many houses in that part of Bridgewater, New Jersey, his nearest neighbors couldn't even be called neighbors . . . just houses on the same street separated by long stretches of manicured lawns. Only his brother woke up, but a few choice words sent him scurrying back into his bedroom. He was on the highway within fifteen minutes, heading south and then west. Putting as much distance between himself and his house as possible.

He had been afraid that he would have trouble staying awake and so he pulled into the first rest stop off the highway and bought an old-fashioned bottle of Coke. He needn't have worried, though. Even without the caffeine, adrenaline was coursing through his veins at what he was about to do. He drove straight from ten p.m. until morning. Around eight a.m., he pulled slowly off the highway into a little town in Ohio. He chose randomly. It didn't matter what town or what state because all towns had schools. It wasn't fair for him to spend his whole life living in gray. It wasn't his fault that he was born the way he was born (and it definitely was nature, not nurture, as the court psychologist hinted in his questions before the sentencing: "Were there any times your parents touched you in ways that made you uncomfortable?"). The truth was, he had had a nice childhood, and his parents had done everything right. His mom read him bedtime stories, told him he was special, held his hand in parking lots, helped him with his homework at night. His father never made much of an effort, but he'd never hit him, never screamed at him—the only time his father had raised his voice was when the boy got sent home from school for that essay he wrote and, well, that was understandable. That was also around the time his dad switched from beer to hard liquor at night. He tried to feel a connection, or an attachment at least, to his parents; sometimes he sat on his bed and closed his eyes and imagined them dead. *Feel something*, he told himself. He imagined his parents lying on the side of the road, bodies twisted, glass from the windshield of their car sprinkled in their hair, and he felt about the same as when his favorite cereal ran out. People were born all kinds of ways, but even as a boy he knew his feelings weren't "normal" and he also knew, by the time he was sixteen, that they weren't going away.

He worried that it was too late, that everyone would be in homeroom by now—his own school day started at 8:05 a.m., and most kids were already seated, ready to raise their hands for attendance at eight a.m. But as he pulled into the parking lot, he saw another car pull in, careening around a corner and slamming into the last parking space at the far end of the lot. If it was a boy, obviously he would have to keep searching, but the driver's-side door opened and out stepped a girl, short and chubby with dark hair. *If her backpack is red or blue, I'll keep looking*, he told himself. That was fair, those were decent odds. She ran to the passenger side of her car, threw the door open, and slung a backpack over her shoulder. Green. He drove to the road that separated the parking lot from the school and put the car right in the girl's path as she crossed. He rolled down his window. "Is this the high school?"

The girl slowed her pace and peered into the window, taking in his unfamiliar face. "Yeah. Are you new here?"

"Yeah. My family just moved to town from Chicago."

"Chicago? That's so cool." She laughed, though he didn't know why. "I'm Julia. I'm a junior." She laughed again. "Sorry, I don't know why I told you I'm a junior. I go to school here." The way she smiled when she apologized made her look much younger than a junior in high school. He would have pegged her for a freshman.

"Do you think you could get in and show me where to park? This lot is full."

The girl hesitated. It was almost 8:05 a.m. The boy bet that Julia, with her nervous laughter and desire to please, was not the type to be late to homeroom. He put a half-smile on his face and forced himself to look her in the eye. "Come on. You can tell the principal that you were showing the new kid around. That it was your civic duty." At this, the girl relented, seemed excited even, to be chosen for this task. It wasn't until he left the parking lot and turned down an empty side street that she started to fidget and laughed again. "Where are you going?" When he stopped on the side of the road and told her to get into the back seat, she did. He thought maybe he'd have to force her, pull her hair or something, but he didn't have to; she just silently climbed over the center console into the back seat. In fact, even during it, she didn't really scream, which surprised him. She bit him when he put his hand over her mouth, but even after he took his hand away, bleeding, she didn't scream or yell. Only quiet crying, the whole time. When he was finished he told her to get in the passenger seat again.

It wasn't until after he dropped her off at the school that he noticed she had completely ruined his dad's car. The blood had soaked right through her jeans, pooling in the fake leather seat. He turned away and kept his eyes on the road ahead, but the smell wafted into his nostrils and made him gag. From the school, he drove to a deli in the small town center and ate a sandwich and waited.

He rubbed the memory out of his mind and moved his eyes back to the girl in the cabin, got up from his crouched position, and moved slowly across the room.

THE CABIN

ANNE

"Not awake yet," it was between a question and a statement. The man stood right in front of them, staring at Thea. Anne kept her eyes low as the man bent down and picked up a few strands of her daughter's hair, rubbing them between his thumb and pointer finger. She moved her eyes to his hands but stayed as still as possible. "Julia," the name came out in a whisper. Anne jerked her head up to his face. The man's eyes stayed on Thea, and Anne watched his face contort. She read something like regret, maybe even sadness, in his eyes. She didn't realize that she was holding her breath until he stood up abruptly. He walked across the room and this time, instead of pacing, he slumped down against the front door. He kept the gun in his right hand, resting on his knee.

"Excuse me." Her mother's tone caught them both off guard for the second time. "I have to use the bathroom." Rose wrung her hands. "I am going to have an accident." She spoke as if she was a schoolchild, waiting for the bell to ring.

"Just go," grunted the man.

"Sir, we're not animals," she said, almost chidingly. "I'd really rather not sit in pee, and I don't think it would be pleasant for anyone else, either, considering how small this room is."

Nice try, Mom, Anne thought. The man didn't care whether or not the cabin smelt of piss.

He grunted again. Tapped the gun against his leg. Ran his eyes over Rose's plump sixty-five-year-old body. "Fine. Let's go."

Anne erased the surprise from her eyes and stared blankly as the man came to get Rose. He took her mother's arm roughly and pulled her to a standing position. She met her mother's eyes for one second and Rose looked at her hard. She didn't have time to figure out what her mother wanted her to do before they were out the door. She heard Rose take a few steps off the deck, but the man stayed close to the cabin door and said loudly, "I have my gun on you. Hurry it up."

Anne was already wasting time. Her heart beat in her chest. She whispered her daughter's name several times and ran her fingers across Thea's face. Nothing. Though it seemed like hours ago, it had been only a handful of minutes since Thea and the man collided; Anne was not going to panic yet, Thea could still wake up on her own. She gently shrugged Thea out of her arms and placed her daughter carefully on the floor. She couldn't make too much noise—if she could hear him out on the deck, then he could hear her inside. She scanned the cabin quickly. The sun was almost fully set and her eyes strained against the shadows. She heard a clicking sound and spun around, peering into the dark corners of the cabin, before realizing the sound was coming from her teeth. She bit down hard, pressing her molars together, and the chattering stopped. She stood up slowly and moved to the closest window. Ran her fingers along the ledge. Nothing. She kept moving, scanning the floor for rocks. There was only grit and small pebbles from the hundreds of boots that must have walked the floor over the years. Shit. Time was running out and she had accomplished nothing. She heard the man say, "Hurry the fuck up, lady," right as her eyes landed on one of the wooden chairs. It was across the room. Anne didn't know if she had enough time, but she was already moving quickly, squinting her eyes as her boots crunched over the dirt on the floor. She squatted down in front of the chair. One of the bottom pegs, connecting the legs, hung loose and had almost snapped in two. She thought she could snap it the rest of the way but it would certainly make a sound. "Oops!" she heard Rose exclaim outside and then a *thud*. She heard him muttering "God fucking dammit" and used their voices to mask the noise of stepping on the piece of hanging wood and pulling. Her fingers were numb and she couldn't feel the wood but she kept pulling. A chunk broke off and she shoved the wood, sharp point up, into her boot. She heard the man grumbling, dragging Rose up the steps; their boots against the old wood stairs made loud scraping sounds. She took large, quiet steps back to Thea. Her head was light with adrenaline. She had just pulled her daughter back into her arms and shut her eyes when the door opened. She kept her eyes shut tight as she felt her mother slide down beside her. She forced her breaths in and out of her nose evenly.

Anne opened her eyes. The man stared at her. She stared back. The wood rubbed against her calf. She waited until his head was bent between his knees before she stole a glance at her mother. She talked to Rose with her eyes. *I'm ready*, she said.

THIRTEEN YEARS
BEFORE THE CABIN

ANNE

It was early May, right before Anne found out she was pregnant, the days were warm and the nights felt hours longer than they had in March and April. Ethan was in the office until after dinner most nights, arriving home around nine p.m. or later—Anne already tucked into bed with a book—but that was normal, the way it had been since Anne quit her job three months after the wedding. What wasn't normal were the angry outbursts and snide remarks that had seeped into their interactions over the past few months. *He* had been the one to convince *her* to quit her job at the law firm, saying nothing would make him happier than to support her while she figured out what she really wanted to do.

"And if that turns out to be lying in bed with you, drinking coffee?" she'd joked (half joked) the Saturday morning he'd brought it up.

"Then I say . . . lean in," he'd responded and kissed her neck. "Seriously, babe, I make more than enough money to support us and it would make me happy to come home to a happy wife, instead of a miserable, grumbling monster."

Anne had burst out laughing and climbed on top of him. "I'll show you a monster."

So, she'd done it—she'd quit the law firm. Why not take a few months, or a year, to figure out what she really wanted to do? And in the meantime, she could spend more time with Ethan, cook in her new kitchen, decorate, do all the grown-up things that were suddenly a part of her life. But over the past month—or was it the past several months?—something had changed in her marriage. She couldn't pinpoint when, but Ethan stopped kissing her when he got home from work, instead throwing out a quick "Howwasyourday?" before jumping in the shower. Rather than telling her in detail about his meetings, he'd turn on the television. "I just need to zone out, babe."

It was a phase, obviously. Her husband was stressed and on edge because of work, but unlike in the past when their relationship seemed to be his respite from a stressful workday, suddenly everything she did and said made it worse. She couldn't figure out how to make herself into the person she had been when she made him happy. First, she tried to do more, to be more funny and more talkative and more affectionate. Then she tried to be less, like a pleasant shade of soft gray blending into the walls.

It all started because she had gone to Whole Foods and spent two hundred dollars on groceries. Ethan had never cared, had never even noticed before when she bought the groceries, but she didn't realize that his company hadn't been doing as well and he was worried about their finances. When he saw the Whole Foods bags, he asked her to show him the receipt. She told him that she'd already thrown out the receipt but that the groceries came to around two hundred dollars.

She didn't think anything of it at the time, because they'd never been on a budget before.

"You spent two hundred dollars on groceries for two people?" Ethan laughed.

Anne laughed back. "Well, Whole Foods is expensive, but I got the normal stuff."

"Are you fucking kidding me?" His voice changed. "Two hundred dollars for two people," he repeated. "Return it."

"What? I can't return—"

"Those groceries need to be out of this house tomorrow."

They argued until her husband screamed, "Goddammit, Anne, I'm sick of this shit. Do you even realize how entitled and spoiled you are?"

She walked into Whole Foods the next day, carrying two bags overflowing with food; her face sweaty and hot, her arms burning. She told the manager she hadn't remembered that her husband had done the grocery shopping the day before. *Silly me, so forgetful.* The manager was gracious, looking down when she had to brush away tears and wipe her nose on her sleeve.

"So sorry, I've just been spacey lately," she said as he credited the two hundred dollars back to her credit card.

After that, Anne learned to read Ethan's energy as soon as he walked into a room. There was the fun, brilliant, kind man she had walked with for miles on their first date, and then there was this second Ethan, the on-edge Ethan, the one she learned to be careful with—but he was temporary, a creation of circumstance. He'd only materialized for the first time in the past few months, since they had married, in fact, so he couldn't be an actual part of her husband; she was certain he would disappear completely once things at work settled down. She truly believed this.

The last time they'd gone out—an effort to get Ethan out of his work-TV-bed routine—they'd met Lana and Steve at the same Lower East Side bar where Anne had introduced Ethan to her friend more than a year ago. This time, Ethan texted Anne, saying he'd been held up at work and he'd meet her there. When she arrived, she found Lana and Steve cuddled up on a couch near the back of the room. Anne greeted her friends, mentioning that Ethan would be joining them from work, and then went back to the bar for a drink. After she had grabbed her drink and left her credit card with the bartender, she sank down onto the couch next to Lana. It felt good to be out with her friends solo. She listened to Lana go on about her first art exhibit the following week. Lana's paintings (gorgeous, vibrant colors splattered across huge canvases—the opposite of her somber personality) were being shown at a small, hip gallery downtown.

"It's a big deal," Lana acknowledged flatly. "I'm excited."

"This is huge. I'm so proud of you." Anne grinned; she knew that her friend had worked for years for an opportunity like this. "I promise that I will be the first one in the door and the last one out. Actually, hold on." She downed the rest of her whiskey and ginger ale in one gulp. "We're taking shots to celebrate."

"Yes, tequila!" Steve yelled as Lana smiled the tiniest bit in approval.

Anne put three shots of tequila on her tab and moved back through the crowd to the couch, balancing the three shot glasses between her fingers. The smell wafted up and burned her nostrils and her body felt loose from the strong cocktail she'd downed a moment ago.

"To Lana," Anne declared. "A star will be born next week," and the three of them carefully clinked their shot glasses together and then poured the liquid back. The alcohol, smoky and sweet, ran down Anne's throat and she closed her eyes as it made its way to her stomach. When she opened them, Ethan stood before her, watching her with an amused expression.

"Babe! You're here!" Anne threw herself into her husband's arms. "We're celebrating Lana's gallery showing next week." She kept her voice elevated, happy; she couldn't force her husband to have fun, but she could at least set the tone.

"Oh, congrats." Ethan gave Lana a quick peck on the cheek and shook Steve's hand hello. "Next round is on me," he said with a wink, and Anne relaxed and let out a breath. Over the next couple of hours, Anne sat with her back touching Ethan's and talked with Steve about his work as a project manager for a marketing start-up. She leaned her head against the back of Ethan's neck as she sipped her third cocktail. This was going to be a good night for them.

Eventually, they parted ways, Lana and Steve set off for the L at Fourteenth Street and Anne and Ethan strolled a half block to catch a cab.

"That was so much fun." Anne nuzzled her head against Ethan's shoulder in the car and let the nice, warm feeling of the alcohol spread through her head.

"That was fucking humiliating."

Anne lifted her head, too quickly, and saw stars before her vision cleared, and then, her husband's face, dark, angry, his jaw clenched, working against nothing. "What are you talking about?"

"I had a nice little chat with Lana. About your ex-boyfriend. The guy you dated before me. She went on and on about how into him you were, but how he messed with your mind and how glad she was that you *settled down with me.*" Ethan spat out the words.

"Ok . . . I'm sorry, I'm confused. Why—why is that a bad thing?" The car was speeding up Sixth Avenue, lurching around slower vehicles, and Anne's stomach flipped as the driver sped up and then slammed on the brakes repeatedly.

"I'm glad I could be your fucking consolation prize, Anne."

"What? I'd broken up with Drew, like, six months before I met you. I think Lana misspoke or you misunderstood . . . You're not a consolation prize. You're my husband." Anne tried to laugh, but her heart was drumming too hard in her chest and she felt queasy.

"We're not talking about this right now." Ethan took out his phone and started typing, shifting as far away from Anne as possible in the small back seat.

"I'm sorry," Anne whispered.

That night, Anne woke up at three a.m. to Ethan kissing her shoulder. Even in her half-asleep state, she felt relief course through her body; she could tell by the way Ethan was kissing her shoulder that he knew he'd fucked up. The fight, and his anger, had been fueled by alcohol and stress. She brought his head up to hers and found his lips. They started to kiss softly at first and then Ethan brought his mouth against hers forcefully, pushing his tongue through her lips. He climbed over her and pinned her hands over her head. Before she could react, he used his knee to open her legs and entered her roughly, abruptly. She closed her eyes. He thrust into her sharply, grunting. It was over in a minute. Afterward, he rolled off her and fell asleep immediately. She rubbed her wrists and made no sound at all as tears slid from the corners of her eyes to the pillow.

The next morning, Ethan kissed her gently before he left for work. "I love you so much. You make everything better." He didn't mention the night before and neither did she. They'd both had too much to drink, and in the light of day, she couldn't even remember what had happened exactly. It all felt like a blur. The next week, her Ethan was back, the guy she fell in love with. He was affectionate and giddy, and the night of Lana's art show, Ethan surprised her by coming home early with tickets to *The Phantom of the Opera*. Anne typed out a text to send to Lana and then erased it. She didn't have a good enough lie and there was a tiny part of her that was angry at Lana, why the fuck had she been talking to Ethan about Drew anyway? She felt sickening guilt but told herself that she had to focus on her marriage right now—her friends were important to her, of course, but Ethan was her life partner. She couldn't explain to her friends why she kept missing dinners, why she couldn't meet up with Whitney when she visited the city, and why she'd become unresponsive on text threads.

Theresa finally called her and demanded to know what was going on. Anne's face burned as Theresa's voice blared through the cell phone, finishing with, "We're really worried, Anne." So, they'd all been talking about her behind her back. Anne didn't even try to defend herself. They wouldn't understand the pressure that Ethan was under at his job and how he needed her undivided attention. Instead she'd replied coldly, "Thanks for your concern, but I just have a lot going on. And, Theresa, you can tell everyone not to worry about my marriage. I can take care of myself." She'd hung up and cried. When things were truly back to normal and stable, she would reconnect with Lana and Whitney and Theresa. She told herself this over and over, but even so, Anne was lonely and when a Facebook message popped up from an old college friend, a friend who didn't know Ethan, who she hadn't spoken to in years, asking if she wanted to grab a coffee, she hungrily accepted.

She met Joseph for a four-dollar cup of Stumptown coffee in

downtown Manhattan. Joseph was tall, lanky, and lean in college. He always walked into their English lit class with his contradictory lazy but purposeful gait. When he made his infrequent comments in class, the whole class sat up straighter and listened. Joseph had a way of seeing not just additional layers or subtext in a piece of writing but another universe, and as soon as he pointed it out, Anne would go back and reread passages, amazed at what she had missed. She'd had a crush on him in college, but they'd been alone a couple of times—studying, walking home from an apartment off campus—and nothing physical had happened, and so they settled into a solid friendship, but still . . . Anne sometimes wondered if Joseph had ever felt the same attraction she had.

She spotted him right away when she walked through the door of the small coffee shop—still tall, lanky, and lean, his limbs folded on top of each other to fit into a delicate wooden chair. Two coffees sat on a white marble table. She got to him before he could get up and motioned for him to stay sitting. "You'll upend three tables if you move," Anne said, leaning down to give him a quick kiss on the cheek. He smelled the same, like oak and pepper (she never knew if this was his body's natural smell or if he wore some kind of mildly musky cologne), and she felt light-headed as she came away from his cheek.

"It's really good to see you." Joseph smiled.

"It's good to see you, too. You look exactly the same." She scanned him from the top of his head to his feet.

"Well, how long has it been? Not that long, right? We're not that old yet."

"Four, five years?" She laughed. "No, we're not that old." She took him in from across the table. She had such a strong urge to get up and hug him again that her hand shook as she picked up the coffee and brought it to her mouth. "I was happy to hear from you."

"I've thought about you a bunch since college."

Anne felt herself flush. "I know, we shouldn't have lost touch."

"Well, I've moved to New York, so now we have no excuse." He smiled. "So. Anne."

"Joseph."

"You're married! How does that feel?"

It was a chemical reaction, she couldn't control it; she felt her eyes filling and then tears were making their way from the corner of her eyes down her face. "Oh god, what the fuck, I'm sorry." She laughed and grabbed a napkin from the table.

Joseph looked at her. "I'm sorry . . . I didn't know—"

"Oh no, no, I'm still married. To Ethan. And things are fine, pretty much. I guess just . . . It's just harder than I thought it would be?" Anne laughed again and felt blood rushing to her face. "I'm so embarrassed. I don't know why I started crying. Honestly. It must be hormones or something. Things are really fine."

"Yeah, it looks and sounds like things are just dandy." Joseph gave a quick grin. "But if you don't want to talk about it, let's start with something else, huh? How do you like working for a fancy law firm? I'll admit I've stalked you online a bit," he said with a smile.

"Actually." She thought about lying or stretching the truth for a split second, and then, "I quit a few months ago. I always thought I'd be a lawyer for some reason—I guess just because it seemed like a se-cure job, a job where, if I worked hard enough, I'd get ahead, you know? A straight line. But Ethan wants me to figure out what I *actu-ally* want to do and . . . I have no fucking clue." She laughed and looked down at the table, embarrassed. She must sound like a spoiled brat to Joseph.

"Jesus." Joseph paused. "I think that's partly why I applied to this PhD program. To stall entering the real world for a few more years." He shook his head, took a gulp of coffee. "I'm not sure anyone really has a clue, if it makes you feel better."

They talked for two hours that morning, or sixteen dollars' worth of fancy coffee. Anne felt that she could be completely herself with Joseph; there was no pretense, nothing to be gained or lost. The ease of their conversation put into sharp contrast Anne's fraught dynamic with Ethan. They met up for coffee or lunch a half dozen times in May and June. And they really were just friends, Anne told herself. She felt light and good when they were together, but there was no flushing of the cheeks or racing of the heart. Of course, the question must be posed then: Why didn't she tell Ethan about Joseph?

The day Ethan found them together was the first time Anne invited Joseph over to the apartment. They were supposed to meet for coffee and a walk, but she woke up to the sun already scorching through the windows at seven a.m. and air-quality alerts flashing on her phone.

"Unbelievable. It's not even July yet and it's supposed to reach the mid-nineties today," she mumbled to Ethan, reading her phone with one eye open.

"Stay inside today." Ethan was already dressed and about to leave for work. He came over to the bed and kissed her on the forehead. "Do you have any plans today?"

"I'm just going out briefly around nine"—she yawned—"to meet Nicole for coffee."

"Well, stay hydrated." He paused at the bedroom door. "I'll see you tonight at eight for dinner. Text me when you decide on a place."

"Yes, I will. Can't wait. I love you."

"I love you, too, baby."

She stretched in bed for a few minutes, thinking about how Ethan seemed better the past couple of weeks. In fact, she hadn't seen on-edge Ethan since the beginning of the month. The thought was immediately followed by the anxiety of wondering when the other Ethan would be back. She pushed it out of her mind. Today would be a good day. That was all that mattered. She got up, took a shower, and pulled on a loose dress. She looked at her phone again. Eight a.m. and eighty-two degrees. She was meeting Joseph at nine a.m. near Central Park. She stood in the kitchen, fixing herself a pre-coffee coffee.

Want to come here instead? It's going to be hot as balls today. I have air conditioning, and a Nespresso maker. She tapped out her address and pressed Send.

Joseph replied a few minutes later. On my way ☺

She gave Joseph the tour of the apartment. The interior was minimalist but inviting with clean lines and a color palette of gray and white. She tried to hide her pride as they walked from the kitchen with a large marble island, over the soft white rug in the living room, down the hallway lined with black-and-white photos and into the master bedroom, sunlight streaming over the tan duvet cover.

"And then there's a small guest bedroom as well over there," she said, pointing farther down the hall.

"Can I grow up and live in a place like this?" Joseph walked over to the bedside table and picked up the book on top. "Do you like it so far?" He flipped open to the dog-eared page of the *The Road*. "It's pretty intense, huh?"

"It's good," Anne agreed. She moved backward out of the bedroom, suddenly dizzy. She couldn't remember why they were here, in her apartment, in her bedroom. "Do you want a fancy coffee or a regular coffee?" she called to him, making her way to the kitchen.

"Black coffee is good, thanks." She heard him moving out of the bedroom and down the hallway. "Your place is really great," he said again as he walked into the kitchen.

She turned from the coffee maker to hand him his mug; he was closer than she expected, and she almost bumped into him. "Thanks," he said. His mug was still in her hand. He took the coffee from her with both hands, brushing her fingers. They took their coffees from the kitchen into the living room. She sat on the far end of the couch and he sat right next to her, so close that their legs touched. A shock went through her body and she drew her legs to her chest and cupped the coffee mug on her knees.

Joseph turned and met her eyes. "I've been wanting to ask you, but I wasn't sure if you wanted to talk about it. Ever since our first coffee date." At the word *date* Anne's stomach flipped. "Are you doing ok, really?"

She opened her mouth to laugh and brush his question aside, but when she met his eyes, she said simply, "I'm leaving Ethan." She didn't realize it was true until the words were out of her mouth. All of the stress and anxiety she'd been holding in her body the past few months dropped away with the thought that she could simply leave. It would be difficult, but she could, she *would* leave Ethan. She put her cup down on the coffee table in front of them and took Joseph's hand. She felt the warmth of his palm and closed her eyes. The air was thick and a slow pulse started in her temple. Joseph leaned closer; she could see him in her mind's eye, feel his body moving through the heavy air, closer, closer, and then his lips were on hers. She placed one hand against his chest, nudging him backward and his face came away, his eyes wide.

"I'm sorry. I shouldn't have—"

Before he could finish, she pushed him against the back of the couch and climbed on top of him, pressing herself against him, biting her lip to keep from screaming or groaning or sobbing—one of the sounds buried deep in her stomach, trying to claw its way out. She looked down at him, her eyes open now and laser focused. They watched each other, and then she brought her mouth to his again. His hands moved up her legs, under her dress. She lifted her body so that he could put his hands wherever he wanted. There was so much noise in her ears—the crackling of the air, the blood drumming through her body, their breaths coming fast and strong—that she didn't hear the door to the apartment building open. She didn't hear someone clomping up the stairs to the second floor. It wasn't until the jangling of the keys right outside the front door that her head cleared, her pupils shrank back to their normal size and she jumped off Joseph, whispering, "Fuck. Fuck. Fuck."

"Is that?" The color drained from Joseph's face.

"Yes, that's—" The door swung open and Ethan walked in with force, his face peering down at his phone, swinging his briefcase onto the entry bench.

"Hi!"

Ethan snapped his head up and a look of bewilderment mixed with panic flashed on his face.

"Ethan, this is Joseph, my friend that I was meeting for coffee this morning." She was talking quickly, stringing words together. "But then it was too hot. You know, the warning? Um, the air-quality warning? Anyway, we decided to meet here instead." She turned to Joseph and forced her mouth into a smile. "Joseph, this is my husband, Ethan." She looked from Joseph to Ethan. Her husband had rearranged his face into a neutral expression and he strode over to Joseph and extended his hand. "Nice to meet you, Joseph. Annie's told me all about you."

"Great to meet you, man. You guys have a beautiful place here." Joseph shook Ethan's hand with the hand that had just been inside her dress. She couldn't look at either of them. She wondered if Ethan could smell the guilt. She willed the blood to flow out of her cheeks downward.

"Thanks. We know we're very fortunate." Ethan smiled at Anne. She smiled back. "Well, I just stopped by to grab this phone charger," he said, yanking Anne's phone charger from the wall. "I have to head back to work. Nice to meet you, Joseph. Always nice to meet one of Anne's friends." He picked his briefcase back up. "Annie, don't forget to text me about dinner. I'm really looking forward to it. It's been so long since I've had you all to myself."

"Ok, I will," she stammered. "Love—" The *you* got lost in the sound of the door slamming shut.

THE CABIN

ROSE

It was getting dark outside. Rose stepped down onto the first step off the cabin porch. She took her time, trying to give Anne time. She saw a rock, the size of a closed fist, near the front door of the cabin as she exited with the man. *Anne,* she thought, willing her toward the rock in her mind, *move.* The man yelled at her to hurry up and she picked up her pace a bit, climbing the rest of the way down the stairs. She wanted to draw him out, away from the front door, but as she moved toward the woods, he stayed back and warned, "I have my gun on you. Hurry it up."

Fine. She would squat down right there, a few feet from the porch. As she was about to undo her pants, she saw a rock a few steps forward, sticking out of the snow. It was shaped like an Indian artifact. An arrowhead—that's what her third-grade teacher called a similar-looking rock she found on the playground. She remembered because he had turned it over in his hand. "I'll ask my friend at the museum about this, Rose." She had been ecstatic, had seen fame and glory in her near future—only years later did she realize that he had only been kindly humoring her. This one had the same shape—curved on one end, flat and sharp at the other. She unzipped her pants, hunched down, tilted forward, and tumbled.

"I'm ok," Rose called over her shoulder. Her fall landed her within reach of the rock. She shimmied her pants down around her ankles and fluffed her coat out behind her so that her backside was covered. She drew in a breath as the cold needled her skin. She used one hand to steady herself, placing it directly over the rock. The urine came fast and strong, surprising her. She didn't think she would be able to go at all. When she finished, she stood slowly, clutching the rock in her hand and tugging her pants up. She clumsily zipped her pants, still grasping the rock in front her body, her back to the cabin. As Rose turned toward the man, she slipped her hands into her coat pockets, opening her palm and letting the rock fall into the bottom of the pocket. She hoped the darkness and the distance were enough of a shield.

She felt the man's eyes on her and shivered convincingly. At the bottom step, Rose lifted her foot. It was dark, and the steps to the cabin were coated with a sheen of ice. Her foot came down, half on the step, half off. She wobbled, pulled both hands out of her coat, and just barely caught herself, fingers splayed on the second step. "Oops," she said loudly. She imagined her daughter inside the cabin.

The man grabbed Rose by the elbow and pulled her the rest of the way up the stairs and into the cabin. She saw Anne, sitting against the wall at the back of the cabin, eyes closed, in the same position. She could have been sleeping if it weren't for the flush that Rose could make out, even in the dusk light. She sank to the floor beside her daughter and granddaughter. She felt Anne look at her, but she didn't meet her daughter's glance. She thought about Sam telling her that her mind was her most potent weapon. "You need to be one step ahead, always. The ability to surprise your opponent will give you the advantage." She put her hand into her pocket and rubbed the smooth stone.

THE MAN

He watched the grandmother with a smirk as she clumsily grabbed hold of the rock and pocketed it. He felt something akin to respect as she moved past him into the cabin. The old woman was angry; she wanted to fight. These were feelings he understood. Maybe he would let her have a go at him—to let her feel that she had tried. The man smiled to himself. He could be generous to the women, even in these circumstances. The anger he felt, the things he had done, it had nothing to do with them—he almost wanted to try to explain to them, that this was fate, it was something being done to all of them. They were all in this together.

The man studied the women huddled together. He looked at the gun. Counted in his head. He could use the bullets right now, easily, and it would all be over. Or he could just use one bullet, like he was going to do in the parking lot. He contemplated this. Ran his fingers over the gun, popped the cartridge out, and looked at the top bullet. He felt the air shift across the room before he saw her move. She was slow, the old one, but she made a good effort and she was almost to him by the time he had shoved the magazine back in. He held up the gun and pointed it at her chest. She froze, put her hands in the air, wheezing. The other woman was crying softly. He smiled. "Sit down."

The grandmother turned slowly and walked back to the wall. She didn't remind him at all of his own grandmother, the only one he ever met, who was scrawny and put plastic over the furniture so that his bottom would make a squeaking sound every time he sat down.

"You're not all bad, you know," she'd said gruffly once. He had thought he'd misheard because it came out of nowhere—he hadn't kicked his little brother in the ribs or thrown a glass ashtray across the room. They were just watching TV, side by side on that squeaky couch.

He looked at her, contemplating her words. "How do you know?"

She didn't look back at him, just kept staring at the TV. "Because no one is all bad."

"But." And with a rush of something that he'd never felt before, a feeling close to regret but not quite, he asked, "But how do you know?"

His grandma reached for the remote and pressed down on a button until the voices on the TV drowned out the thoughts in his head.

Now, he watched as the older woman slid down beside her daughter and granddaughter. The man could hear whispers between the two women. He shook his head and yelled, "Shut up!" The women fell silent, but he could still hear the whispers in his head and he slammed the gun on the ground and yelled, "Shut up!" again.

The man's head throbbed. He wanted it to be over. He could do this small kindness for all of them, but especially for the girl. His grandmother was wrong. If she'd been right, he would have found someone by now, just one person, who was like him, whom he could talk to. It was a different kind of loneliness he'd lived with his entire life. Physical loneliness, he could stand. He did fine by himself in a cell. In fact, he preferred it when he didn't have a cellmate. But the loneliness in his head, the loneliness of knowing he would never, ever be seen by someone else. That's what made him want to claw at his temple until his head split open. The girl was supposed to be the answer. He looked at her again. She was still a lump, barely breathing. She wasn't going to make it. If she hadn't woken up by now, she must have some kind of brain damage. He'd come this far for nothing. He thought about the bullets in the gun again, more than enough, and stood. When he reached the women, he saw that they knew. The grandmother's face was stone, but the mother's face was relaxed, accepting. He looked down and his finger paused on the trigger. He lowered the gun.

The girl was waking up.

THE CABIN

THEA

She was between awake and asleep. She'd felt this before—this out-of-body feeling, of being here but not here. She was dreaming of being on a warm beach, the water lapping at her ankles. She'd never been to the Caribbean, but she thought this must be what it would feel like—the aqua water, smooth, tickly sand against her toes, and hot sun soaking into her shoulders. Someone was walking toward her from the other end of the beach. Closer, closer. A man. Light brown hair, handsome and lean. He wore white shorts. As he came closer, Thea could see that his lips curved up in a smile.

"Mr. Redmond," she said. "I mean, Ted." She laughed with him. "What are you doing here?"

"Thea." He was so happy to see her. She beamed. "You're such an old soul." He beamed back.

Now they were in his classroom and this was real—not a dream—a memory. She looked around the room, touched the desk lightly with her fingertips, transferring her weight into the tops of her fingers. "Is this real?" she asked him.

"Thea, what can I do for you?" He stood up from behind his desk; he didn't hear her question.

"I just thought you seemed kind of sad in class today and I wanted to make sure everything was all right," she replied.

He smiled a sad smile. "You're very perceptive, Thea. I have a family member who isn't doing very well, and . . . sometimes I just can't turn off my brain." Mr. Redmond took off his fine, silver glasses and rubbed his eyes. "I'm sorry. I know I probably shouldn't be telling you this." His voice broke. Thea's heart broke at the same time. He was so sad. She had never seen an adult man so sad.

"I'm sorry." Her eyes filled with tears, too.

"Oh god, don't you cry, too," he said, and then he stepped toward her and put his arms around her. His hand rubbed a small circle on her back. He pulled away. "Thank you for asking. You're a very special person. An old soul."

Thea felt something nice spread through her body, but she didn't smile because this was a serious moment. "I'm so sorry, Mr. Redmond," she said again. She hid her shiver. "About your family member." Before she could stop herself, the words were out of her mouth: "I lost my dad. He died when I was little."

"I'm so sorry. Look, you can call me Ted when we're not in class, ok?" He scribbled down something on a piece of paper on his desk and handed it to her. "Here," he said with a smile. "In case you ever need to talk."

She felt warm, like a sudden fever had overtaken her body. Her stomach hurt a tiny bit. "Ok."

The classroom and Mr. Redmond faded away and she tried to hold on to the memory. Now she was in a cold, dark room. She heard a loud voice. She struggled to open her eyes. For a moment, she wanted her mom, then the feeling of betrayal snapped back into her body with force. She stopped struggling, sank back into the blackness. She was alone.

ANNE

Thea was born on December 10, this much Anne had told her, always with "Christmas came early that year!" tagged at the end. What she always omitted was that Thea's due date was not really December 25 (though it made a cute story). No, her daughter's scheduled due date was February 5. Two months away. They hadn't even assembled the crib, put together the changing table, or procured diapers. Anne thought she had so much time.

She was going to leave Ethan, she really was—what she'd told Joseph that morning was true. That night at dinner, Ethan hadn't mentioned a thing about finding her with another man on their couch; he had played the warm, doting husband as she sat there replaying Joseph's skin against hers. Over the next weeks, she started to plan her escape, scrolling through craigslist ads seeking roommates, saving as much as possible from the weekly transfer from Ethan's checking to hers, refreshing her résumé. She was going to tell her parents and her friends, too, to make it real, so there was no going back. And then she'd found out she was pregnant.

She took a pregnancy test while Ethan was at work, realizing with a start that she hadn't had her period in more than two months. She'd been so preoccupied with her plan and thoughts of Joseph . . . But no, she was on the pill so she couldn't be pregnant; it was impossible, or only .01 percent possible, according to the white leaflet. She held the pregnancy test between two fingers, one hand clutching the side of the bathroom sink, and when the second line appeared, she felt her groin clench in protest. She stood rooted to the tile floor, sobbing, and then she splashed water on her face, looked into the mirror, and made a decision. She would give Ethan one more chance. Maybe this baby would change everything.

The day of Thea's birth was a Saturday. She and Ethan were sitting on the couch, his hand resting on her stomach, her feet resting on the coffee table. It was morning and he was in a good mood. He had closed a big deal that week at work—an investor he had been pursuing for months had finally caved, dumping millions into Ethan's asset management company. That morning, he couldn't stop smiling. "Let's go to brunch at Mars. I think a celebration is in order," he said. The fancy place down the street with a five-course tasting menu. "One mimosa's ok, right?" he asked, kissing her forehead. They were going to have a good weekend, she could feel it. And then a good week. And then a good month. He hadn't always been angry, Anne told herself. In fact, in the years since they'd met, he'd been in almost a perpetually good mood. It was a joke at first that she used to make, "Euphoric Ethan." Anne found it perplexing at the beginning, that he was always so cheery, so optimistic, and then, when she grew accustomed to it, it was intoxicating. It became one of the things she loved most about him—Anne was a worrier; the slightest hiccup could make her spin into obsessive thoughts (as a therapist she would label this as a pattern of *unhelpful thinking*)—Ethan could always convince her that everything was going to be fine. "Love," he would say, "is this going to matter in a year? Or three months even?" He gave her the perspective that she so often needed; he was like a constant flow of Lexapro into her bloodstream. And since she'd announced she was pregnant, things had been better, much better, between them. Anne was starting to feel silly that she had come so close to leaving, to ending her marriage because of a rough patch.

That Saturday morning, two years after they met and six months after their wedding, her phone buzzed and jumped on the coffee table. If she hadn't picked it up, or if she'd left it in the bedroom where it usually stayed on weekend mornings, things might have turned out differently, but the phone was right there, in front of them and couldn't be ignored. She reached out, her head still resting on his shoulder, and opened the message. Just thinking of you . . . hope all is well. Her cheeks involuntarily flushed. Ethan looked down and she felt his body still. "You're still talking to Joseph?" His voice was measured, calm.

"No, not really. I haven't heard from him in a while." Her voice came out high. She was trying too hard, overcompensating. But it was the truth. She'd met with Joseph one more time after that morning to tell him that she couldn't see him again, that she'd made a mistake. He tried to convince her otherwise until she finally interrupted, "I'm pregnant. Almost three months." They'd only texted a few pleasantries since.

"Right," Ethan said and stood up. He walked into the kitchen. "Come here."

With the flick of his wrist, the gas flame burst up under the grate of the stove. That was one of the reasons she'd wanted this apartment—it was on her "pro" list, the gas oven. She'd always loved fire. She watched him slowly turn the dial back until the tops of the flame barely grazed the top of the grate. "Annie, come here," he said again. "I've changed my mind about going out. Come keep me company while I cook." She got up stiffly from the couch, pulling her feet from the coffee table to the floor and standing slowly, stretching her hands toward the ceiling, prolonging the moment. She watched him rummage in the refrigerator; he pulled out a half-used stick of butter, the paper lazily crumpled around the end. She slid into the kitchen; it was a bright morning, the sun shone so hard that even with the blinds only half open, the kitchen filled with pools of light. He opened the cutlery drawer and pulled out a butter knife. The dull blade sliced into the butter, cutting away a chunk. Ethan tossed it onto the griddle and it sizzled, the air filled with the smell of fire and butter. To this day, she can't smell burning butter, a smell she used to love, without bile rising into her throat and tears pricking her eyes.

"I thought we were going to Mars," she said, her voice bright, trying to match the pools of light on the kitchen floor.

"I'm not in the mood to go out anymore." He picked up the heavy griddle with one strong hand and the butter slid around, coating the bottom uniformly. He took three steps toward her and closed the distance between them. He put one hand on her stomach, the other caressed her face. She looked into her husband's eyes and smiled. "Why are you crying?" he asked.

She rubbed her eyes with her hands and laughed. "I'm not." In truth, Anne couldn't say why her eyes filled with tears that morning. Perhaps she already knew what was coming. Up until that day, he had never hurt her, not really. There were those few times he'd gotten angry, an anger that took her by surprise, an anger that sometimes seemed to come out of nowhere. But all couples fight (isn't that what they say?), and Anne wasn't wholly innocent; she had yelled back, sometimes egged him on even. And the fights had ended; things were back to normal. The darkness had evaporated so completely that she'd convinced herself it was gone for good.

"I really was looking forward to brunch." Anne forced her eyes from the sizzling griddle back to her husband.

"Fine." He turned around quickly, flicked off the flame. The hair rose on the backs of her arms, as the griddle crashed into the sink.

"Oh come on, Ethan," she snapped back. "You don't have to make such a big fucking deal." She was angry now, too, and she felt safer in her anger.

"You want to go to brunch, so we're going to brunch." He walked past her, grabbed his coat from the hook on the wall, and opened the door. "Let's go."

She crossed the threshold of the door without looking at him, anger radiating from her body. At the top of the narrow metal stairs (one of the items that made the "con" side of the list while they were apartment hunting), she half turned her head to say something—she can't remember now what she was going to say. "Lighten the fuck up," maybe or, if she's being more generous with herself, perhaps she was going to try to make amends with a kiss, a kiss that would have turned the morning back to what it had been before her phone buzzed—but she never said anything. Her scalp was on fire, her hair yanked so hard backward that she gasped and her eyes bulged and then shut tightly.

"Did you fuck him?" She heard her husband's voice, soft, calm, in her ear.

She could have said no. She could have said of course not, don't be silly. But even in that moment, the moment before she lost consciousness, she was more angry than afraid, and she spit out a "Fuck you" before her head jerked forward and the ledge of the first step slipped beneath her boots; her body followed her stomach down, down to the landing. She felt a snap followed by enormous pressure. She lifted her head slightly and said, "Help me," before she threw up out of the side of her mouth.

THE MAN

He wondered what it would feel like, to feel for another human the way the mother felt for her daughter. He understood what it looked like. He saw the anguished look in the mother's eyes while she watched her daughter's limp form, and he saw the hot rage when she stole glances at him; yes, he understood the look of it, but he still wondered what it would *feel* like. He had warm feelings toward his own mother; he appreciated her cooking and the way she adjusted his hat in the winter, pulling it down over his ears and then sweeping his hair under the sides. He was grateful when she pretended not to notice the bruises and bite marks on his little brother. He was surprised when he went away and didn't miss her, barely even thought of her. The man looked at the mother now, sitting across the cabin, her eyes closed, head against the wall, hand on her daughter's forehead, and he thought about how weak it made her, to have these feelings for another person, but still . . . He tried for a second to feel what she felt. He directed his eyes toward the girl—but as soon as he looked at her form, it was all images and sounds in his head, thrashing and screams and groans and his breathing sped up and his hands shook a bit. He made himself sick with these thoughts but they kept coming, and they were stronger than him.

The man put his head in his hands. It was the mother's fault. That bitch drove into the parking lot at the exact moment he was about to end it. That wasn't *his* fault at all. He was trying to do the "right" thing, to be good. "Be good today," his father had said to him every day before school, and he heard his father's disappointment, fear, and hope all mixed up in those words. As if it were that simple, as if he could simply turn off the thoughts and the voices. He had learned how to hide them from other people, but he couldn't find the switch to turn them off. And even when he tried to do the right thing, it always turned out to be not the right thing. Like the parking lot. He had gone back to a parking lot a second time; it felt like divine intervention, when he saw the sign for the nature reserve. He would do it in the parking lot, except this time to make things right. And then the woman had messed everything up. No matter what, he was going to suffer, either by doing the wrong thing or by doing the right thing that turned out to be wrong.

He had met a man in prison who told him that everyone, at least every man, wanted to do what they did, deep down in the most buried parts of themselves. It was nature, the nature of man, he said. Only not everyone was brave enough to go after what they wanted. "We're being punished by a society that doesn't want to admit what people really are," his friend had preached, his voice booming over the din of the cafeteria. "We are the sacrificial lambs, so they can all go around pretending, living normal lives, but never really *living*. They're all like us deep down, at the core. We are pure, my friend. We are what nature intended." The man had listened, spooning soup into his mouth, and wondered if that was really possible. Maybe he wasn't so different from other people after all. Did everyone have a little bit of what he had? The types of thoughts and voices he'd heard since he could remember? He didn't ask to be filled with thoughts of dragging women to dark places and watching the fear in their eyes as he held them down. But the thoughts came from a place he couldn't control and he felt like a bottle his whole life, being shaken up, until he was ready to explode. Up until the age of twelve, he was able to mostly lash out at his little brother, who would scream and cry but not tell anyone when it came down to it. Then he began to notice girls in a different way and the urges morphed. It was difficult to imagine other people having those urges. Maybe if they had, he would have had friends.

The only person he'd say he got along with was his mother. She seemed to understand him or at least she didn't think he was beyond saving. A memory flashed into his mind. He was eight and his brother was six. They were alone and then suddenly his mother was there; she must have run toward his brother's screams. After she checked his little brother's neck and made sure he was ok, she sent his brother to go find their father. "Don't tell him what happened, honey," she'd said to his brother, "it was just an accident. If you can keep it a secret, we'll get ice cream later." Then she had taken his chin in her hand. It hurt, her fingers tugged so tightly on his jaw. He was ready for her to yell, to tell him to never, ever do that again, but she said, "I am calm." She looked into his eyes. "I am calm," she said again. "Say it."

"I am calm," he said.

"I feel nothing," she said. "Say it."

"I feel nothing."

"Whenever you feel those feelings, the ones that make you do bad things, I want you to repeat that in your head. Do you understand?"

"Yes."

She'd let go of his chin and kissed him on the cheek. "Nothing is wrong with you, my love, you're just different." She smiled and wiped her hands against her eyes. "You're my special boy."

He looked at Thea again. He needed her to wake up. He saw her eyes open before. If she died, if her small body shut down, then this would be all for nothing. He rubbed his hands together on his lap. It was too cold. His hands shook involuntarily, and the gun trembled on his thigh. The man thought he could take it, but the girl's body wouldn't last much longer in the cold. He got up and walked outside without saying anything. He wasn't worried about the women escaping; the women would not leave the girl. As he gathered branches and leaves, he thought about the girl and then his thoughts turned to Julia. He remembered something else the guy from prison said to him, "Women are taught to acquiesce. Since they were little girls. If you find a fighter, enjoy it." The man had had to look up the word *acquiesce* in the library a few days later. ACQUIESCE. *TO ACCEPT SOMETHING RELUCTANTLY BUT WITHOUT PROTEST.* He picked up a branch from the ground, mulling the words over in his head. No wonder he didn't get better after Julia; she had barely struggled. That was partly his fault, because of what he'd done to her, but it was over so quickly. Too quickly. Thoughts of Julia swirled in his brain and he couldn't make them stop. The man pricked his finger against the end of a sharp stick he was holding. He thought about his last parole hearing, his third and final. He had told them not to let him out twice before, and twice before he had been denied. He had explained to the board about the hunger—about how it had grown, not diminished. About how he could remember it, the nag in his stomach, for as long as he had memories. This kind of talk had worked twice before. But the third time the man sat quietly, listening to the board discuss his case. When it was his turn to speak, he talked about being a troubled youth at the time of his crime and how he had made progress with the in-house therapist since his last parole hearing. He fixed his mouth into a straight line and said he wanted the chance to redeem himself, or at least to do some good in the world. The woman sitting in the middle of the panel, with her tired eyes, declared, "You've done ten years. You've served your time." As if that meant anything. He had leaned forward slightly, waiting. And then, to no one in particular, she had announced, "The board finds the prisoner suitable for release."

The man fingered the sharp end of the stick again. How would it feel to push it slowly into his eye, through his brain? When he walked back into the cabin, the women eyed his load but didn't move. The man threw the sticks and leaves in the fireplace and felt in his pocket for the lighter. Before he lit the kindling, he took the pack of ciga-rettes out of his pocket and lit one up. He thought again about the girl waking up and felt a mixture of sickness and excitement churning in his stomach, mixing with the smoke.

TWELVE YEARS
BEFORE THE CABIN

ANNE

When Anne woke up in the hospital, the first thing she noticed: Her body was empty. Ethan stood to the side of the hospital bed, gripping her limp hand and wiping a tear from the corner of her eye.

"Baby," Anne whispered, trying to move her head up from the pillow.

"What, love?" Ethan bowed his head down.

"The baby," she said, her throat felt raw and the back of her head throbbed.

"She's fine. Just a little early so they took her to the intensive care wing." He caressed her cheek with his hand. She felt rage bubbling up from her groin into her head. *Did you fuck him?* It all came rushing back. Maybe it was the drugs coursing through her veins, giving her strength, but the next words she spoke came out perfectly clear. "If you ever touch me again, if you ever come within a foot of my baby, I will kill you."

Ethan blinked and when his eyes reopened they were dark and blank. "You're not remembering clearly, Anne. You tripped on your way down the stairs."

"Touch me again and I will scream." She was crying now, desperate. "Leave. Leave now or I will fucking ruin you, Ethan. I'll go to the police."

"Do you really think anyone will believe you? You're a whore, Anne." He said the words kindly. "And if Joseph were under oath . . . Well, it wouldn't look good for you, love."

A nurse came into the room, alerted by the beeping of the monitor. "Ok, ok, calm down, honey," was the last thing Anne heard before she sank into blackness again. When she woke up, her husband was gone, and Rose was there, holding her hand. Her father sat in a chair at the foot of the hospital bed, his hands placed firmly on his knees. Anne told her parents about the stairs and what Ethan had said about "not remembering clearly." She didn't tell them what he had said about Joseph.

"I'm going to kill him," her father said. "I'm going to—"

"Sam," Rose cut in. "Please." Anne watched a look pass from her mother to her father. "Everything will be ok," Rose continued. "We'll figure all this out. Right now, you need to rest so you can be strong for . . . Does she have a name?"

Anne thought about the name she and Ethan had picked, Madeleine, for his grandmother.

"Thea." It had been Anne's favorite after she'd stumbled upon the name on a baby name website. Ethan had already decided on Madeleine but Anne carried the name and its meaning in the back of her mind. Thea: goddess of light.

"Beautiful." Rose smiled. "Sleep. Everything will be ok. I promise."

For the moment, as she plunged back into darkness, Anne believed her.

For ten weeks, Thea lived in a tiny incubator in the NICU and then in the neonatal wing of the hospital under close supervision. Anne was technically discharged a few days before Christmas, but as soon as she could move around, she spent her days and evenings in the NICU, staring at her daughter's tiny form and then, when the doctors and nurses gently shooed her away, sitting in the waiting area until she could go back in. The baby weighed three pounds ten ounces at birth—Anne was told that was big and strong for her gestational age, in the eightieth percentile. She looked like a featherless baby bird that had been thrown from its mother's nest, translucent skin wrapped too tightly around tiny bones, fingers like little claws. Anne wasn't allowed to touch her daughter for the first twelve days of her life, and so she watched. She watched the nurses open the side of the Plexiglas box, checking the IVs, the tube under Thea's nose, the monitor over her heart. She watched for something to go wrong, even as Thea began to gain weight and the nurses assured Anne that the baby was doing great, as healthy as possible under the circumstances. She watched Thea's chest, convinced that she might stop breathing at any second. She stood for hours, eyes on her stomach as it jutted up and down with each breath, sure that as soon as she looked away, the tiny body would fail.

Anne spent nights at her friend Nicole's, whom she'd worked with at the law firm before quitting (Rose had had to return to the bakery but visited every week for a night or two, staying at a cheap hotel in Queens). Anne was never particularly close to Nicole, but she was quiet and kind and offered her couch without asking any questions. Anne had grown apart from all of her friends since marrying Ethan, and she wasn't ready to explain why she had come out of the hospital without a baby, without a husband, and without a place to sleep. She set her alarm for midnight and three a.m. and pumped milk in the dark.

A few weeks after Thea came into the world, Anne left the hospital for a couple of hours in the middle of the day. She took the subway to the Upper East Side and got off at her old stop, Eighty-sixth and Lex, determined to grab her passport and birth certificate from the safe, and some changes of clothes. She hadn't been back to her apartment since the day of Thea's birth. She had been living off her dwindling checking account; she no longer had any of her own credit cards— she was an authorized user on several of Ethan's credit cards, but they had all been canceled the first night in the hospital, three e-mails in succession alerting her that she had been removed from the accounts. A lump formed in Anne's throat as she threw a duffel bag over her shoulder and walked up the subway stairs to the street. It had only been a few weeks, yet the neighborhood felt completely different— the green awning on the deli that she passed every day looked fluorescent and the people and buildings came into hyper focus.

She hadn't seen Ethan since the first day in the hospital. That first night, she dozed in and out of sleep, startling awake at every sound. Her eyes moving to the door of her room every time it cracked open, expecting his face to appear, heart accelerating and then slowing to a steady thud each time a nurse's head popped in instead. When he didn't show up that night, and then stayed gone the next forty-eight hours, Anne knew he wasn't coming back. A wave of relief mixed with sadness washed over her, and she cried with relief and then she cried harder, as it hit her that she was on her own, fully and completely.

She made the trek to their apartment on a Wednesday. Her husband would be at work, and Anne, of course, still had a key. She knew there was a possibility that he had changed the locks but, walking down the street, toward their building, she was almost certain he hadn't. Anne had been in charge of house stuff; if anything around the house needed to get done, she was the one who took care of it, from calling the plumber to setting up the automatic utility payments. It occurred to her once or twice how odd it was that Ethan had managed to build an extremely successful career yet couldn't seem to figure out how to get the mail.

She walked slowly, with one hand protectively placed in front of her abdomen where the incision area still smarted. She slowed her pace even more as she made the left onto their block. They lived on a quiet tree-lined street surrounded by an odd assortment of large luxury buildings with ornate lobbies and doormen, antiques dealers, and small buildings, like theirs, that didn't have fancy trappings but housed only two or three spacious (by New York standards) apartments. Anne chose the apartment, but the apartment was his—everything signed in his name. It was his money, after all, and when they'd bought it they weren't even married, just engaged. She took out her keyring and climbed up the front steps to the building door, inserted the key into first the outside glass door and then the interior wood door. The entryway was completely silent. She unlocked the mailbox and quickly sorted through the letters, pamphlets, and magazines that spilled out of the slot. Nothing of importance. She climbed the stairs that she had crashed down a few weeks earlier, gripping the railing and keeping her eyes looking up and ahead. When she got to the front door of their apartment, her entire body was shaking—half with fear, half with expectation. He wasn't going to be home. She knew he wasn't. But still. There was a slight possibility. Just in case, she knocked softly, ready to bolt—nothing. She slid the key in and the latch clicked. She pushed the door open.

"Hello." It came out barely above a whisper, hardly loud enough to alert anyone to her presence, but she could tell from the still air that the apartment was empty. She averted her eyes from the kitchen and walked down the hallway that ran the length of the apartment, toward the bedroom. The quiet felt suffocating and the surroundings suddenly foreign. Even though Anne had picked each piece of furniture and decoration, down to the forks and spoons, Ethan had had final approval over everything. She'd felt the tiniest bit silly standing idly at Restoration Hardware, sending him picture after picture, and waiting for his thumbs-up or thumbs-down, but they were a team, he'd said, and they were building this home together. She tiptoed into their bedroom like an intruder and went straight for the safe in the closet, quickly dialing the code and exhaling when she saw the documents stacked neatly inside. She stuffed a few pairs of underwear, bras, socks, three shirts, one sweater, and two pairs of jeans into the duffel bag. Next, the bathroom. Since she was there, she might as well load up. She walked over the plush beige carpet of the bedroom into the black-and-white tile of the bathroom. The bathroom was her favorite room in the apartment—open, crisp, and clean with an old claw-foot tub and a large window that let in the soft afternoon light. She grabbed a small travel case out of the vanity and filled it with deodorant, toothpaste, and a toothbrush. The balance of her checking account flashed into her mind: $106.58. She reached for an expensive face cream and shoved it into the bag. Color rose to her cheeks as she realized that the weekly transfer from Ethan's account to her own would most likely never be coming through again. The medical bills were mounting, her daughter was in the NICU and she was worried about face cream. She shook her head and shut the medicine cabinet door. She couldn't help but exhale sharply at her own reflection. She'd been avoiding the hospital bathroom mirrors, at least close-up, and this was the first time she'd truly stopped and taken in her face since the "accident." Her eyes were sunken and dull, her cheekbones jutted from her face, and her skin ranged from gray to deep purple. She was about to tear her eyes away when she saw something in the cabinet mirror. Not her skeleton face, but something in the foreground, a speck of bright white, in sharp contrast to the black tile, peeked out from underneath the claw-foot tub.

Anne walked over to the tub, got down on her hands and knees, and pulled it out, holding it in front of her, pinched between two fingers. A piece of notebook paper, small and lined, as if from a diary. There were numbers written neatly all the way down the page. And beside each number, three letters. Initials? She stared at the numbers. Some looked like they could be phone numbers, but some were longer, too many digits. Her head felt hollow, unable to piece together what this meant. She stayed kneeling on the floor for several minutes. Perhaps it was nothing. Just some work document that had fluttered out of Ethan's briefcase . . . in the bathroom. Before her brain understood fully what she was doing, Anne was on her stomach inching under the tub, one hand placed flat against the scar on her abdomen, the other pushing along the floor. Cold sweat ran down her face as her body protested. She took a deep breath and reached as far as she could, running her fingers along the side of the wall where the lip of the tub touched the window, feeling around for . . . what? More pages from a diary? There was nothing, just dust rubbing off onto her fingers. She started to inch her way back out from the under tub. The slit in her lower belly ached and she paused for a moment and then turned carefully onto her back. She began to shimmy out from under the tub and then had to stop again. "Ok, you're ok," she whispered to herself. The incision area throbbed and she waited for the burst of stars to clear from her eyes. A small black notebook, secured directly on the underside of the tub, stared down at her. It blended almost completely into the underbelly of the tub. She ran her fingers around it, feeling under the edges. She heard a small ripping sound as the notebook came away from a Velcro base. She opened to the first page. And then the second and the third. She flipped all the way through, squinting in the half-light. Every single page of the notebook was filled with numbers, like the first scrap of paper. After each number were three letters. Some of the letter combinations showed up frequently. Some only once. She put her head against the cool floor, closed her eyes, and lay absolutely still. For a moment, the pain coursing through her body felt secondary. Her husband had a secret diary Velcroed to their claw-foot tub containing nonsensical codes of numbers and letters. Anne tried to open her mind, to allow for all the possibilities of what this could mean. She had underestimated her husband once. She wouldn't do it again.

Tears pricked her eyes and trickled down the sides of her face to the floor. A few weeks ago, she was expecting a baby with the man of her dreams, living in the home they'd made together, wanting for nothing and now . . . She took a shaky breath in and found her lips starting to curve up. The smile turned into a laugh and then she was laughing hysterically on the bathroom floor, still halfway under the tub. It was absurd, unimaginable, how much had changed in the past month. She felt suspended in between two realities—on one side, her old life, polished and serene, and on the other side, a mangled funhouse mirror image. It hit Anne that she hadn't come back to her old apartment for underwear, or her passport even. She was looking for something, she didn't know what, but something that would fill in the gaps between the husband she knew and the man he had morphed into over the past year. What she found didn't exactly fill in the gaps, in fact she had no idea what was in the pages of that notebook, but it reinforced what her gut had been telling her: she had never known Ethan at all. A sick feeling came over Anne as she realized she was choosing the second reality, the fun-house one; she pictured her old life oozing out of the mirror and evaporating like mist. Even if she wanted to, she couldn't go back to something that had never existed.

Once the manic laughter stopped, Anne stuffed the loose page into her back pocket, pressed the notebook back against the underside of the tub, and eased herself out from under the bathtub. She tentatively lifted the full duffel bag. "Fuck." She winced at the pain that shot through her body, and took one step and then another toward the front door. She paused on the way out of the apartment and let her eyes slide over the living room and kitchen. Takeout containers littered the countertops and dishes overflowed out of the sink. She shivered to see happy photos of the two of them still lining the walls. She took one last look and then locked the front door and slipped out of the building.

She turned left, the opposite direction of the subway, and walked east for several blocks, pulling up Google Maps to check she was headed in the right direction. It was a ten-minute walk, straight into the wind. She entered the building, tan and plain, and approached a woman at the front desk. She was led to a sparse room with two chairs and a table where she waited for an hour and a half. Finally, there was a short rap on the door and, as the door opened, she suddenly felt she was playacting an episode of *Law & Order*.

"What brings you here today?" "Today" came out as *TAday* in the officer's Brooklyn accent. He was short and chubby, with jet-black hair and an open face. He introduced himself as Officer Thomas. Anne wasn't sure if he meant his first name or last name.

"I need to report a crime. I mean, I need to report my husband." On the word *husband* her voice cracked, and the officer said, "Take your time," in such a kind tone that she almost burst into tears. She swallowed a few times and then explained everything that had happened—the stairs, the push, the hospital. She told him about going to her apartment and the notebook full of random numbers under the tub.

Officer Thomas listened quietly and then said, "What I'm about to say, I'm not saying to dissuade you from pressing charges. I just want to"—he wove his fingers together on the table—"be real with you. I want you to understand the reality of what's ahead, ok?" He explained that with no corroborating evidence such as past documentation of abuse or witnesses or past injuries, it would be her word against Ethan's—the process could be lengthy and expensive, depending on Ethan's resources. And, with no hard evidence, would most likely end in a plea deal—six months of anger management counseling and a fine. "And I'm not gonna lie, that notebook sounds real sketchy, but it wouldn't be enough to make an arrest or secure a search warrant." Officer Thomas looked past Anne's shoulder as he asked the next question, "Is it possible that the notebook might be related to . . . indiscretions that your husband might have had during your marriage?" He leaned back in his chair and gave a sympathetic smile. "I'd be angry, too, Ms. Thompson, your husband sounds like a grade-A jerk, but this might be a case better suited for family court."

Anne stood and thanked the officer for his time, exited the police building, the wind pushing her forward, and made her way back to the NICU.

ROSE

Rose left Anne's bedside at the hospital, pulled on her winter coat and hat, and walked from Lenox Hill Hospital twenty blocks south to Ethan's firm. She had listened to Anne's recounting of what had happened at the top of the stairs. Rose believed her daughter—Anne was terrified, that much Rose was certain of—but she also knew her daughter had a tendency to . . . love passionately. She thought of her daughter's only other long-term relationship, the boyfriend right before Ethan. It had been tumultuous—starting and stopping every few months, terrible fights followed by flowery apologies, breaking up, always for the "last time," and then getting back together.

Of course, the circumstances now were unmistakably serious. Anne had fallen down a flight of stairs. Pregnant. She could have died. She could have lost the baby. Which was precisely why Rose just couldn't reconcile the Ethan she had known for the past two years with the man from Anne's memory of that day. Rose had never been able to completely shake her misgivings of Ethan; he was too helpful, too cheerful, too polite (not exactly characteristics she could complain about aloud), but he loved Anne fiercely, unwaveringly. He might have given Rose an odd feeling on occasion, but he surely wasn't capable of *this*. It was too jarring, too sudden, and she couldn't make sense of it. Wasn't there typically build up to this sort of catastrophic event? A slow burn before the dynamite went off? Anne hadn't said a word to Rose about things souring between her and Ethan; as far as Rose knew her daughter had been blissfully happy with Ethan. It didn't add up. Rose felt that she had to see him, look into his eyes, and then she would know.

She strode south on Park Avenue. The morning sun glared down on tall buildings and warmed the bitter air ever so slightly. Men and women walked quickly past her, hands stuffed inside pockets of heavy winter coats covering slacks and smart suits. Rose marveled at the women wearing high heels, expertly navigating the slippery sidewalk with their stiletto points. The walk went quickly and even though icy air whipped her face, she looked at her surroundings, up at the gleaming buildings and around at the people, as often as she could. She could only stand visiting Anne in the city for a few days at a time, not enough space and too much noise to live with, but she appreciated the food, the architecture, and all the different types of people living together on one little island.

She slowed as she approached Fifty-fourth Street, the street where Ethan worked. She had visited Ethan's building several times with Anne, picking him up in the lobby and then strolling to Aquavit for lunch, where businesspeople paid fifteen dollars for a smoked salmon appetizer the size of her pinkie. Rose paused across the street from Ethan's building and looked up the silver structure, her eyes resting on the dark windows of what she thought might be the twenty-sixth floor. She made her way to the crosswalk and waited for the red hand to turn into a white dotted figure. And then she saw him.

Ethan stood across the street. He had just stepped out the front doors of his building. He was on his phone, talking animatedly. Even from this distance, Rose could see his hair was perfectly coiffed. A woman tagged along beside him, dressed in a fitted tan coat with fur trim, texting on her own phone. Rose recognized the woman. Ethan's firm was relatively small, albeit luxurious, taking up only one floor of the building. Rose remembered walking past the reception and Anne saying a cheerful "Hello" to the woman now at Ethan's side. Ethan got off the phone and said something to the woman. She threw her head back and laughed. Rose stood completely still. Her daughter was in the ICU and her granddaughter was fighting for her life in a small box and Ethan was cracking jokes to his receptionist. Rose balled her hands into fists and started to trail them from across the street when they disappeared into the Starbucks next door. Rose stopped again. There was something about the way they moved together, the woman and Ethan. So familiar. But then again they were coworkers; they had probably spent countless hours together in the office. They *were* familiar.

Rose walked a few more feet down the sidewalk, positioning herself directly across from the coffee shop. She strained her eyes, trying to see through the glass walls, but the windows were tinted and all she could make out were indistinguishable shapes on the other side of the glass. A few minutes later, Ethan walked out, holding the door open for the woman. Rose held her breath. They walked to the front doors of the building. Rose started back toward the crosswalk. She would go into the lobby and confront him. She didn't know what she was going to say, but she was suddenly furious. All the worry and fear from the last few days channeled into hot, red rage. She was practicing the words in her head when Ethan took the woman's hand. It was so casual, so intimate, as if he'd done it a thousand times before, that it took Rose's breath away. He pulled the woman toward him into a kiss; his hand dropped to her backside before the woman pulled away and looked around guiltily, laughing. She brushed his hair from his forehead and then swatted his hand from her rear. They separated and strode inside the building, both smiling.

Rose didn't go inside Ethan's work that day. She did not confront him, did not curse him out in front of his coworkers like she'd been planning. She stood still, turning over in her head what she had seen, and then she unballed her fists, put her hands into her coat pockets, and started the walk back to the hospital. By the time Rose got back to the hospital, she was, surprisingly, filled with a sense of relief and calm. Ethan was having an affair. Which meant he would leave her daughter and granddaughter alone.

TEN YEARS
BEFORE THE CABIN

ANNE

After Thea was released from the hospital, Anne quietly moved them from New York to her hometown in Vermont. Everything she owned at that point fit into a backpack. It wasn't until she lost Ethan that she realized how completely she had folded herself into his life and given up so much from her own. She had quit her job, given up her room in the cozy, sunlit apartment she was renting with two other college grads, and fallen out of touch with the majority of her friends. All of those parts of herself, gone in a few months. At the time, though, it hadn't felt rash or stupid. It had felt like she was falling in love and starting a new life with someone. And now it seemed she was back to square one—a football field behind square one, in fact. No job, no apartment, no money, no husband, and a newborn baby that required a feeding every hour and a half. Her daughter cried and cried those first months. Anne couldn't blame her—she'd had to leave her comfortable home two months early and she was letting her indignation be heard. Rose was the only one who could soothe Thea in those early days. Rose was born to be a mother and grandmother. While Anne would often break down into sobs herself, Rose would walk Thea back and forth across the living room for hours, humming softly, coaxing her wails into slack-mouthed snores. Eventually Thea grew from a featherless baby bird to a wispy, towheaded toddler who laughed at everything and had three arm rolls of insulation.

They lived with Anne's parents for the first year and a half of Thea's life. A few weeks after Anne got a full-time job, Sam knocked softly on her bedroom door. Thea had been asleep for an hour and Anne was sitting in bed reading a thriller she'd borrowed from Rose.

"Come in." Anne's loud whisper floated through the silent room. She could tell by the knock that it was her father.

Sam opened the door slowly and peeked in cautiously, scanning the room first before directing his attention to his daughter.

"Dad, you don't have to do that anymore. I'm pretty sure he's not hiding under the bed." Anne kept her tone light.

"I know, I know, just a habit." He stepped into the room and stood awkwardly in the middle of an area rug next to Anne's bed. "I wanted to talk to you about your future. Your mother and I feel it's time for you and Thea to become more independent. Get a place of your own."

"Oh." He was right. She was almost twenty-nine, she had a full-time job, and Thea would be starting daycare next month. It was time. But she felt pressure behind her eyes and her throat grew dry and suddenly she couldn't speak for fear of crying.

"Honey." Her dad never called her pet names. "You've been through a lot. We've all been through a lot, but now it's time to move forward with your life. You're young. You shouldn't be living with your old geezer parents." He forced a laugh that sounded more like a bark. "I just . . . I don't want you to get stuck."

"I know. I know, you're right. I'll start looking for an apartment."

She didn't want to admit she was scared. Feelings and sharing were not her dad's territory. So instead, she smiled. "I'll look at craigslist tomorrow."

"You're going to be fine, Anne," her dad answered the question she hadn't asked aloud. He cleared his throat and uncrossed his arms. For a moment, Anne thought he was going to touch her forehead. "Well. Good night. Get some sleep."

"You, too, Dad." He was almost through the door, just his hand still visible, pulling the door shut. She had to say it. It was now or never. She swallowed and then: "I'm sorry. For everything I've put you and Mom through."

His face reappeared quickly. Anne braced herself for the anger she knew he'd been holding in the past year. She had disappointed him by choosing someone like Ethan and she'd disrupted her parents' life, what was supposed to be their first "golden years" of retirement. She shrank against her pillow, wanting to get his bitterness toward her and what she had done to all of them by bringing Ethan into their lives out in the open.

"This is not your fault, Anne." His voice was low and sharp. "That man is a parasite. A con artist. He tricked us all." Anger pulsated from her father and she realized with confusion that it was not directed at her but at the invisible presence that had been sharing her parents' house for the past year and a half. "If I can, I will kill him. I will—"

"Dad," Anne interrupted. She was about to tell him to calm down, but instead, she simply said, "Thank you." After her father closed the door, for the first time in a year, she cried tears of gratitude.

Three months later, Anne and Thea had moved into their own apartment, a small one-bedroom in the center of Charlotte, Vermont.

Anne slept on a pullout couch in the living room and set up Thea's crib in the small bedroom. She decorated with furniture she found at Goodwill that Rose helped repurpose—they stained and painted side tables and a small bookcase while Thea dug for worms in the yard. The apartment was tiny and bright with gleaming hardwood floors in the living room and a soft gray rug in the nursery. Anne worked during the day as a paralegal at a local firm specializing in domestic abuse and at night studied for her master's of social work. Most days, and nights especially, it felt impossible—working, school, and Thea. The first few weeks, Anne was terrified, not of Ethan suddenly reappearing, but of being on her own with her daughter. She didn't have her mother's skills in the kitchen or her father's ability to make Thea giggle by flipping her upside down and swinging her in the air. Steadily, though, they fell into their own routine—perhaps lacking in decadent home-cooked meals and acrobatics, but theirs, nonetheless.

She found a therapist who would take her on as a sliding-scale patient. During their first session, the therapist, a woman named Grace, listened intently as Anne spewed out the events that led to her and Thea moving back to Vermont. She recounted the days and nights in the NICU and that now—even though she was on Zoloft for anxiety and Klonopin for panic attacks—every sound Thea made at night, every time her daughter cried, brought her back to the hospital, to the fluorescent lights, and to the fear that the tubes and machines wouldn't be enough to keep her baby's tiny heart beating. She confessed to Grace that she thought about Thea's health constantly and had started wearing face masks to the grocery store, terrified that she might bring home germs, even though Thea was proving to be a healthy, hearty toddler. She revealed the nightmare that woke her about once a week—the same one over and over, seemingly benign: Ethan cradling Thea in his arms, humming. Anne had had an idea of therapy from movies and TV shows—that the therapist would sit across the room, nodding her head, scribbling down notes, mostly silent except for the utterance of phrases like "Go on," and "How does that make you feel?" But Grace was animated during their first session, her face warm and open, her voice strong yet soothing. She wore her black hair cropped close to her head and a simple gold chain with a heart pendant. Rather than sitting silently, Grace interjected her thoughts often: "So this sounds to me like a sort of 'emotional reasoning'—letting a purely emotional response dictate what you think is going to happen, i.e., 'I am scared and anxious about Thea's health because of a past event and therefore she is going to get sick again'—it can be a very normal part of the healing process. But let's keep an eye on it and work in more healthy and helpful thinking styles." Hearing this woman put a label on and dissect some of the particular roots of her anxiety helped Anne to feel moored for the first time since Thea's birth.

It was Anne's time with Grace that led her to enroll in a master's of social work program to become a therapist herself. She still saw her therapist on an as-needed basis, but between work, school, and Thea, it was rare that she could make the time. She was tired, yes, but she was happy. Life felt busy but also simple and full in a way she had never known before—her daily routine was set, she was working toward a career she was deeply passionate about, and she was raising an extraordinary person who filled her with a love that often took her breath away. The nightmares about Ethan had subsided to once every few months. She stopped checking his LinkedIn and Facebook page—though he hadn't posted anything new in the past year anyway.

She still found herself imagining Thea getting sick or falling off her high chair once in a while, but she was able to pull herself out of these thoughts by doing breathing exercises and focusing on the present. She began to relax into this new life. She was so occupied, so involved in the day-to-day, that when she got the letter from Ethan's lawyer, she barely glanced at it, assuming it was junk mail, a solicitation. Her eyes skimmed the page and then stopped on the familiar name. "On behalf of our client, Mr. Ethan Mills . . ." Her breathing slowed, her vision became blurry. She couldn't take in full sentences, only words. *Motion. Petition. Custody. Daughter.*

He showed up at her front door a few days later.

"Annie, how are you?" His eyes were warm, the eyes of the husband she knew and his tone was that of a long, lost dear friend. His hair was now sprinkled with salt, streaking through the same thick, dark hair. He had a five-o'-clock shadow and new lines creased his forehead. He looked good. Tired but good.

The absurdity of him standing there, of him appearing as if nothing had happened, made her feel slightly punch drunk and she fought a giggle. "Ethan." She didn't know how to say his name, how to act, what role to play. A terrified single mother? A merely annoyed ex-wife? The person standing in front of her was so unlike the man in her nightmares, the man who pushed her down a flight of stairs.

"What do you want?" *Who are you?* is what Anne really wanted to ask.

"I've moved to town," he said with a smile. "I'm going to be working remotely so that I can be in Thea's life." He leaned against the door frame.

"It's been two years," she said, her mouth felt dry, full of cotton.

"I have sole custody. You didn't show up to any of the custody hearings. You haven't paid child support." She faltered, thoughts rushed into her head and she couldn't form another sentence that made sense. "It's too late," she finished weakly.

"I know it's been a while, but I've missed you. Both of you," he responded. He looked down and when he looked back up, his eyes were filled with tears. "I'm going to be the father she deserves." His eyes cleared just as suddenly and he remarked casually, "I think they call it a substantial change of circumstance, me uprooting my life for my daughter. It's one of the main reasons for revisiting a custody agreement. And here." He dropped a piece of paper and it flittered to the floor, landing print-side up. A check. *FIFTY-FIVE THOUSAND AND* $^{00}/_{100}$ scrawled in capital letters. "Child support for the past two years. I deeply regret not being in Thea's life until now, but I was working on myself. I've been in a bad place, Anne. I wanted to be the best version of myself for her. That's why I'm here now." He held her gaze and smiled.

Anne couldn't speak. Her heart thrummed in her ears. She tried to take a deep breath in but her lungs stayed closed. Ethan was back, showing her what he could do, how convincing he could be. Thea started to shout from the kitchen, where she was perched in her high chair, shoveling Cheerios down her throat. "MAMA." The color drained from Anne's face. "I have to go."

Ethan's face lit up. "There's my girl." He took a step forward; Anne kept her feet planted just inside the door frame. The last two years disappeared in an instant. She was going to collapse. She was weak and Ethan was strong. He would win. She pulled a breath in through her mouth and managed to say: "You can't see her."

"Well, I'll see you soon in court then," he replied cheerfully as she shut the door and fastened the chain lock in place. She paused in the entryway and rested her forehead against the wall.

She gathered herself and walked slowly from the front door to the kitchen.

"Who that, Mama?" Thea reached a chubby hand toward the table, clamped down on several Cheerios, and brought her fist to her mouth; all but one Cheerio fell to the ground.

Anne smiled at her daughter and waited a moment, swallowing down acid that had crept up her esophagus. "Just a man, baby."

THE CABIN

ANNE

They'd all seen it. Thea's eyes had opened, just for a moment, and then flickered back shut. Anne's teeth were no longer chattering; her body had gone numb some minutes ago. She watched the man across the cabin. He was pacing by the door and then, suddenly, he opened the door and walked outside. Anne turned to her mother and whispered, "You can*not* do that again, Mom. You can't just run at him—"

Rose cut her off. "You're right. We should make a plan. I have a rock in my pocket."

Anne paused, surprised. "I have a piece of sharp wood, from the chair, in my boot," she whispered back.

"Take the rock." Her mother pressed the smooth, jagged edge into her hand. "Use them both. When he's not expecting it. I'll take Thea and run."

Anne looked at Rose and nodded slowly. "Yes." Her brain felt slow—she couldn't think of another plan, something more sophisticated, less clunky. She knew she had a better chance of taking down the man than her mother. Rose was smart but soft. Her mother's arms and hands were better used for holding babies and kneading dough than for gouging a man with a piece of wood. Rose would only make it a few hundred feet with Thea, but maybe they could hide in the woods. Anne didn't think past what would happen to them in the woods, overnight. Thea would get out, away from the man, that's all that mattered right now.

"You have to knock the gun out of his hand, Anne."

"Ok." The matter inside her head felt warm and thick. "It's possible, though, that he's going to let us go. He looked sad before, or confused or . . . Maybe I can try to talk to him again . . ." Her voice trailed off.

Rose snapped, "Anne. I'm pretty sure his intentions aren't great." Her voice was ice. "We need to act now. This is important. If this is going to work, if we're all going to get out of this, you must knock the gun away from him."

"Ok." And then more forcefully, "Yes, ok."

Anne's mind flashed to a day when she had picked up Thea from daycare, just a few days before Ethan came back. They were driving home when Thea asked from her car seat, "What's a daddy?" The question came out of nowhere, and in the moments that followed, five seconds that felt like an eternity, Anne went through a catalog index in her mind. She'd thought this out. She had many different answers stored away, thoughtfully analyzed and studied during the past year and a half. But she hadn't expected her daughter to ask that question before she turned two years old. Anne thought she had a few more years to construct her answer into something honest yet gentle, forthright yet sparing. And so, in those five seconds, she sorted through her answers, but nothing came out; her mind an abyss. Her hands tightened around the steering wheel, time slowed down, and right as she began to stutter some nonsensical reply, Thea screeched in joy, "Mama's my daddy!" Anne's shoulders loosened, she glanced back in the rearview mirror. Thea was pleased with her answer, repeating it several times while pounding her knees. "Mama's my daddy. Mama's my daddy. Mama's my daddy."

Anne looked down at Thea's ghostly white face now, her daughter's breath made a whistling sound as it came out. The door creaked open and the man reentered carrying sticks and leaves, for a fire, she presumed, though he tossed the sticks on the hearth and lit up a cigarette. A few minutes passed. The man was deep in thought, like he had completely forgotten that he was going to create some warmth in the cabin. *Fuck you.* Her body suddenly felt hot. She wanted to growl, scream, claw his eyes out. But she stayed still and waited for the right moment.

The man finished his cigarette. Tossed the butt in with the sticks and twigs. Flicked the Bic with his thumb. A flame danced out of the top of the lighter. He lowered it to the end of a skinny stick and waited for it to catch. He spread the flame from the end of the skinny stick to the other sticks, twigs, and leaves; he reached up into the chimney and yanked open the flue. It took a few minutes but a fire started to catch. The leaves crackled as they burned and withered and smoke billowed up the chimney. The man tucked the gun into the waist of his pants. He spread his hands out over the flames, rubbed them together. Anne looked down at Thea, her daughter's face dappled in shadows by the light of the fire. She looked at Rose quickly and her mother gave her an almost imperceptible nod.

She shrugged Thea gently out of her arms and moved her daughter to Rose's lap. The man looked at Anne, curious, and raised the gun so it was level with her head. "What are you doing." It was not a question but a threat.

"I have to pee." Her voice was steady; her heartbeat slow and rhythmic.

"No."

"But . . . you took my mom before and I really—"

"I'm not taking you." Even as he was saying it, she was slowly inching her way off the floor, sliding up the wall. The man looked to Rose, as if to say *It would be in your best interest to convince your daughter to stop moving.* "I said I'm not taking you." He said it louder this time, and a tingle of fear shot through Anne's body. She made a split-second decision. "Fine, then I'll go by myself." She needed to get close to the man. She stood up fully and pushed herself off the wall. Eyes on the floor, she headed toward the door. Her heart pounded faster as she recalibrated the plan. The man moved toward her with long strides and put himself between her and the front door. She kept going. He aimed the gun. "Goddammit. No one is leaving this—"

Before his lips formed another word, in one motion she bent down to her boot, closed her fingers around the shard of wood, pulled up, and lunged forward. A scream escaped her throat as she brought the stake down. He jumped back right before she made contact, and instead of stabbing his stomach, the stake sank into his upper leg. Anne fell to the ground, thrown off-balance. She climbed to her hands and knees on the ground, breathing heavily, hands flat on the floor, ready to spring. She looked up. The wood protruded from his thigh. Her eyes darted around the floor. The gun. Where was the gun? She looked back to the man. He peered at the wood sticking out of his leg and then, with a grunt, wrenched it out. He took two steps forward and his knuckles connected with her cheekbone and she was off her hands and knees, flat on her back. She didn't know if it was the cold or the adrenaline, but she barely felt a thing, only a ringing in her ears. "You fucking bitch." He lifted the gun, still in his right hand, aimed it at her face. She heard a sound from across the room and a thought flashed through her mind, *Mom, protect her,* before she closed her eyes and prepared herself for nothingness.

"Get the fuck up."

She opened her eyes. The man was staring at her, the gun inches from her face. She pushed herself off the floor and then almost collapsed back down as blood rushed from her head down her body. She steadied herself against the wall, averted her eyes from the dark circle forming on his pants where the shard of wood had punctured his skin. The fire crackled from across the cabin, casting shadows and sharp patches of light onto the floor. The man walked over to her slowly. He looked at her intently, as if searching for something he lost in her face. He raised the gun, pressed it against her forehead. "I didn't want to do this," he said, more to himself than to Anne. "Why are you making me do this?" He looked to her as if for an answer, but she didn't know what he wanted her to say. There was still a ringing in her ears and she tried to play his question back in her head, so she could figure out how to answer, but there was only static. They were inches away from each other, his breath hot and sour on her face. He was staring at her hard, and she knew that whatever she said next would determine whether he pulled the trigger. Anne opened her mouth to speak even though she didn't have the right answer when Rose said, "You need her." Her mother's voice was strong and sure. "When the girl wakes up, she will want her mother." Anne felt the cold metal leave her forehead. It didn't matter that she still couldn't form words, because Rose had answered correctly. He took a long breath in, the gun hovered for a moment, level with Anne's head, and then he lowered it to his side. He grabbed her arm and dragged her back to the wall where her mother and daughter sat.

"If you move again, you're dead," he said.

It was not until Anne slid down into her place against the wall that she realized Rose hadn't tried to run with Thea. Her mother had not moved an inch.

ROSE

Rose clenched and unclenched her jaw as she listened to Anne's hurried whispers on the other end of the phone. She heard Thea in the background yell something and then Anne yelled back, "Thea, NO, that is NOT to eat. Mom," her voice came back into Rose's ear, "I gotta go, but I just can't believe he's back. How can this be happening?"

Rose wrapped her fingers tight around the cord of the old house phone she refused to get rid of and breathed in deeply through her nose before she spoke. "Honey, everything is going to be fine. Your father and I are here for both you and Thea. We will figure this—"

"Sorry, Mom, I gotta go." Rose heard "Thea Rose Thompson, spit it out" before Anne's voice cut off and Rose was left standing in the kitchen, listening to a dial tone. She stood like that for a few seconds, thinking, phone pressed to her ear, cord dangling down to the kitchen sideboard. It had been two years since she'd last seen Ethan, since she'd watched him with his mistress, girlfriend, whatever she was. She remembered the sense of calm she had felt, walking back into the hospital, into Anne's room, placing a kiss upon her daughter's clammy forehead, knowing that Ethan was gone for good.

Of course, she realized now, she had been mistaken. She wasn't thinking far enough ahead. She hadn't thought that eventually his workplace fling would come to an end and he would get bored. Her ex–son-in-law was a parasite, hopping from one host to the next, sucking the blood up until the host lay parched, a hollow shell of what she once had been. Rose had seen what he'd done to Anne, and she'd watched as her daughter slowly but surely came back to life. And now Ethan was here, in their hometown, about to take a wrecking ball to everything that Anne had built for herself and Thea during the past two years.

Rose gently put the phone down on its base and then picked it back up again. She dialed a cell phone number she knew by heart and listened to the deep voice come through on the other end.

Rose didn't even say hello. "I need you to teach me how to shoot."

THE CABIN

ROSE

Rose was torn between wanting her granddaughter to wake up and wanting her to stay unconscious, dead to the world, or at least to the man. On the one hand, if Thea were to regain consciousness, it would mean she was improving physically, and it would also mean they had a chance of running. All three of them. On the other hand, if Thea were to wake up, the sick son of a bitch would take her and . . . Rose didn't finish that thought. She knew what the man wanted, what he was going to do. Rose could tell that Anne's brain was stuck, wasn't letting the information in, but Rose knew right away from the way he looked at Thea. Pedophile. Rose was thankful that Anne hadn't made the connection yet, wouldn't allow herself to make the connection, because she needed her daughter as calm as possible.

The first attack had been unsuccessful, Anne had barely injured the man and the gun never left his possession, but Rose was already pushing forward in her head to the next steps. As long as Thea's eyes stay closed, she still had time to plot. She calculated that they had been in the cabin for less than twenty minutes, though it was already getting dark outside. The sun had disappeared from the gray sky, the night waiting to take over. The man had brought in larger chunks of wood from outside and steadily built a fire. It provided a flicker of warmth in the small room, enough that she thought Thea's body wouldn't give out from the freezing cold. She turned her head slightly to look at her daughter. Anne stared at nothing, as if in a trance, and rubbed Thea's arm.

After the failed attack, Anne had turned to Rose while the man collected more wood and whispered, "Mom, why didn't you move? You were supposed to run with Thea. At least try to. You didn't even try."

Rose had had to look away from Anne's stricken face. She couldn't answer truthfully, there was only so much she was willing to tell her daughter, and so she said simply, "I'm sorry. I froze." She thought of Sam and wished she could ask him what to do. Of course, if Sam were there, beside her, they wouldn't be in the cabin in the first place. She shook her head and smiled bitterly at her own twisted logic. Sam wasn't here and wouldn't be swooping in to rescue them, no matter how often her mind traveled to him.

Rose turned her attention back to the man, who was smoking again by the fire, when she felt the energy shift beside her.

"It's not fair," Anne said aloud. "To you, I mean." Rose snapped her head to look at her daughter, but Anne's focus was solely across the room.

"What?" the man responded gruffly, his back to them. Rose noticed he did not call her *bitch* or use another four-letter word. Rose's body tensed, waiting for Anne's reply. She did not know what her daughter was doing.

"You said you didn't want to kill anyone," Anne replied.

He turned slowly. "You don't know shit."

"That may be true, but I can sense you're struggling and I'm sorry for that. It must be difficult," Anne said calmly, smoothly. She was in therapist mode. Rose flicked her eyes between Anne and the man, as if she was watching a tennis game.

The man turned toward them. His eyes looked down to the floor and he nodded once. When he spoke, his voice was so low that Rose had to close her eyes to hear every word. "I was going to end it. I was gonna do the right thing. And then you drove in." The man flicked his cigarette into the fire and muttered something else that Rose couldn't hear. Rose was still unsure what Anne's intentions were in engaging the man, but this was the most the man had spoken since he took them, and Rose held her breath, waiting for Anne's next move.

"I'm sorry. I shouldn't have chosen that parking lot. I put you in a difficult position." Anne's voice was genuine without a hint of condescension, and even though Rose understood that her daughter was trying to engage the man or appeal to him in some way, she was impressed nevertheless.

The man turned his back to them again and spread his hands over the fire. Rose thought he had shut down, but then she heard him say something in a whisper.

THE CABIN

ANNE

"She had blond hair, so I had to," the man said, or at least that's what Anne thought he said—his back was to them again and the words came out in a whisper. She didn't have much time to process before she responded back to the man; it was important that she kept him engaged and she'd like to keep this specific energy going. She couldn't be sure that he said what he said or that he was referring to Thea but she went on instinct.

"Why did you have to? Why her?" She flicked her eyes toward her daughter and kept her voice level, interested but neutral. The more he talked, the more opportunity she would have, if things kept progressing, to find a way in, to flip a switch in his brain, to get him to see them as people rather than objects—she didn't know where that switch was yet, but she thought she could figure it out if she had some time. The man was not a straight-up psychopath, of that she was fairly certain, and the thought gave her some hope.

"She had blond hair," he repeated to himself, as if Anne's daughter's hair color was both the problem and the solution. "She's the one.

That's just the way it is," he muttered. His back was still to them and she feared she was losing him. He was retreating, so she asked another question to keep him talking.

"'She's the one'? What do you mean by that?" Anne kept her voice soft.

"You wouldn't understand." His voice dropped again and he turned to them and said loudly, "I don't have a fucking choice." She felt Rose tighten beside her. Anne's eyes inadvertently dropped to the dark patch of blood on his pants, and she forced herself to look at his face, forced herself not to stop on the gun. "I'm sorry you're struggling. Sometimes"—she thought for a beat—"sometimes it's incredibly difficult to control negative thoughts."

"Do you have thoughts you can't control?" The man was staring at her. She blinked. She wasn't expecting a question from him.

"Yes. I do," she answered. "Or I did for a long time after my daughter was born." She pointed with her chin. "Thea," she annunciated and the man flinched, "was born very early and I became obsessed with her health. I would wear a mask out in public and use hand sanitizer fifty times a day so that I didn't bring any germs home when she was a baby. It was mentally and physically exhausting." She felt Rose look from the man to her and back to the man again. Her mother must have been hopeful that she was making progress and she allowed herself the same hope. Anne opened her mouth to keep speaking but the man had begun to move in their direction. He crossed the room quickly and knelt down.

THE CABIN

THE MAN

The man tried to hide his smile while the mother therapized. She thought she was a hotshot. He had met people like her before, people who thought, if they could just get inside his mind and tinker around, they could fix him. He had had a guidance counselor named Ms. James who would sit down with him every week for an hour. During the first five or six sessions, he kept quiet, hardly said a word. Ms. James was young, probably the same age he was now, he realized, and it was her first job out of college. She told him that right away, as if that revelation, her incompetence, might bond them together. She asked him about the essay he wrote, the one that got him in trouble with his English teacher. She asked him why he never raised his hand in class, why he didn't have any friends or participate in any extracurricular activities. For weeks he had sat silently, doodling on pieces of "draw your feelings" paper, but Ms. James, with her thick glasses and hippie skirts that looked like blankets, was so steadfast in her questioning that he finally began to answer. It was better than being bored for an hour. He told her that he wrote that essay because he fantasized every day and dreamed every night about what his classmates' expressions would look like if they realized that he was in control, if he was the one deciding their fate. He told her that he wasn't interested in school, no matter how much his mother wanted him to study; and no matter how hard his father pushed football on him, he just didn't care. Ms. James still wanted to help him for a while; she tried to get him to "open up" about where these feelings were stemming from and she questioned him about his past, searching for evidence of trauma or abuse ("It's possible you don't even remember the traumatic event, that you blocked it out entirely," she told him earnestly). He finally told her, a few days before he met Julia, exactly what his fantasies consisted of: what it would feel like to have complete control over someone else, to be able to look into her eyes and know that he alone was causing her fear and pain, how it would sound to hear another human begging him to stop. The man explained to Ms. James that he'd had these urges, to inflict pain on other people, since he was a young child, but that only in the past few years had the fantasies evolved to include sex.

He became fixated on girls when he turned twelve, and by the time he got to high school, sex was all he thought about. Sophomore year, there was one girl in particular. Her name was Molly. She sat in front of him in chemistry and had ringlet curls. She was voted to be a "student helper" and sometimes she talked about the third graders she tutored on the weekends.

One time the teacher paired them up to do an activity. They were handed a packet on the periodic table of elements. They had to draw the table from memory and answer multiple choice questions. He didn't know any of the answers and Molly kept laughing at him, brushing her arm against his as she circled the answers, and telling him he should study more. He asked her if she would help him pre-pare for the test at the end of the week since she was a know-it-all. He said it with a half-smile, like he'd practiced in the mirror. She laughed again and said sure, she could help him after school the next day. When he got to the place they'd decided upon, near the swimming pool building and across from the tennis courts, Molly was already there, sitting on the grassy hill, books splayed open in front of her, waiting for him. He was ready. He had practiced in his head all last night, what he would say and do, how it would go. He watched the videos he had found online over and over. He started looking for vid-eos of men doing to women what he imagined doing in his head— there weren't any videos that got it exactly right, but watching every night helped him feel calm.

He studied Molly as he approached her spot on the hill. She sat Indian style on the grass, twirling a pen through her fingers like it was a baton. He felt all the crackly fuzz leave his head, and his thoughts became very clear. As soon as he was close enough he asked if she could come over to his house instead. He had forgotten that he had to walk his dog. They could study there; it would be better any-way, quieter, they could get more done. Molly stared at him and then she laughed. The dumb fucking bitch laughed, just like she'd done in class every day for the past year. Like all the girls did. Laughed at him every time he got an answer wrong, every time he was forced up to the chalkboard, every time the teacher pointed at him and said, "We haven't heard from you in a while . . . any lights on in there?"

"Why are you laughing?" he asked. The fuzz started to trickle back into his brain.

"I'm not going to your house." She closed the books in front of her and stood up. "Nice try, though."

That's when he knew, he told Ms. James, that if he wanted to have his way, he would have to make a decision. "If you couldn't do the one thing that made you feel alive, what would you do?" He had genuinely wanted to know, but Ms. James just shook her head and told him quietly to leave her office. That night he heard his mother on the phone with the school, her voice breaking as she set up a time to go and sit down with the principal and Ms. James. He heard his dad ask, "What was that about?" And his mom said, "That was about our son. Again." Then, "Oh, good, Rich, pour yourself another drink. That will really help."

Now, the man listened to the mother go on about her anxiety over her daughter's medical history. She said her daughter's name. *Thea.* He rolled the name around in his head. This girl was not like the others. She was different. If she woke up, everything would be different. He got up off the half-broken chair and walked over to the women. He knelt beside the older one, the one who knew what he was, and whispered in her ear exactly what he did to Julia.

THE CABIN

THEA

The room was dark and cold. She was still in between sleeping and waking but thought she was closer to awake. She could feel that her body lay on a hard surface and her head was in her mother's lap. She knew this because, even in the cold air, she could smell her mother, a mix of lavender and sage. She wanted to open her eyes, wanted to break out of the foggy place she was in, but her eyelids felt so heavy. She let herself sink back into her body. She felt a hand on her head, her mom's fingers, warm against her forehead. There were voices talking above her head. Her mother's voice and one she didn't recognize, a man's voice. There was something wrong with his voice, though—it wasn't like Mr. Redmond's voice, silky smooth, it was gruff and scary sounding. The words blurred together. She heard her mom respond to the other voice, but her mom sounded like she was talking to a friend and the other voice was fighting. There was something about the other voice that reminded her of something that she didn't want to remember—a memory at the very edge of her mind. It didn't make any sense, this memory—it was comprised of shapes and sounds and fear in the pit of her stomach. She didn't want to remember this, whatever it was. Thea stopped trying to listen; she blocked the voices and drifted back into half-sleep.

She let her mind wander back to another memory from Mr. Redmond's classroom. She sat at her desk. She was early, one of the first students to arrive for class. She pulled out her book, not really seeing the words, waiting for Mr. Redmond to notice her. A popular boy, one of the most popular boys in her entire grade, entered the room and broke the tension. Thea kept her eyes on the pages, but she felt that the popular boy was moving toward her instead of his own desk across the room. Her stomach fluttered as he approached her. He was coming over. He was going to talk to her for the first time. She looked up from her book, anticipation filled her stomach. She said, "Hey," right as he said, "I've never seen you from the side before. You have a pointy nose. Like a witch." He kept walking. Deep shame welled inside her. She looked up at Mr. Redmond, but he was riffling through papers at his desk. He didn't hear, thank god. Her face burned and she fought down the lump that was rising in her throat. She couldn't cry. She spent the rest of class in a daze, trying to work out in her head what to do, but there was nothing she could do about her nose. She didn't even know it was pointy. She hadn't ever looked at her own profile. At the end of class, she stood up numbly and walked out the door. She felt someone tug on her backpack and spun around.

"I wanted to tell you before you ran out of class—I saw that short story you wrote. The one that made it into the school paper. It's brilliant, Thea. I was very, very impressed." Mr. Redmond's eyes sparkled with admiration. Before she could respond, he had turned around and walked back into his classroom. She spent the rest of the day fighting a smile.

Her mind ricocheted further back to a memory from when she was seven or eight years old. She was looking out the car window as they pulled into a farm. Wide, open fields and bales of hay and barns scattered all around.

"Are you excited, Thee? You're going to ride a horse!" her mom called from the front seat.

She was excited, and a little scared. She loved horses more than anything, but horses were big in real life. "Yes," she said, still looking out the window as their car rolled into the dirt parking lot, kicking up dust. "How many other kids will there be?"

"I don't know, honey. Maybe five or six?"

When they got into the ring with the horses and the instructor and the other kids, Thea watched her mom pull the instructor aside. She could hear bits and pieces of their conversation. She tried not to listen but she heard the word *condition* and the instructor nodded vigorously. She looked at the other kids standing with their parents and then down at the ground.

"Ok, one at a time, guys," the instructor called out. "Get into a line. I'm going to help you onto the horse and then walk you around the ring, ok? Slow and easy. I know for a lot of you this is your first time on a horse. Let's have some fun, ok?"

Thea watched the first three kids go, each of them scrambling up onto the horse with the help of the small, sturdy instructor. When it was Thea's turn, her mom got on the horse first and she heard someone yell, "Hey, why does she get to go on with her mom? That's not fair." The instructor helped her up and then her mom pulled her the rest of the way. As the horse started to move, she jolted forward and panic flooded her body. She was really, really high off the ground. The horse was even bigger from this perspective. Her heart started to race.

She wanted to get down. She could feel tears starting behind her eyes. Her mom leaned forward, a warm pressure against her back, and wrapped her arms around Thea's middle. "You're ok, Thee," she whispered in Thea's ear. "You're on a horse, Thea. You're doing it." Thea's heart slowed. She felt her mom's warm cheek against her own. For a moment, she let herself believe that her mom wasn't riding with her because of her condition, because she was "different," but because she was special. By the time they had walked around the circle, Thea was glowing and she gave her mom and the instructor each a high five as she dismounted the horse.

The nice memory dissipated and her mind and body snapped back to the cold floor and the dark room. At first she didn't know why, and then she heard a voice, not her mother's, say very clearly, "It's time to wake up now, Thea."

ANNE

Six months after Ethan showed up at Anne's door, he showed up again, for his first court-ordered overnight with Thea. Two court hearings, in which Ethan had played the genuine, loving father, had resulted in the judge's granting Ethan supervised visits and then one overnight every other weekend. The week prior to the first overnight, Anne burst into tears eating a tuna sandwich, typing out an e-mail, walking to get a coffee, on the toilet, folding laundry. She couldn't eat more than a couple of bites before the food going into her mouth would feel like sludge on her tongue. She told Thea several times that the man, who was a friend of Mommy's, the one who had played with her in the children's room of the library, was going to be picking her up for a playdate and that she would be coming home in the morning and everything would be fine. Everything would be fine.

The night before, she took Thea's hand in hers. "So." Anne searched for the right words. "Remember how you're having a sleepover tomorrow with the man from the library? He's an old friend of mine, and he had to go away for a bit, but he's back now. Technically, he's your father," she finished, the words stilted, too adult. Thea cocked her head to the side. "Technically he's my fathah?" she repeated in an accent that varied between Boston and Scottish on any given day.

"Yes," Anne said. "You're having a sleepover with your dad. It's going to be fine!"

The next morning, Anne was waiting on the other side of the door, pacing, when the doorbell rang.

She opened the door, sweat coating her palms. "Hello."

Ethan flashed a bright smile. "Is she ready?"

"She is." She gripped the doorknob. "Thea!" She couldn't keep her voice from swinging up at the end; the sickly sweet intonation glaringly disingenuous even to her own ears.

Thea came bouncing into the entryway. Anne could see immediately her daughter was in one of her "I Love Everyone" moods. Thea ran to Anne's leg and peeked out from behind up to Ethan, wanting to stay hidden and be seen. "Hi," Thea sang. "I'm feeling shy." She bounced out from behind Anne's leg. "Ah we going to have a sleepovah?"

"You bet we are." Ethan crouched down to Thea's level. "How's my baby girl?" Anne watched as a tear formed in one eye and rolled down his cheek. She thought about how her knee was level with his nose. How her booted foot could easily smash down. Ethan straightened up. "Is she ready to go?"

"Mama." Thea looked up at Anne. Anne ran her hand along the top of her daughter's head, through her hair. Anne's chest tightened. Thea was going to leave, just like that. She knew it could have been the opposite just as easily, sobbing and screaming, having to drag

Thea to the car, that was what she had prepared for, and this was better; she knew that logically.

"Of course!" Her voice came out in a falsetto again. "Do you have
a car seat installed?" She couldn't look at him, her eyes were starting
to blur over, but she kept the smile plastered on her face.

"Yes, Anne, I have the car seat installed," Ethan drawled. "Thea,
want to ride in Daddy's cool car?"

They walked to Ethan's car, a black Maserati, with a car seat jammed
in the back seat awkwardly. When they reached the car, she thought, *I
can't do this.* Then she picked up her daughter, kissed her on the head,
buckled her in, and handed her overnight bag to Ethan. She told Thea
that she loved her and she'd see her in the morning, and then she walked
back to the apartment building, through the front door, into the
kitchen, and squatted down in front of the kitchen sink. She opened the
cabinet and pulled out the Windex, all-purpose counter cleaner, and a
bucket and spent the next hour scrubbing down the kitchen. *Everything will be fine.* She mopped and vacuumed, used a roll of paper towels on the windows, scrubbed the fridge with a sponge. She got down
on her hands and knees and scrubbed the tub, sprinkled blue powder
into the toilet and flushed it down. She even took the grates off the stove
and rubbed the grease and soot from the hidden crevices of the oven.
She looked at the clock. Nine p.m. She peeled off her sticky, dirt-stained
clothes, showered quickly, and then climbed into bed, exhausted.

She tossed and turned all night. It was too hot, so she threw the
covers off, and then too cold, so she got up and rummaged around for
pajamas. She must have finally fallen asleep for a few hours because
the next thing she knew she jolted awake, upright in bed. The clock
read seven a.m. Three hours until Ethan returned Thea. She called

Rose but the phone rang and rang and then her mother's machine came on. Rose had been working nonstop at the bakery lately. Rose's Sweets had taken off years ago after a write-up in *Bon Appétit* magazine (THESE ARE THE TEN BEST NEW BAKERIES YOU HAVEN'T HEARD OF), and she was always working, either at the bakery in the kitchen, baking and supervising, or in the basement of the bakery, creating new menu items, redesigning the layout, strategizing growth for the booming business. Lately, she was working even longer hours and never home. Rose's coping mechanism for Ethan's reappearance seemed to be to ignore it completely and hope for the best—"Don't worry, honey, everything is going to be ok"—a technique that had apparently trickled down to Anne.

She sat down on her couch/bed and opened her laptop, determined to pass the three hours by working on an essay due the next week. She had been doing the bare minimum for her master's program since Ethan reappeared, and it was starting to show. On her last research paper, the professor merely wrote, *This is lacking, Anne.* Anne stared at her notes, tapped the space bar a few times. *Think.* There was a big rock sitting on top of her brain, making her eyes feel heavy and her breathing shallow. She stood up, walked into the kitchen, poured herself a glass of water, sat back down at her laptop. She tapped the space bar again and then slowly bit each of her fingernails down to the quick. When she finished with her fingernails, she picked up her phone and dialed.

"Grace, I'm so sorry to call you like this, I know it's early and a Sunday and—"

"It's ok, Anne. What's going on?" She sounded like she'd been awake for hours.

"Ethan's come back and he had Thea last night for the first time and there's nothing I can do. It's a nightmare—" Anne paused for a moment to catch her breath and realized why she had really called Grace. "I need to tell you something—something I never told you during our sessions that I probably should have told you."

"Ok, I'm listening." A soft creak suggested she had sunken into a chair. Anne imagined Grace's hand cupped under her chin, assuming the same position she did in her office.

"I had an affair." Anne blurted the words out, wanting suddenly for them to be out of her body.

"When was this?" Grace asked, her voice smooth and neutral.

She recounted everything: the coffee dates, Ethan's mood swings, the morning at the apartment with Joseph and Ethan walking in. When she finished her chest burned and she inhaled deeply, starving for air.

"So," Grace said through the phone, bringing Anne back from Joseph's face and hands to the hard sofa bed. "Did you continue your relationship with Joseph after that?"

"No, Jesus, no. But"—she felt herself finally losing composure and the next sentence came out broken by sobs—"a few weeks later I found out I was pregnant." She wanted to tell Grace all the fragmented thoughts racing through her mind. She had been so close to leaving Ethan, then standing in the bathroom that morning holding the positive pregnancy test—before she made the decision to try with Ethan—her first impulse had been to grab her phone from the back of the toilet to google nearby clinics. The thought now, at how much her body and mind hadn't wanted Thea, filled her with shame. She felt certain that everything that was happening now was karma, the universe's way of punishing her for so desperately wanting to escape her marriage and the baby that grew inside her.

She wanted to tell Grace all of this, but instead she said, "I decided to make it work with Ethan. Of course, that ended up not being the right choice, either." She let out a bitter laugh. "I have these thoughts, though"—she paused, twisting a thread sticking out of the couch between her fingers—"that everything that's happening . . . is because of what I did."

"What you did?" Grace repeated it as a question, genuine curiosity lacing her voice. Anne heard a car engine and looked out the window.

"Oh shit, Ethan is three hours early," Anne said to Grace. "I'm so sorry, I have to—" She dropped her phone and ran out of the apartment, out of the building, and down the sidewalk, where Ethan's car idled at the curb.

"What are you doing here? Is everything ok?" she panted when she reached his car, yanking open the back door. "What's wrong? What's wrong, Thee?" Thea's face was red, sobs erupted angrily from her throat every half second, and her body convulsed in shudders. Anne unclicked the seat belts, pulled Thea from the car seat, and rocked her daughter. Thea buried her head into Anne's shoulder. Her daughter's body was sticky with sweat and her hair was matted.

"What happened?" She tried to keep the panic at bay, but her voice came out high and thick.

Ethan leaned against the side of the car. "Nothing *happened*, Anne," he said with a cold smile. "She just wouldn't stop crying. So I brought her back."

She felt Thea calming in her arms, her sobs turning into quick hiccups. She looked at Ethan. "Give me her bag." Anne took the overnight bag from his outstretched hand and turned toward her building.

"Thea," Ethan called when they were halfway up the path. "See you in two weeks, baby girl."

THE CABIN

ANNE

Anne watched her mother's face as the man talked into Rose's ear. Her mother's face was steady, not betraying a thing, until the very end when she pursed her lips and Anne could see her jaw moving, her molars biting down on the inside of her mouth. The man swiveled and his eyes fell on Thea. Anne lowered her eyes slowly, painfully, because she knew what she would see; Thea had started to moan softly while the man spoke to Rose and to roll her head back and forth on Anne's lap. Anne looked down now and saw her daughter's eyelids fluttering up and down, struggling to stay open. Thea's mouth opened slightly. "Mom," came out in a hoarse whisper. "Shh," Anne said as quietly and calmly as possible. She told her daughter with her eyes that she needed to stay quiet, that everything would be fine, but Thea's eyes flicked around wildly, from Anne to Rose to the man.

"Thea," the man was saying softly. "It's time to wake up." Anne looked at him quickly and then forced her eyes away because, with a jolt, she recognized exactly what it was she had seen before—not regret for what he had done, but for what he was going to do. She tasted blood and realized that her tongue was between her front teeth. Thea was shivering now. Anne could hear her gathering saliva to coat her parched mouth and throat and then she swallowed with a clucking sound. "Where?" she asked. Anne replied, "Shh," again. She brought her hand to Thea's forehead and cheeks. They sat like this for a few minutes, Thea's head still on her mother's lap, her eyes taking in the room, looking from Anne to Rose for answers.

"She needs to be closer to the fire," Anne said to the man. "She's too cold. Let me sit with her by the fire so that she can warm up and"—her voice caught but she continued—"get stronger."

The man's eyes never left Thea and it wasn't clear he even heard Anne speak. She tried again, "She's freez—"

"Fine," he cut her off. "Go."

Anne didn't look at Rose as she got up slowly and moved to the fire; her daughter's arms clutched her neck, her legs dangled almost to the floor. Anne pushed her mouth through Thea's hair, finding her daughter's ear. "Hold on to me. Don't let go." She lowered them both slowly to the floor in front of the brick hearth. The sides of their bodies facing the fire grew warm quickly. There was no grate, but the fire stayed contained in the hollow brick box. The larger pieces of wood burned steadily; soot and embers formed red, glowing clumps at the edges of the hearth. She felt Thea's heart beating against her own, felt Thea opening her mouth to speak. Anne shook her head, *No.* Thea nuzzled her head into the crook of her mother's neck. Anne didn't know how long she had so she forced her body to stay tense, ready. She could feel Rose across the room, and her mother's words echoed in her head, *If we're all going to get out of this.* She quieted her mind and waited.

She did not have to wait long. A few minutes passed and then the man began walking toward them. He stopped, barely a foot away, and stared at the back of Thea's head. He circled around them, like a child watching an animal through glass at the zoo, and lowered himself down behind them, in front of Thea's face. Anne felt her daughter's hot breath come faster into her neck. She heard him whisper, "Thea," and then it was time. She reached into a clump of embers, felt their hotness searing her skin. In one motion, she spun her feet and body toward the man and threw the soot and ash into his face. He shrieked from what sounded like far away. She was already on her feet. "Hold on, hold on," she told Thea, and her daughter did what she was told, her body went rigid and tight. Anne ran to the cabin door. She didn't know where the man was. It was quiet behind them now. Thea's arms and legs were wound tightly around her and so she used both hands to pry open the front door and then they were out on the porch. It was pitch black outside, or looked that way at first, coming from the bright glow of the fire, and she couldn't see anything, but she didn't stop. She found the outline of the railing and took the steps quickly, tripping on the last one and coming down hard on one knee; she got up, with hardly any time lost, and kept moving, through the open clearing outside the cabin and into the woods.

Anne paused, eyes straining against the darkness and turned her head left and right, staring into nothingness. "Mom," Thea breathed into her ear, and she whispered "Shh" again. She took a few steps forward, reaching her arms out in front of her and to the side. Her eyes had started to adjust, and she realized it wasn't quite night yet. She could make out the branches that surrounded them and snagged on their hair, coats, and legs, a tug of resistance before they sprung backward, back into the night. She had no idea how far they'd traveled from the cabin. She tried to keep moving in the general direction of the main path, but with each step their location became muddled in her mind. She stopped again, opened her eyes as wide she could; she could make out the dark shapes of the larger trees and branches, and she searched for a path snaking its way through the woods. Thea was starting to sag down her thighs, and she placed both her hands under her daughter's butt and boosted her up higher. She started walking again, ignoring the tight pinch in her lower back.

"Thea."

Anne froze at the sound of the man's voice.

"Thea, you have ten seconds to come back here before I shoot her." His voice cut through the air, closer than she would have thought; they must only have been fifty or so feet from the cabin.

"Mimi." Anne heard the anguish in Thea's whisper and a silent scream ripped through her body.

"Thea, no," she said, their cheeks pressed together. "We can't go back. Mimi wouldn't want us to go back." She felt hot wetness dripping down her face, her daughter's tears. "Thea, please," and now she was crying, too, silently, their tears mixing together.

"Ten," the man called out.

Anne closed her eyes while the man counted. Rose at her side in the hospital filled her head. Her mother washing her face and chest with a thin white washcloth when she couldn't yet bathe and braiding her greasy hair into a thick French braid. *Beautiful, Anne, you're just beautiful.*

"Six." The man's voice had an edge to it now. Rose scooping Thea from her arms when Thea was two months old, still so tiny and fragile, wailing for hours for something she couldn't provide. *Rest, Anne, you need to rest.* She felt Thea shaking against her. "Mimi," her daughter cried again, louder.

"Three!" he yelled, anger vibrating in his voice. The same tone that crept into Anne's voice when she used the ten-second rule to get Thea out the door in the morning, *Thea, I'm warning you.*

She felt Thea pushing against her, her daughter's hands shoving against her chest, Thea's legs kicking to the ground, and she knew it was over. "No," she pleaded. "Thea, no." Anne dropped to her knees, taking her child with her, trying to hold on to Thea's limp form, but her daughter struggled free, just like she'd been able to since she was a toddler, tensing and relaxing her body into spaghetti, slithering expertly out of her mother's grip.

"Two." The man's voice was calm now, accepting, and in Anne's mind, she saw him placing the gun against Rose's temple.

"Mimi, we're coming!" Thea's high voice cut through the air. "We're coming back, wait!" A moan floated through the trees. Rose.

Anne crawled for a few seconds and then staggered to her feet. Turned back toward the cabin, she could already see the dim outline of the building, lit from within by the glow of the fire. She heard Thea crunching through the woods ahead of her and took long strides to catch up. She got in front of her daughter and put her hands under Thea's armpits; Thea struggled for a moment until Anne said, "It's ok, Thee, it's ok."

It only took a few minutes to reach the clearing where the man stood with Rose. Thea wriggled out of her grip again and threw herself around Rose. Anne couldn't look at her mother. She failed her by leaving and she failed her by coming back.

The man looked at them. No, didn't look at them, looked at Thea.

"Good decision," he said with a smile.

THE CABIN

THEA

The cabin was freezing and it felt like someone had smashed a hammer into Thea's forehead. The last thing she remembered was running; she was racing her mom, and then . . . nothing. She looked around the barren room, eyes stopping briefly on the man with the gun. Raggedy facial hair covered most of his face, but she was sure she'd never seen him before. The man had separated her from her mom and Mimi so she sat alone at the back of the cabin. Her mom was toward the front door with the man, and she and Mimi were on opposite sides of the back wall. She pulled her legs toward her chest and shivered. It was freezing, even with the fire going. Thea knew from the silence in the room that her mom and Mimi were really scared. There was a thickness to the air. She wanted to ask questions but she didn't dare open her mouth.

Thea took some deep breaths through her nose and tried to stay calm. "Don't panic," her teacher had said during the last active shooter drill. "It's really important to keep a clear head in these situations." *Ok*, she released a breath, *don't panic*. She took stock of what she knew. There was a man with a gun: bad. But they were alive: good. The fact that they were still alive must mean that he didn't want to kill them. Thea clung to this thought. She knew from school exactly what to do if there was ever a bad man with a gun. She had been doing lockdown drills since kindergarten. If she was in a classroom, they would hide in the closet while the teacher barricaded the door and the windows. If she was in the cafeteria, she would run to the storage room with the orange door that could fit a few dozen kids. Except both these plans hinged on having a spot to hide. Thea looked up again, moving her body as little as possible. There was nowhere to hide in the cabin. The man with the gun caught her eye. Those plans also hinged on the man with the gun not yet being in the same room, staring at you.

Thea closed her eyes to shut out the creepy man. She tried to focus on her breathing, pushing air in and out of her body. She couldn't feel her hands or her feet and she tried to imagine the sun on her body, warming her from the outside in. She was going to die from the cold, she thought, and tears formed behind her eyes. She imagined herself on a beach, somewhere warm, and then, without meaning to, her thoughts were filled with Mr. Redmond. She scolded herself again; thinking of him right now was stupid, but she couldn't help it and the more she tried not to think about him, the more she thought about him. She squeezed her hands into balls and remembered the first text she sent him, the week after he complimented her short story.

Hi Mr. Redmond/Ted (lol), it's Thea. How are you doing? Just saying hi . . . I hope it's ok for me to text . . .

Thea, hi! I'm doing ok . . . of course it's ok. How is break going? ☺

Great! I'm in Florida with my mom.

Oh wow, that sounds great. I'm jealous ☺

Yeah, there's a pool and everything. See?

Have a great time, Thea. See you in class soon.

She had sent a picture of herself in the hotel pool, the water up to her waist, in her first two-piece bathing suit. Her mom bought it for her in anticipation of their first trip to Disney World—the zip-up top had Mickey's face plastered across the front. An older man had walked past her at the pool, his flip-flops smacking against the wet concrete. He smiled, eyeing her up and down. "You're going to be quite the heartbreaker, honey." She had laughed and turned red. It wasn't a big deal, he meant it as a compliment, but she'd plugged her nose and sank underwater for as long as she could hold her breath, and when she came up for air, he was gone.

Her first day back at school, after winter break, she stayed after class, heart pounding, to ask Mr. Redmond a question about the Spanish homework he'd assigned for that night. She spent the last twenty minutes of class rehearsing the question in her mind, over and over, so that it sounded casual but real. She kept thinking about the bikini picture and his response, the dot dot dots, how they had started and stopped several times, while she held her breath. Had she made a huge mistake? Maybe she'd gotten it all wrong. Of course, she'd gotten it wrong. She was a huge idiot for thinking a man like Mr. Redmond would ever be interested in a gangly loner girl. But maybe . . . maybe he felt the same way. She had to know for sure.

"Thea?"

The word snapped her out of her reverie, and she adjusted her face from the angsty expression she was sure she'd been making to neutral.

"Class is over," Mr. Redmond said with a smile. "You might not have noticed but everyone else has left."

"Oh, yeah, ha. I just—" She pushed her chair back and stood, the groaning of the chair's feet against the linoleum filled the silent room. "I wanted to ask you a question about tonight's homework. You said to start on page 274, but I looked and the lesson actually starts on the next page, so I wasn't sure if you wanted us to do the last part from the previous section or maybe you made a . . ." Her face filled with color, she hadn't gotten this far in her head. She didn't want to accuse Ted of making a mistake. *Shit.* "Um, maybe the book is wrong or something?"

Mr. Redmond walked over to her desk, brushing against her shoulder as he peered down at the textbook. He flipped it open and fanned the pages to page 274.

"Look at that. You're absolutely correct, Thea. Start on the next page." He turned and looked her straight in the eye. "Good catch."

"Sure, no problem." She backed away from him, breaking the contact of their shoulders. Her stomach flipped. She tried to think of something else to say. *Do you like me?* "I guess I'll see you tomorrow!" God, she was a loser. She couldn't even figure out how to flirt with a guy. She walked quickly to the door, her face burning.

"Oh, by the way, Thea, if anyone ever bothers you. If any guy . . . gives you any trouble at all. Please tell me."

She stopped and turned back. Mr. Redmond's eyes pierced hers. He was jealous of other guys. He did like her. She was right. Her heart thudded loudly in her ears. The air felt thick with static electricity.

"Of course . . . Thanks, Mr. Redmond."

"You can call me Ted, remember?" He winked. "See you tomorrow, Thea."

"See you tomorrow . . ." *Do it. Don't be such a scaredy-cat. Do. It.* "Ted."

Thea shivered and snapped back to the reality of being trapped in a dank, freezing cabin. She tried to imagine that she was back at Disney World with her mom, the sun beating down, sweat pooling under her arms, and her mom asking discreetly at the end of the day, "Sweetie, you know you can borrow my deodorant, right?" Thinking about being warm was not working, if anything it was making her colder. She tried to get Mimi's eye. They should all charge the man at the same time. Even with Mimi's hands bound and her mom's ankles tied, it would still be three against one. She just needed to somehow relay this thought to her Mimi and her mom. *Mimi,* she thought, staring a hole into her Mimi's head. She coughed a tiny cough. *Mimi.* Mimi didn't budge. Thea tried to see what her grandmother was looking at—from this angle she could only see the side of Mimi's face, but when she followed her gaze, Thea found her own eyes traveled to the man. Thea looked at Mimi's eyes again. They were looking at the man but they were angled slightly, not at the man's body but at what he was holding in his hand. She followed her grandmother's gaze again. Mimi was staring straight at the gun.

ROSE

The first three times Rose asked her husband to teach her how to shoot, he said no. By the fourth time, though, he just looked at her, shook his head, and sighed. Sam knew, and Rose knew, that when Rose wanted to do something, she would do it, one way or another. Sam learned this on their third date. He took her to Echo Lake Aquarium in Burlington. She had mentioned that she'd never been to an aquarium even though at one point growing up she'd lived only an hour away from the Boston aquarium. She said that her mother had tried to take her and her brother once, when she was thirteen years old and her brother eight, but when they got there, the discount coupon her mother tried to use turned out to be expired. Instead of arguing or appealing to the college kid's sense of compassion, Rose's mother had turned quickly on her heel. "Let's go," she called to Rose and her brother, as they trailed behind her teary-eyed.

On their first date, Rose told Sam that she loved sharks, it was close to an obsession growing up—she'd had a shark lunch box, a T-shirt with a picture of an openmouthed great white across the front, and shark bath toys (all bought in the boys' section of the Renys in her hometown), and she'd always wanted to see one in real life. When they pulled into the parking lot of the Echo Lake Aquarium, Sam turned to Rose. "Unfortunately, they don't have sharks here, but the person I spoke with said they have a giant sea turtle, one of the biggest ever found. I thought that might be interesting—"

"Wonderful!" Rose cut Sam off. "I can't wait. Let's go."

They walked through the building slowly, looking at the colorful fish in the tanks lining the walls, stopping to watch how one exhibit mimicked the ocean current, and peering into a touch tank with a starfish suctioned to the glass and minnows shooting through the shallow water.

"Let's go see the turtle," Rose said, increasing her pace up the ramp to the next floor. They followed signs pointing to CHARLIE, THE LARGEST SEA TURTLE IN NORTH AMERICA all the way to the top floor of the building.

"I'm sorry, miss," the attendant in a blue jacket said with genuine pity in his voice. "The last show is just about to finish up and then Charlie's off duty for the day."

"Oh no!" Rose exclaimed.

Sam blushed. "I'm sorry, Rose. I should have checked the time."

"Oh, it's all right," Rose said. "It's not the end of the world. You go ahead. I'm going to use the ladies'. I'll meet you outside."

Rose came galloping out of the building fifteen minutes later, right as Sam was about to reenter to look for her. "Where have you been?" Sam asked with a laugh at his date's expression.

"I was at the sea turtle exhibit!" Rose said with glee. "It was marvelous."

Sam laughed again. "Rose. How did you—"

"I have my ways," she said, hooking her arm into his.

Sam looked at the glowing young woman beside him and felt his insides constrict with longing. He had thought she was kind and pretty before, that's why he frequented her bakery every morning and spent seventy-five cents on coffee that he really should have been saving toward new tools, but that afternoon he saw her sheer force of will come out for the first time.

When Rose found out she was pregnant, three months after they were married, she was thrilled and terrified. She had been told after her miscarriage that it was very unlikely that she would get pregnant again, due to scarring in her fallopian tubes, and even less likely that she would carry a baby to term if she managed to get pregnant. "Look at the positives," the doctor had told her. "Once you settle down with the right fellow, you won't need to use protection." So she had managed her expectations; she took the pregnancy week by week, never allowing herself to truly believe an actual baby would be arriving at the end. Sam, on the other hand, was overjoyed from the day she walked out of the bathroom, pregnancy stick in hand, with a look of disbelief on her face.

"There is a strong, healthy baby girl in there with an iron will. Just like someone else I know," he'd said and pressed his ear to her still-flat belly. "Yep, there she is, chattering away."

"I told you what the doctor said two years ago." Rose placed her hand on his head. "This probably won't stick." She knew exactly what was coming; she'd experienced it before.

Rose never quite let her guard down, even when they passed the three-month mark, and then the six-month mark. She didn't truly believe she was carrying a baby until Anne was placed in her arms, silent with blue eyes wide open. Rose took to motherhood immediately.

She commiserated with her next-door neighbor who also had a newborn, nodding her head in agreement when they discussed the exhaustion, the physical toll, and the mental drain, but secretly she loved every moment, even the long nights when Anne seemingly couldn't get enough to eat and woke every two hours.

As Anne grew up, Rose observed how her husband's love for their child morphed—Sam loved baby and toddler Anne easily, bursting through the front door after work and swinging her up onto his shoulders, practicing numbers and letters with flash cards before bed, and then, bit by bit, something changed. As she aged into a young woman, his love became muted. The pure joy in his face upon seeing his daughter turned to assessment, as if, in order to mold her into a proper human being, he had to put a barrier between the two of them. Rose understood, though she wasn't sure that Sam himself did, that he made a choice to steer the course of his relationship with his daughter from a full, deep love to shallow waters, where they stood safely. As Anne grew up, Rose would sometimes catch her husband looking at their daughter, as if he knew a painful truth that she had yet to learn. Rose always wondered what he was picturing when the cloud came over his face. He spoke very little of his time overseas, but Rose could sense that the way physics, or fate, had unevenly distributed the shrapnel weighed on Sam every day. There were things that Sam could not explain to anyone, not even himself, about what he had experienced in Vietnam, and so he distanced himself from Anne, the child he loved so wholly, but also the person who might be able to unearth those unnamed things.

Sam looked at Rose now and sighed again. "Rose, I'll do this under one condition."

Rose cocked her head and let out a noncommittal "Hmm?" not

giving any indication of agreement or disagreement but encouraging him to continue nonetheless.

"Before you take any action, you come to me first. If we're going to do this, I need to know in advance."

"Fine."

"Rose. I'm serious. With my background, I'll be the one—"

"Sam." Rose took his hand in hers. "Think about what life will be like if we can pull this off. Think about Thea." She watched Sam's face as he made the calculations. She knew within three seconds that her husband would acquiesce.

"When can we start?" Rose asked.

"Let me talk to a friend. I'll want you using something that can't be traced. Give me a couple of weeks."

Rose's heart thrummed as the reality hit of what she was asking her husband to do.

"Good." She nodded and released his hand. "Sam . . . I'll only . . . take action if there's no other choice. I just want to be pre—"

"Give me a couple of weeks," he said again. "If we're going to do this, we're going to do it right."

ANNE

She checked Thea all over for marks, bruises, cuts. Nothing. When she asked her daughter what happened at Mama's friend's house, Thea's face crumpled and she asked if she was going back again. "No. No, you're with Mama now. Everything's ok." Anne couldn't bring herself to tell her daughter that she was going back in two weeks.

The next day she cut over to Ethan's house after work, before picking Thea up from daycare. A warm breeze followed her up his front walkway, lined with manicured shrubs and white and pink roses. The sweet smell wafted into Anne's nostrils and she held her breath. Her body shook as she stood on his front porch and rapped on the door. Heavy footsteps sounded and then the white wooden door swung into the house. Ethan stood on the other side of the threshold in gray sweatpants and a dark green sweater.

"Annie." He said it like she was the last guest to arrive for a dinner party. "Come on in."

"If you ever touch Thea, if you ever hurt her, I will fucking kill you." She recited the words she had practiced on the way over, but tears were already forming beneath her anger and she clenched her jaw, determined not to show weakness.

"I will never, ever"—Ethan paused and smiled, taking his time—"leave any marks on Thea. You won't be able to prove anything. I'll make sure of that."

She stared at him, unable to take in what he was saying for a moment. "What are you?" she finally asked.

"Don't be so dramatic, Anne." Ethan laughed. "I'm merely a father trying to get to know his daughter. His daughter who has been kept away from him for the first two years of her life. We have a lot of catching up to do. Thanks to you." He crossed his arms over his chest and waited. "Is there anything else you want to talk about?"

Words flashed into her mind, but she couldn't form a coherent sentence. She stood there, staring at him, studying him, and oddly a sense of calm flooded her body. She was right about her ex-husband; a tiny part of her had wondered if it was possible that she *was* misremembering, that perhaps Ethan hadn't pushed her, that she had, in fact, slipped down the stairs. That part of her was erased as she stood looking at the thing in front of her. Somehow *this*—whatever this was—felt better than being in limbo.

"No," she said, the tremor had left her voice. "There's nothing more to talk about."

"Right, bye then." Ethan shut the door.

She walked down Ethan's perfectly paved path, surrounded by his sprawling, perfectly buzz-cut lawn, and got into her car. She called Rose on the way to daycare and told her mother about the confrontation with Ethan.

"Thea and I have to go, Mom," she said, one hand gripping the steering wheel. "I'm going to start researching tonight. I probably won't tell you where, at least for a little while." She waited and then brought the phone away from her ear, checking to make sure she was still connected.

"Yes. I think you're right," she heard Rose's voice float out of the top of the phone. Anne brought the phone back to her ear.

"What? Mom, what did you say?" She was prepared to list out the reasons why this was her only choice—the slowness of the courts, the broken legal system, the futility of trying to prove psychological abuse. She couldn't believe that Rose would condone running away with Thea without trying to convince her to examine all of her options.

"I think you're right," she heard Rose say again. "Ethan is dangerous, and we can't wait for him to actually hurt Thea in order for the court to strip his visitations." Rose's voice was calm, hypnotic. "Why don't you start planning, get together the documents you'll need, money, an extra cell phone, think about changing your physical appearance, just in case. It's going to take a few weeks, maybe longer, to get everything together, so start now."

Anne realized with a start that Rose had already been anticipating this—the moment this call would happen. Listening to her mother list out everything she would need to do to disappear made her suddenly hesitant that this was the right choice. She went through the other possibilities in her head, down the other paths they could take, but each time she arrived at the spot where she would be required to wait on a judge to decide Thea's future. She thought of what Ethan had said, he wouldn't ever leave marks on Thea, he would never do anything she would be able to prove. No, there was no other choice.

"Thanks, Mom, I'll keep you updated as much as I can," she said, pulling up to the small white house where Thea went to daycare every day. "I gotta go. I love you."

"I love you, too."

That night Anne took Thea's hands in hers and lifted her daughter's body slowly into the tub, like a crane plopping down a concrete slab.

"Doop doop doop and you're in!" she said as Thea's feet hit the water.

Thea yanked two dinosaurs out of her toy basket and began walking them slowly toward each other on the rim of the tub. "You be him, Mama," she said, eyes concentrated on the imminent collision of the dinosaurs. "Mama, you be *him*." She jerked the pterodactyl toward Anne.

"Give me one second, Thee," she said, pulling her phone out of her back pocket and bringing up the page she had been looking at before. "Safety Plan," the website said in red letters at the top. She heard Thea let out a sigh. "Just . . . one . . . second." Thea chattered in the background as she scrolled down the page. She was so absorbed in trying to memorize the main bullet points on the page that for a minute, maybe more, she didn't notice that anything was wrong. It was the lack of sound, the silence, that finally broke through her concentration. Anne's head snapped up. Thea's face jerked in small movements. "Thea?" Her daughter's eyes were open but glazed, looking down into the water. "Ok. Ok, you're ok." Anne grabbed her shoulders and pulled her body out of the water. Thea's arms lay stiff by her sides and Anne wedged her fingers into her armpits to keep a hold of her. Thea's body was stiff, frozen, and her head still moved slightly back and forth on repeat. Anne's first frantic thought was that her daughter was choking, and she thumped her back quickly before realizing Thea hadn't been eating anything and her face was pale, not bluish-purple. "Thea." She tried to connect with her child's eyes but they stayed glazed and down. "Thea, baby, can you talk to me? Can you say something?" she pleaded. Anne reached backward with one hand, searching for a towel on the rack behind her. Her hands touched soft fabric and she yanked the towel down and spread it clumsily on the floor and then placed Thea on it. She wrapped her up, blotting water drops from her face with the edges of the towel, and heaved her daughter into her arms. She got halfway to Thea's bedroom and then ran back for the cell phone, reaching down, careful to keep one hand secured under Thea's head, and scooped up the phone from the bath mat. As she jogged back toward Thea's bedroom, she brought up the keypad and dialed 911. Right as she was about to hit the green call button, she felt her daughter's body softening in her arms and then "Mama" came from within the bundle.

"Are you ok? Thea." Anne peered into the towel. "How do you feel?"

"Gud," Thea replied. "Tired."

"But, love, what happened?" Anne asked her daughter, knowing she wouldn't be able to give an answer, that she seemingly wasn't even aware of the convulsions that had overtaken her for . . . a minute? Twenty seconds?

"Don't cry, Mama."

"I'm just happy you're ok," Anne said, wiping her face. "These are happy tears."

"I'm ok." Thea nodded. "Book and bed."

As Anne read *The Missing Piece Meets the Big O*, Thea drifted to sleep. Anne listened to her daughter's breath come in and out of her nose and watched her chest rise and fall. She deposited Thea into her crib, hovering over her for several minutes before backing quietly out of the room.

She walked into the living area quickly, dialing the pediatrician's office on the way down, pressing 1 for the after-hours nurse. After ten minutes of describing Thea's movements and asking and answering questions, the nurse said that it sounded like a shuddering spell.

"It's actually pretty common in kids her age. It looks scary but it's a normal developmental occurrence that, to be honest, we don't even really know that much about. These shuddering attacks fall into the medical category of 'undiagnosable but normal.'" The nurse let out a husky laugh. "There are more of those than you might think. You know, it could also be something like a pinched nerve. There's a whole slew of things that could have caused it and most likely it'll never happen again. If she's acting normally tomorrow and doesn't have a fever, then you don't need to bring her in. Just keep an eye out, ok?" Anne's breathing slowed at the nurse's assured, cut-and-dry tone. As soon as she ended the call, a text message flashed across the top of the screen.

Grace: Checking in. Is everything ok?

Shit. She had completely forgotten about hanging up on Grace the day before. She responded, fingers flying across her phone, asking if now was a good time to finish their conversation. Grace wrote back asking Anne to call her in five. Anne sat on the pullout sofa, tapping her fingers against her leg. She wondered if what she said in their last conversation changed how Grace thought of her, and her face burned as she dialed.

"I'm so sorry to have hung up on you before—Ethan showed up early with Thea and I thought something was wrong. I'm sorry I completely—"

"Is Thea ok?"

"Yes, she's—" She thought about her daughter sobbing on her shoulder outside Ethan's car. And the tremor in the bathtub. The page still up in her phone Internet browser about putting a safety plan in place. "Yes, she's fine. I think he just didn't know what to do with a two-year-old."

"Good." Grace let out a deep breath. "I'm so glad to hear that. Look, I have to ask again, have you thought about reaching out to some of your friends? Lana or Whitney? It would be really good for you to have some support. I know you've said that—"

"No." Anne shut Grace down. "Those friendships are too far gone. I was . . . What I did, missing Lana's show and not seeing Whitney all the times she visited the city after I married Ethan. Never responding to messages or phone calls. I was horrible. Just trust me on this."

There was silence for ten seconds before Grace asked, "Anne, what did you mean when you said before that 'everything that's happening now is because of what I did'?"

Anne licked her lips. They were so dry that the saliva burned. "I didn't want Thea. My whole pregnancy, I resented the thing inside me . . . And this . . . Ethan coming back, getting custody . . . it feels like karma." Grace took a sharp breath; Anne braced herself.

"Anne, there is no such thing as the universe punishing someone. Do actions have consequences? Absolutely. But the only thing we have control over is how we move through life and what we learn as we go along. I always want my patients to look within themselves and try to be brutally honest about how they can make healthier choices and really guard their own emotional well-being, but—" Grace paused to take a breath. "Sometimes you're also dealing with some really fucked-up shit. Ok? They're not mutually exclusive."

Later, Anne hung up the phone and thought about her conversation with Grace. She stretched out on the sofa, too tired to pull the front out into a bed. She turned over in her head what it would feel like to believe that Ethan returning wasn't punishment for what she did with Joseph, but rather another lesson that she was going to have to fight her way through, making the best decisions she could with the information she had. *Pretty fucked-up lesson*, she thought as her eyes closed. That night she dreamed of Thea's head jerking to the side in rapid movements, her arms and legs stiffening as she toppled to her side. "Thea, tell me what's happening," she cried. Her daughter's eyes stayed glazed, but this time she spoke through the side of her mouth, crystal clear, "Mommy. I can't tell you. I'm sorry. You have to figure this out yourself."

THE CABIN

ROSE

Rose hadn't touched a gun in ten years. Truth be told, it never made her feel safer when she carried a gun on her body, the opposite in fact, and she was glad when she no longer had use for it. But when she looked at the man's gun, snug in his hand, she could feel its weight, the cold smoothness against her palm, the power beneath her fingers. She closed her eyes and breathed in the sour air through her nostrils and felt the burn in her throat after the trigger was pulled. She saw from the way the man held the gun that he'd only used it once or twice before, a handful of times at most. He treated it as a foreign object, separate from himself, and he gripped it tightly but awkwardly, as if it might wriggle out of his hands at any moment.

Rose thought about the night she went to Ethan's house ten years ago. How she had looked at Sam after that phone call from Anne, and he had known immediately. That was the night.

"But am I ready?" Rose had asked, the blood slowly draining from her head.

Sam had surprised her by saying without hesitation: "Yes, Rose, you're ready."

He'd packed an overnight bag and called an old marine friend, the one he had dinner with once or twice a year and usually ended up staying the night if he had too many beers. When Sam hugged Rose goodbye, she felt his body tremble and, for the first time, wondered if she was making a mistake.

"When it comes down to it, it's just another day in the woods. Just like yesterday, and the day before," Sam said, standing in the kitchen with his arms wrapped around her. "The first time I took someone down, it messed me up. I had panic attacks and I kept thinking about the guy I shot. Who was he? Did he play sports? Like to read? Did he have a family? Racing, obsessive thoughts." Rose listened quietly, her head on his chest, their soft bellies touching. "Before the next mission, my sergeant took me aside and asked me, 'What was the alternative? If you hadn't gotten your shot off before him. What was the alternative? It's not going to get easier, so you need to decide whether you can live with this better than you can live with the alternative.'" Sam backed up and looked at Rose. "I guess what I'm trying to tell you is: What you're about to do . . . it's not like in the movies. Afterward, you're different; it stays with you, it seeps into you, and it's a heaviness that you'll carry. Always." Sam sighed. "But don't second-guess what you're about to do. Unless you can live with the alternative."

They never spoke outright about what all the practicing and training was for—Sam's speech was as close as they ever came to putting it into words, and Rose understood that, in his halting way, he was giving her his blessing. After she heard his car start up and back out of the garage, she got ready slowly and methodically. She laid out the ninja ensemble she had stored in her bottom drawer: black turtleneck, black leggings, black gloves. She dressed quickly and then undressed, deciding on jeans and a blue sweatshirt blotted with coffee stains. She wound her hair into a tight bun and secured it, watching her face in the mirror like she was looking at a stranger, waiting for it to break into a smile or start talking, but it stared blankly back at her. She walked into her bedroom and slid her fingers into one glove and then the other, testing the fit, scrunching and straightening her fingers into the nylon material.

Rose looked down at her hands now, bound tightly at the wrists with her own shoelace from her Bean boots. She glanced to her left and caught Thea in her periphery—huddled against the wall a few feet down, knees to her chest, arms circling her legs, head resting against the points of her knees. Rose moved her eyes carefully to the right without moving her head and saw Anne's legs and feet, tied together at the ankles with Rose's other shoelace. Rose shivered involuntarily at the section of Anne's naked skin showing between her thin socks and leggings that ended just above her calves. She silently scolded her daughter for not wearing long underwear and thick socks. Anne's zip-up boots laid on the hearth, the tall trunks curled over onto themselves, empty. Anne hadn't looked at Rose since the man had dragged her back into the cabin and thrown her against the wall. Rose wanted to tell her daughter that she did the right thing, she had come so close to saving Thea, and it was not her fault that they were all back in the cabin now.

Rose kept her eyes straight ahead on the fire and shifted her hands slightly, feeling how much leeway she had. The boot lace was wrapped tightly around her wrists twice and the prickly fibers cut into her skin. She rubbed her wrists against each other, keeping the back of the man in her sight. The thin rope cut deeper into her flesh but gave a tiny bit. She straightened and scrunched her fingers, testing. For now, she had full range of motion in her limbs but she feared they might fall asleep. As long as she could move her fingers she thought she was still good.

Her stomach rumbled for the first time since they entered the cabin and she wondered about Anne and Thea. It had only been a few hours since lunch, but Thea had barely eaten, pushing her burger around her plate, sucking the ketchup off a few fries. Rose pictured the large water cups dripping condensation onto their table and her insides suddenly screamed for water. She blocked the image immediately. They would last another few hours in this cold before they started to get sluggish from dehydration, and Rose didn't think the man intended on keeping them another few hours anyway, from the looks he'd been giving Thea. The words the man had whispered in her ear ran through her mind. *"I used a glass bottle, so that the bitch would stay nice and still."* Rose shuddered and flexed her fingers again.

THE CABIN

THE MAN

The man was almost done waiting. His whole body vibrated with anticipation. But when he looked at the girl, a sickness formed in the middle of his stomach and he wanted to smash his head against the floor. She looked only half alive, huddled by the fire, but he didn't care. He was tired of waiting. He started walking toward the girl. He licked his lips and pressed the end of the gun on the crescent-moon scar.

"I know what you want." The mother's voice jerked him out of his thoughts and he stopped abruptly in the middle of the room. "I can give you what you want," she continued in a low voice.

The man let out a sharp laugh. The bitch was trying to crack his code again. "I already told you. You don't know shit."

"It's not your fault that the girls in your school didn't understand you," she replied. He let out another laugh, but his face burned as Molly's ringlets flashed into his mind.

"It's because they were so young. They couldn't understand." The woman's voice was cold and she looked straight into his eyes. "I get it. You want someone to see you for what you are. I see you."

The man turned his body away from the girl, toward the mother. "What do you see?" he asked.

"I see a powerful man. A man who knows what he wants. You want control. Complete control. I can give you that." She leaned toward him, off the wall as far as she could. "I can give you exactly what you want."

The man felt his body responding to her words. He walked toward her until the tips of his boots touched the soles of her feet. He extended his hand and the woman took it, hauled herself off the ground awkwardly, tipping to the side. He pushed her back against the wall and she almost fell again. "Not here," she said in his ear, leaning on his arm. "Untie me so we can go outside."

The man admired her, what she was trying to do, and for a moment he considered it, examined the offer. But it wouldn't be real with this woman; it would be like the videos he used to watch, where even the violence seemed practiced and orchestrated. He pressed against her harder and felt himself go soft. Rage coursed through his body as he remembered the back seat of the Saab, Julia, and the same feeling he had now of not being in control of his own body. He'd held Julia down, but he couldn't do it; he could feel her beneath him, judging, probably pitying him, smirking to herself, that bitch. He'd finally grabbed the Coke bottle he'd gotten at the rest stop. Now, his admiration turned into anger as he looked into the mother's eyes and saw a glint of laughter.

He didn't know he was going to do it until his knee connected with soft flesh, but once it happened, it felt right. The woman buckled over on herself, a half moan escaping her lips. He heard "Please" as he brought his fist down on her back, but he couldn't stop now. It felt good and he wanted her to be quiet. The child screamed and he yelled, "Shut up or I'll kill her." The woman was on the ground, legs curled to her chest. He kicked her once, a sharp kick to somewhere in the middle, it was hard to be precise with her arms in the way, and he heard a crack. She was still now.

"Shut up," he said again into the room, even though it was silent. "I need quiet." The man pointed the gun first at the old woman and then at the girl.

There was a woman doctor at the prison who told him over and over that his feelings of rage stemmed from growing up in a society that didn't allow boys to be vulnerable, to emote. "You will only begin to heal when you acknowledge that it's ok to experience emotions and have insecurities. Try to accept those feelings instead of repressing them. And let someone else accept you as well," she said, leaning toward him, almost tipping out of her black plastic chair.

He lowered the gun from the girl to his side. He studied the lump of the mother in front of him. It was her vulnerability, her emotions that put her in the position she was in now. He wanted to tell that prison doctor that he may never be healed, he may never be normal, but he felt pretty fucking good right now.

TEN YEARS
BEFORE THE CABIN

ANNE

Two days before Thea's next overnight with Ethan, Anne broke out into hives. Her boss tapped on the side of her cube and asked if she should maybe go home. "I won't count it as PTO, Anne . . . Just, you know, a freebie," he said, leaning his body slightly away from her.

"Oh! No, it's not contagious. I'm having an allergic reaction"—she laughed loudly and it reverberated through the small office—"to sushi." It was the first thing that came into her head. "I had it for lunch and I totally forgot that this happens when I eat raw fish." The truth was, she couldn't go home, couldn't be alone with her thoughts. It felt like she was carrying a grenade around in her purse. She knew it was going to explode. But she couldn't do anything about it. She just had to wait and bear it.

Ethan came on Saturday morning again. This time she didn't say a word to him. She held Thea closely and whispered into her ear, "You'll be home tomorrow. You'll be home tomorrow," as Thea clung to her and sobbed. She watched his car speed off and then she sat on the floor, motionless, for hours. She didn't eat or drink. She didn't cry.

She just sat, muscles tight, waiting. The plan to leave, to take Thea and flee, was still taking shape. She had withdrawn almost her entire balance, eight hundred dollars, from her bank account in four chunks of two hundred dollars, driving through the ATM wearing large, dark sunglasses—even though it was her money and she could do with it as she pleased. Still, she looked into the rearview mirror nervously each time, fingers shaking as she typed in the passcode. Anne had researched countries without formal extradition agreements with the United States, but the ones that came up in her search—Algeria, Serbia, Lebanon, Afghanistan—weren't realistic options, especially not for a woman and a girl. She shifted the plan to disappearing inside a new country once they arrived there. She started looking at countries where they wouldn't set off red flags at the customs counter, places a mom and her daughter could be vacationing for some bonding time and Instagram-worthy photo memories—Italy, Portugal, the Netherlands. It was taking longer than she had anticipated. Rose was right. This part, laying the foundation, would take weeks or months, not days. They couldn't just up and leave. Everything had to be in place. She had one chance, she realized, to execute the plan correctly, to board a plane and disappear completely.

As she sat on the floor and waited, she wondered what risk was greater, leaving without sufficient planning, or staying and handing Thea over to Ethan again and again. She kept her eyes on the clock on the kitchen microwave, fluorescent green numbers burning through the dark. She thought if she could stay awake and stay focused on Thea, it would protect her daughter somehow. She knew it was irrational, just as she knew her clenched hands on the armrests of the plane weren't the force keeping the plane aloft during takeoff, and yet she always remained in that position for the first few minutes of a flight, only relaxing her fingers once the plane leveled off. She stared at the clock and thought of Thea. Her daughter's face burned in her mind. She carefully studied her from top to bottom, encasing Thea in her mind. Her eyes must have closed at some point in the early morning because when they opened, her head lay against the prickly carpet and sun streamed in through the kitchen windows, shining a spotlight on her body. She sat up quickly and looked at the microwave. 9:45 a.m. Thea would be home at 10:00 a.m. She resumed her vigil. The clock turned from 9:59 to 10:00. She willed her ears to pick up the rumble of Ethan's engine. At 10:05 a.m. she told herself it was only five minutes past—the difference of putting on Thea's sneakers versus her slip-ons. At 10:10 a.m. she felt a lump in her throat rising and knew something horrible had happened while she'd slept on the floor, oblivious. At 10:15 a.m., she picked up the phone and dialed Ethan's number, ready to scream, sob, and then throw herself at his mercy. It rang. No answer. At 10:30 a.m., she grabbed her purse and walked out the door right as Ethan's car sped up the street.

Anne ran to his car and pulled open the back door. Thea sat in her car seat, quiet, perfectly still. As Anne unbuckled her daughter, Thea stayed quiet. "Thea," she said, fumbling awkwardly for words. "How are you?" In Thea's silence, Ethan spoke, "The kid cries a lot. You should do something about that."

Anne lifted Thea out of the car seat, turned, and walked back to their apartment, barefoot on the warm concrete walkway, talking to Thea the entire way, asking her questions, naming the insects buzzing in the air and moving through the grass, in hopes that her daughter would suddenly animate. She sat with her on the couch, stroking her hair, checking her face, the top of her head, her arms, discreetly, telling her about the trip they were going to take soon, until finally Anne stopped talking as well, and they sat silently together, resuming the vigil from last night.

"I'm tired, Mama," Thea said, breaking the silence. She reached her arms toward her bedroom and Anne carried her to her crib.

"You'll feel better when you wake up," she said, lowering Thea down. She cupped her hand under her daughter's head and placed it on the pillow. Before she could straighten her body, Thea screamed and clawed at her, climbing back up into her arms. "No, no, no!" She had never heard this voice come out of Thea before—the marrow of the tone was not anger but fear.

"What's wrong?" Anne asked, pulling back the blanket, ready to smash a spider with her bare hand. She lifted the pillow next and looked underneath; Thea's fingernails dug farther into her neck and Anne felt a tremor run through Thea's body. There was nothing in the crib but a white fitted sheet. Anne held the pillow by her side and then dropped it. "No," Anne said out loud. She kicked the pillow out of the door. Thea's breathing started to slow and she released her grip on Anne's neck. "Thank you, Mama," she whispered. Anne kissed her hair over and over. "Go to sleep, love," she told her as she set her back into the crib.

She walked into the bathroom and threw up. Then she called her babysitter—she knew it was last minute, she said, but she was desperate to do some grocery shopping while Thea napped. The babysitter said she was free for a couple of hours. Anne hurried to get ready. If Megan, the eighteen-year-old babysitter, thought her outfit was odd, she didn't say anything. "You look so nice," she chirped as she walked past Anne through the front door. "I love those shoes."

"Thanks! I'll be back soon," Anne called over her shoulder. She took the front steps slowly, grasping the handrail. As she drove, she fiddled with her phone on her lap, careful to only look down for more than half a second while stopped at red lights. By the time she arrived at Ethan's, the app had downloaded. All Anne had to do was press play. She tested it in the car, recording herself and then playing it back. She put the phone in her pocket and spoke both loudly and softly. She listened again—static filled the car punctuated by a faint voice; certain words were unintelligible, but this was her last resort, her Hail Mary, and it would have to do.

She checked her reflection in the rearview mirror and then stepped out of the car. At Ethan's door, she adjusted her jeans, the waistband dug into her skin and the material clung to her legs in a claustrophobic way she hadn't felt since before Thea was born. She pulled her phone out of her back pocket, hit Play, and tucked it carefully back in.

Ethan opened the door and Anne took in his surprised expression, saw herself through his arched eyebrows and slight smile. He was seeing the Anne from that first brunch date. Makeup carefully placed, hair falling in waves, white sleeveless blouse open in a V on her chest. She hoped that her appearance would work to her advantage somehow, disarm him.

"May I come in?" she asked. She could taste acid with each swallow but kept her face smooth and pleasant. Ethan stepped back and opened the door wider, the small smile still playing on his face. "Thanks," she said, crossing past him into his entryway. When he closed the door to the outside, she felt sweat drip down her armpits to her sides. "I want to talk to you about Thea again." She made her way into his kitchen, filled with white cabinets that contrasted starkly with a large, black marble island in the middle of the open room. It was immaculate, every surface gleamed and the appliances were all high-end, stainless steel, but it felt cold, like a staged house that had never been lived in. She leaned against the island, feeling the side of it press against the outline of her phone.

"What about her?" Ethan asked. He stood in the doorway to the kitchen. His frame took up almost the entire space and made him seem bigger.

"She started crying as soon as I put her down for a nap. After you dropped her off." Anne took a breath and then let the pain spread through her voice. "She started crying when her head touched the pillow in her crib." This had worked the first time—Ethan had responded to her raw emotion, had seemed proud even that he could get away with abusing their daughter. She kept going, her voice mounting. "What the fuck did you do to her, Ethan?"

His voice, when it came out, did not match his mouth, which was set in a wide grin. "Anne, she's still getting used to coming here. And being away from you. Please, you have to understand that it will take some time for us to bond, for her to grow comfortable with me." His reasonable tone made hers seem harsh and dramatic. "I'm sure the more time we spend together, the easier this will be, for all of us." He walked toward her slowly until he was right in front of her, pressing her into the island. His placed one hand on her chest and one in between her legs.

"Ethan, stop." Her voice was caught somewhere in her body, and she could barely get the words out. She struggled to move against him but he pinned her harder into the island.

"What? What are you talking about?" He sounded confused, concerned. He leaned into her harder, bending her back over the island. His face was inches away from hers, and he stared at her and said, "Anne, what's wrong? Are you ok? What's going on with you?" He grabbed her harder with both hands and she inhaled at the sharp pain and then he let go abruptly. She pushed past him, breathing hard, focused on getting to the front door.

"Don't worry about Thea," Ethan called after her from the kitchen. "She just needs more time with me." Anne got to the front door and pulled. Her hands were so sweaty that they slid off the doorknob. She wiped them on her jeans and pulled again; this time the door flung open and she raced through, gulping the rose-scented air as she ran down the walkway. She started her car and drove as far as she could before she had to pull over and wait for the shaking to subside. She cried into her steering wheel and then she called Rose.

ROSE

Rose hummed softly as she walked the four miles to Ethan's. The humming made her feel less alone in the darkness of the night. It was only eight p.m. but the street was quiet, the only sounds were Rose's humming and the click of toenails on the pavement. She held the leash loosely that connected to Sal, the border collie that trotted ahead of her. The cars that normally took this road had long since pulled into driveways, the drivers tucked away in cozy, softly lit houses. Even on a warm fall night like this one, the residents of sleepy Charlotte hunkered down as soon as the sun set. If a car were to drive by, she merely looked like a woman taking her dog for a stroll, stealing some moments of solitude for herself before heading back home to join her husband in front of the TV. There were streetlamps hovering over the road but only every hundred feet or so, leaving large swaths of sidewalk dark; their flickering dim light fell directly onto the parts they serviced. She thought of Sam driving to Burlington. He'd be there by now, on his second or third beer, talking to Bob on the couch. She wondered what they talked about—memories from their time serving, surely, or maybe not at all; she realized she had no idea if her husband made these trips to Bob's house as a way to remember the past, or as a way to bury it—paper collaging new memories over the old. She pictured his face in her mind and his lips moving beside her as she aimed. "One shot, Rose, that's all you'll need if you do it right." She thought how it felt, during their last lessons, when everything else fell away and it was just her and the target.

The first morning that Sam took her into their woods, six months ago, she'd barely said a word. Her stomach was twisted into knots and every time she felt the gun against her side, her heart sped up and she felt dizzy. She'd followed him out into the middle of their woods, crunching past the NO HUNTING, PRIVATE PROPERTY signs.

"Little farther," Sam had called back to her. She didn't respond, just followed, trusting that he knew where to go, exactly how to do this. She smiled now at the thought, placing one black sneaker in front of the other, as if a man could know exactly how to prepare his wife for something like this. Before he took her into the woods, Sam had spent a week teaching her about the gun. Each night they sat at the kitchen table with the blinds closed and two guns in front of them, his and hers. "What kind of gun is that?" Rose asked, nodding to the one Sam had positioned in front of her. She wasn't sure why she asked; the answer wouldn't mean anything to her, yet she felt the need to know anyway.

"It's a glock 26. I picked it because it's light and compact."

"Picked it? Where did you—" Rose paused.

"It can't be traced to me," Sam said, answering her unspoken question, and then, with a sheepish grin, "Yard sale."

He showed her the correct grip: pointer finger on the frame, thumbs one over the other, pointing toward the target. "We'll start shooting when you can load this in under ten seconds."

He told her to carry the gun around with her that entire week, just to get a feel for it, and she did, checking to make sure the magazine was empty and then shoving it into her waistband before she left for the bakery each morning. She hated having it on her body, this cold, solid thing that wrought death, violence, and tragedy. She was sure that her employees, a couple of kids just out of college and the manager who'd been with her since she opened, would immediately be able to sense the gun tucked away under her baggy clothes. Rose could feel the foreign bulk with every move she made, chafing against her stomach; it felt wrong, like a part of her body had been lazily sewn on and the threads were threatening to unravel with every step. The first time she went to the bathroom, she reached for the gun while unzipping her pants and it slipped out of her hands, dropping to the ground with force and then skittering across the small bathroom beside the sink. She froze, listening for her employees, but there was silence. When she emerged a few minutes later, face burning, no one said anything about a strange thud.

That afternoon, Rose drove to a sporting goods store a couple towns over. She found the section she was looking for and marveled at the selection. She picked out a light blue bra and brought it behind the small dressing curtain in the middle of the store. "Oh, that's nice," Rose said softly to herself as she adjusted the bra on her body. Underneath the cups, an additional six inches or so of material fit snug around her rib cage with a pouch opening diagonally across her body. She dropped her gun into the pouch. "Oh!" she exclaimed again, pleasantly surprised at the Velcro band that secured the gun in place.

"Well isn't this nice." She picked up one more bra on her way to the register, a light pink, and paid cash to the skinny ginger-headed boy.

"These are super popular," the boy said as she riffled through her purse, his newly postpubescent voice cracking upward on the word *popular*.

Rose smiled and ignored the flush rising to the boy's face. "I can see why. They're very comfortable!"

From then on, Rose rotated between her two holster bras. She tucked the gun neatly into the pouch every morning. The gun lay slanted vertically on her right side, completely undetectable underneath the large sweatshirts she wore to the bakery. She wondered if it was all part of Sam's plan, not giving her any tips, letting her figure it out herself, but either way, after a week of wearing the holster and loading and unloading the magazine every night, Sam handed her a cup of coffee as she was getting ready to go to the bakery. "Call in sick," he said. "Last night I timed you at 9.8 seconds. Today, we shoot."

Rose had hated shooting that first afternoon. Everything about it made her feel sick. The noise, the recoil, the aching in her arms and hands. Half the time, the hot casings flew backward right into the loose neck of her sweatshirt and tumbled along her body, burning her belly and causing her to do a frantic dance each time it happened. All of these things swelled to form a tidal wave of fear in her mind. Every time, right before the bullet left the gun, there was a suspended moment, an in-between moment, before the gun fired and after her finger started to squeeze the trigger; in that moment, the panic rose to a crescendo, thick and oppressive. "I can't," Rose panted after firing all ten bullets. "I can't do this."

"We can stop." Sam put his hand on her shoulder. "You decide."
Rose paused. "No."

"Ok, magazine out. I'll load it this time." Sam looked at the target
on the tree. There were holes in the paper but they were scattered all
over, mostly on the very outside edges. "You're anticipating. It's the
pothole effect. You're bracing yourself for impact. Just let it happen."

Now she cut purposefully off the road and into a field, the last
mile stretching before her as a series of ups and downs over rolling
hills. She forced herself to walk at a steady pace; there was no rush
and no need to expend her, or Sal's, energy prematurely. She shivered
against the warm breeze and reached to her side, instinctively, for her
cell phone that was at her house, pinging its location to the satellites
in the sky. "Almost there," she said to Sal, whose head was held up
regally, nose pointing up in the air to take in the unknown scents
emanating from the field. They both stopped suddenly to watch a
deer wander through the grass ahead of them; Rose held her breath
and Sal seemingly did, too—rather than barking. "Beautiful," Rose
said softly to herself and to reassure Sal that this graceful creature was
a friend.

"Come on," she told Sal. She kept them pointed toward the house
on the other side of the field, pinpricks of light spilling out from the
windows. A few hundred feet from the house, she told Sal to sit. "Stay
here." Rose stroked the dog's head and ears. "I'll be back soon." Sal
was used to waiting for Rose outside of the bakery, and the dog lowered himself to the ground almost immediately, settling in. Rose was
glad to walk the last part alone. When she reached Ethan's porch, she
closed her eyes and pictured herself in the woods one last time, before
knocking lightly on the door. She heard footsteps approach the door
and then stop, and she pictured him looking down at her through the

glass panes at the top of the door, though she kept her body turned away and to the right, as if appreciating the beauty of the structure.

The door opened.

"Rose? God, it's good to see you!" The warm curiosity in Ethan's voice unnerved her. "Please, come in."

"Thank you," she said pleasantly, melting into her past role of mother-in-law. "I'm sorry to drop by unannounced, but I have something important to discuss with you. I'm sorry I haven't come to see you before now," she said, removing her sneakers carefully and placing them on his welcome mat. If Ethan noticed they looked large, men's size 10 to be exact, he didn't say anything. She kept on her gloves. "But, well, you know, Anne . . ." She shrugged and let her voice drift off, as if the relationship between her daughter and ex–son-in-law had morphed into the uncomfortable yet predictable post-divorce calamity.

"Of course, I understand. You have to take your daughter's side, I get it," Ethan said. "But it's too bad there have to be 'sides.'" Ethan crossed his arms. "I'm actually very worried about Anne." He motioned for Rose to follow him into the living room. With his back turned toward her, Rose readied and positioned herself. Ethan stopped abruptly and turned around. "I'm sorry, I didn't offer you anything to drink."

"Oh no. I'm fine, thank you," Rose said, maintaining her stance. "Actually, I really can't stay long. Sal's waiting for me outside."

Ethan stayed rooted to his spot, an expression of amusement spreading over his face. Rose saw herself as Ethan saw her: an out-of-shape grandmother in an oversize old sweatshirt, pointing a gun at his head.

"Rose," Ethan said gently. "What are you doing?"

"Well, I've been thinking about it, I really have, and I can't see any other way around this." Rose wasn't sure why she felt the need to explain herself, but it seemed like the polite thing to do. Ethan was only ten or so feet away, standing perfectly still, and Rose couldn't help but think, *All that training for nothing.*

"This is ridiculous," Ethan said. Rose opened up her peripheral vision to see Ethan's whole body, which was motionless but tensed, just as Sam had taught her. "Anne and I haven't gotten along great lately, but come on." His mouth curved into a smile. "Don't you think this is a little bit extreme?"

"Do you remember what I said to you at your wedding? During our dance." Rose's voice had turned to ice, and Ethan shifted uncomfortably, holding up his hands in surrender.

"Ok, ok, let's calm down." Ethan laughed but his eyes stayed focused on the gun.

"I told you not to hurt my daughter," Rose continued, "or I would kill you. To be honest, I didn't think I would have to make good on that threat, but here we are." Now Rose was talking more to herself than to Ethan, in a low murmur, "The problem is that it seems I have to wait for you to kill my daughter or granddaughter for the courts to get involved. I'm not going to do that."

"I think Anne's been telling you some things that aren't true." Ethan still held his hands up in the air, but he shifted his gaze to meet Rose's eyes. "You know how she is. She has a vivid imagination."

Rose felt doubt creep into her body. She remembered when Anne was in third grade and her daughter told her entire class and teacher that her parents were divorced. Her teacher couldn't hide her confusion when Rose and Sam came in for their parent-teacher conference holding hands.

"I believe my daughter."

"Of course. And I think Anne believes it, too—that I pushed her down the stairs, that I've been abusing Thea . . ." His voice was incredulous. "I would never, ever harm my daughter. The truth is, all I've ever tried to do is be the best partner I could be to Anne." Ethan's face was earnest. He shook his head sadly. "I think it's time we consider that Anne may be a bit unstable. Ever since she had Thea, she's been . . . struggling, and she's taking it out on me. All I want is to help her, Rose."

"What about your coworker?"

"What?"

"The coworker you were having an affair with."

Ethan laughed. "Wow, Anne will really make up anything, huh?"

Rose sighed. It was time. "We did love you."

"Love?" Ethan's voice snapped Rose's eyes from her target to Ethan's eyes; they were dark, almost black. She blinked as he continued in a tone she'd never heard before. "You and Anne don't know the meaning of the word 'love'." He laughed again, a quick, piercing sound; Rose clenched the gun tighter. "You want to talk about affairs? Why don't you ask your precious daughter about Joseph."

"Stop lying," Rose said, trying to keep her arms steady. Something was happening to the room, it was coming in and out of focus.

"If Anne wasn't such a slut, we could have been the perfect family. But she made me look like a fool. And now she's making you look like a fool." Ethan laughed again but it was not her son-in-law's laugh, the one she'd heard a hundred times before. She had the sensation again that Ethan was someone else; that someone else stood across from her wearing an Ethan skin suit. The thought brought a giggle to Rose's throat and she fought it back. She held the gun steady and willed her eyes to focus.

"I know you don't want to do this, Rose. Let's sit down and talk. You and I can figure this out."

"How could you hurt Thea? How could you?" Rose did feel like a fool; her brain told her to shoot. She had a clear shot. But now she wanted answers and maybe this other person, this monster, would tell her.

"I would never hurt a child, Rose. What do you think I am?" Now Ethan was back, the one she knew, his eyes pleaded with her.

Rose looked at her son-in-law carefully. The room came back into focus. "I don't know what you are."

The crack cut through the air; Rose was used to it by now but still internally flinched at the sound. She watched Ethan fall to the floor; blood began to trickle steadily from the small hole in his forehead. She stood there watching for a few more minutes, expecting a flood of emotion, but she felt nothing. She lifted her sweatshirt and reholstered her gun, picked up the casing from the floor, and moved her eyes back and forth over the area behind where Ethan had been standing. She located the bullet easily, in the door frame leading to a small sitting space off the living room. She walked back to the kitchen and rummaged around in Ethan's drawers until she found a corkscrew. She followed Sam's instructions, inserting the point of the corkscrew into the lead base of the bullet and twisting until she felt traction and then slowly wiggling it out. The bullet came out of the wood frame, stuck on the end of the corkscrew. She twisted the bullet free and dropped it into her sweatshirt pocket with the casing. She rinsed the corkscrew at the sink before drying it on a dish towel and placing it back in the drawer. Rose walked to the entryway, slipped on the sneakers, swept her eyes over the kitchen and living room one last time, opened the front door, and walked outside.

"Good boy," she said to Sal, who was whining softly, looking to her for an explanation of the loud sound. "Come on, everything's all right. Let's go home."

ANNE

After Ethan was killed, it took months before Anne started sleeping through the night without waking up multiple times, gasping and drenched in sweat. But the night terrors subsided and there came a point when she didn't think of him every hour, and then there came a point when she only thought of him once a day, and then once a month. It took Thea a fourth of the time; she asked if she was going back to her dad's a dozen times, and each time Anne told her that she was not, he was gone. Thea slept without a pillow for a month and then one day she asked for it, as if she suddenly realized she'd be much more comfortable with something soft under her head. They all healed—Rose and Sam, too. It sank in that Ethan wasn't coming back; he was gone forever. When the realization truly hit Anne, she cried for hours, her whole body shaking. She thanked Sam only twice. The first time was right after. Her father could barely look at her and said only, "Don't thank me, Anne." She never figured out how he did it, how he managed to be in two places at the same time. But even after the police found evidence that Ethan had been laundering drug money through his investment bank—a discovery made after an anonymous tip was called in asking the detectives to keep an eye out for a black notebook containing strange numbers—and marked the case "cold," filing it away as an "unsolved drug-related homicide," Anne knew the truth. And if she had any lingering doubts about Ethan and what he was, they were washed away a few weeks after he was killed. It was evening, and she didn't usually answer calls from numbers she didn't recognize, but she was expecting a call from Grace and answered immediately, before the first ring had even sounded all the way through.

"Hello!" Anne's voice, sure and expectant, was met by one hesitant and soft.

"Anne?"

"This is she," Anne replied, with a rigidity that she hoped shut down the possibility of ongoing conversation.

"My name is Diana. I knew your husband. Years ago." The line went silent. "I'm sorry. Ex-husband." Silence again. "I'm sorry for your loss. I was hoping to speak with you about Da—I mean, about Ethan."

Anne felt a tingle travel up her spine, not entirely unpleasant. "You knew Ethan," she repeated slowly. She became aware of once again standing between two sides of one reality. Whatever this woman said next would force her to step into yet another version of time and space where nothing made sense.

"Briefly, yes." Diana's voice sounded steadier. "We were involved for a period of time over ten years ago. We were both in our mid-twenties when we met. It only lasted a few months, but . . . it was very intense. I've always considered David to be the love of my life. Until now, of course." She ended with a bitter laugh.

"I'm sorry, 'David'?"

"He was David to me. I didn't know that much about him. I knew he worked a lot and that he didn't really have any family—but I thought I knew everything that was important, which was that I loved him and he loved me." The woman seemed to be trying to convince someone, whether it was Anne or herself, wasn't clear. "When he disappeared, I thought something horrible had happened to him. He just vanished. We were so in love, we had plans for the future, so I knew he wouldn't have just left me." Diana's voice came fast and hard now.

"I don't know what to say." Anne chose her words carefully. "I never knew Ethan—David—either. Not really. I'm sorry."

"When I read the article in the *Times* and saw his picture," Diana continued, as if Anne hadn't spoken, "I realized that it was all a lie. *He* was a lie."

Anne paused, letting the other woman's anger settle into the silence between them. *What does this woman want?*

"I don't know how I can be of help. I'm sorry," Anne started, panic setting in. "What my husband did to you, it's not my—"

"I feel free now." Diana's laugh, joyful and clear, rang out of the phone. Anne closed her mouth.

"I've wondered for *years* what I did wrong," Diana continued. "I eventually convinced myself that David had died and was somehow never found, but I always felt deep down that it must have been something I did. That I must have pushed him away. I thought about it incessantly." She laughed again. "But when I read that article . . . about the embezzlement and the drugs and the murder. About his ex-wife and child, Jesus. I realized it was *him*. I hope you can see that now, too, Anne. It wasn't me. It wasn't you. It was him."

Anne started to respond, but before she could get out any words she felt her throat collapse. She heard Diana say, "It's ok. I know," as she sobbed. They talked for another hour, about Anne's almost completed master's degree and raising a toddler, and about the man that Diana eventually married, a good man, and their son, a straight-A student about to enter middle school. After that phone call, Anne felt lighter than she had in years. She wondered how many other women there were out there who had been conned by Ethan . . . or David. It was a strange thought, but also a comforting one, to know she was not alone.

Two years later, she thanked Sam for the second time, in the hospital. He only had a few days left at that point, it was clear by looking at him that the cancer had taken its final hold, but Anne and Rose sat around his bed, talking about Thea starting kindergarten in a few months and how excited she was to get picked up by granddad on her first day. Anne waited until Rose left the room and then she reached for his hand, an acknowledgment that there really wasn't much time left because it had been years since she'd held her father's hand, perhaps not since she was Thea's age, and said it again, "Thank you, Dad. For what you did for me and Thea." This time he looked her right in the eye. He grasped her hand back and said, "There are some choices that are just the least wrong ones."

THE CABIN

ANNE

Anne tried to make as little noise as possible as she sucked tiny streams of breath past her broken ribs and into her lungs. Her chest and stomach were on fire and each breath fanned the flames. She thought back again to the day of the softball game when she knocked the wind out of herself to catch a fly ball. How she loved that game; there was not a more perfect feeling than jogging out to right field on a hot summer day, the wind at her back, the smell of fresh-cut grass in her nostrils. Stretching her arm back, the tendons begging her to stop, and then the slingshot force forward, as the ball sailed from her hand all the way from the outfield to the catcher. Her freshman year of high school, she started every game, and by the time she was a senior, the coach called her "The Arm."

Thea never liked softball, even though Anne signed her up for T-ball and then Little League. Anne was so thrilled to dig out her old worn leather glove that she didn't notice, or ignored, her daughter's boredom as they tossed the ball back and forth on crisp autumn afternoons. She figured Thea would learn to love it, like she had, but her daughter never did. The last afternoon they played catch was when Thea was ten years old. It was a gorgeous day, the sun burned down, and the wind rolled off the lake and infused the air with a fresh tang. They'd only been tossing the ball back and forth for a few minutes when Thea whined to go indoors. Anne's arm was already wound back behind her head, the ball already pushing off the tips of her fingers, when Thea turned her head longingly toward the house and then whipped her head back around and the ball smashed right into her face, right into her mouth. There was blood everywhere. Anne kept saying, "It looks worse than it is. The mouth is full of blood vessels, that's why you're bleeding so much, honey," because Rose had said that to her once, when Thea tripped and fell as a toddler, biting a chunk out of her bottom lip. But there was so much blood this time that Anne didn't really believe herself. She spat out the phrase on repeat and rushed Thea into the house, frantically gathering paper towels and ice. Eventually, Anne mopped away most of the blood. Sometime after that Thea stopped crying. She was fine, other than a cut lip and a chipped front tooth, but for some reason right now, curled up in the fetal position on the hard floor, Anne wanted desperately to tell Thea that she was sorry for forcing her to play softball all those years. It felt so tremendously important and she realized with a sob that stayed trapped in her body that she would never have the chance to tell her.

Anne had always been afraid of Thea. Starting when she was a baby in the NICU. She remembered looking at the machines and the tubes and feeling a heavy panic settle into her body—Anne was not the one who could keep her daughter alive. She was merely an observer those first weeks, and she understood immediately, now that her baby was outside her body, that she could not keep Thea safe. The fear that formed in the pit of her stomach never truly evaporated, it just wormed its way through her body as her daughter grew. Just as she had not been able to save Thea when she was an infant, Anne feared that one day her daughter would look at her and see the truth, that she was not enough then, and she was not enough now. Anne knew mothers and fathers whose greatest wish seemed to be to raise miniature versions of themselves, nudging their children toward the dreams that they themselves never quite accomplished. But Anne knew deep down that Thea would be better off if she grew outward from Anne, rather than parallel, because the truth was, Anne was weak and had always been weak. It should have come as no surprise that Thea was growing to despise her. The only real shock was that it hadn't happened sooner.

These thoughts came easily as she lay on the cabin floor, thoughts she'd never allowed herself to think before. She thought of all the time she had wasted trying to protect Thea from herself and herself from Thea. She wanted more time; she could be better and stronger, more loving, more patient. She just needed more time. Tears rolled down her face as she understood that she would not get a do-over.

The man wasn't going to let them go. That was not how this story ended, of this she was now certain. She should have known, better than anyone, the darkness that lurks inside some people.

The cabin was eerily silent. She didn't dare move, even if she could; she didn't want to attract the man's attention. She saw Thea and Rose in her mind's eye: Thea huddled close to the hearth, her pale face lit by the fire, her knees drawn to her body, and Rose, slumped against the wall, hands tied together and perched on her lap, head back against the wall. *I'm sorry*, she whispered to them both in her head. She was sure that Rose had given up by now and was hoping for a swift end, for Thea at least.

NO.

The voice roared into her head, so loud that she almost flinched. She squeezed her eyelids tighter against her eyes, but the voice was there, beating like a drum in her mind. She may have failed Thea in the past, with Ethan, but she would not fail her daughter now. Not without a fight. The man had been standing over her, she could feel him in the air above her, but now she felt him move away slightly. She took inventory of her body, assessing the damage. Her chest hurt with every breath, her spine ached, and her cheek and eye area throbbed with a deep pulse, but when she tried to straighten her body, ever so slightly, she found that she could move through the pain. She kept her movements small, imperceptible, as she squeezed the muscles in her arms and legs, ankles, shoulders, and neck. Her neck was the only place where a sharp pain shot into her skull and she almost cried out. She forced herself to nod her chin up and down in a slow stretching movement, with each nod the pain seared and then lessened. She was so focused on the pain peaking and then subsiding that, at first, she didn't notice the soft footsteps. She opened her eyes, but from her angle on the floor all she saw were the wood planks straight ahead of her leading to the front door of the cabin. The footsteps stopped and then Thea's voice pierced her brain. "Mom." Anne had heard the word so many times before but never like this. She forced herself into a sitting position, using her hands and arms to take as much pressure off her ribs as possible, but the pain in her chest area was so great that for a moment she was afraid she would lose consciousness. Breathing slowly through her nose, she counted to five and opened her eyes again. The man stood right in front of Thea. His hand was on her shoulder. No, his hand gripped her shoulder, and he was pulling. The word "Mom" escaped Thea's body again. It was not a word but a plea, heavy with fear but also expectation. Her daughter still believed that she would save her.

ROSE

Rose sat on the grass with Thea, waiting for the seizure to pass. They were small, not the convulsions that she'd always associated with the word "seizure," and if Anne hadn't explained a hundred times Thea's specific type of epilepsy, Rose might have just thought her granddaughter was playing a game. Instead of trying to straighten out Thea's arm or grasping her chin in place, like she did the first time it happened, Rose simply held Thea on her lap, stroking her hair. They were quick, twenty seconds, a minute at most, and didn't seem to hurt Thea, but still Rose's heart sped up each time her granddaughter's eyes unfocused and her body became not her own. Anne had explained to Rose that complex partial seizures had no definite cause, or at least the doctors couldn't determine why Thea had developed epilepsy (the neurologist said there was a chance it was related to Thea's premature birth, but he couldn't say for certain), and they were mostly harmless. Anne always said that last part in a sharp tone. When Rose questioned whether the seizures might be linked to what happened during her overnights with Ethan and shouldn't she consult another doctor, Anne retorted, exhaustion lining her face, that she'd seen the best neurologist in Burlington, and that, "He said to give the epilepsy medication at least a year with adjustments. And for the last time, Mom, he said there's no way to know for sure what is causing them. Please, just let me handle it." Rose saw that Anne was seemingly taking the opposite attitude this time with Thea's health— instead of becoming obsessed and anxious, Anne was the voice of reason and logic. "Everything is going to be fine, Mom," Anne said over and over. "Trust me."

"You're ignoring Thea's seizures," Rose's voice swelled. "I know the doctors say they're not life-threatening, but your daughter has epilepsy, Anne, and you're acting like it's just something she'll grow out of. What if we took her to—"

"I know Thea has epilepsy, Mom." Anne's voice was low. Rose braced herself for her daughter's anger. "I've gone to a dozen doctors' appointments and they all say the same things. Try the medication, alter her diet, keep a journal of when they happen." Anne pushed hair away from her face and Rose saw in Anne's eyes not anger but acceptance. "So that's what I'm doing, ok?" Anne paused. "I don't know exactly how to explain this. After Ethan came back, I truly thought he was going to kill Thea, or maybe he would kill me and that would amount to the same thing, right? Because then Thea would go to him, permanently." Tears ran down Anne's face but her voice remained steady. "And I made a promise to God or the universe or whatever, I don't even know what I believe in anymore." She gave a wry smile. "But I said to myself so many times that if I could protect Thea from Ethan then I would never ask for anything ever again." Anne took a deep breath in through her mouth. "So, yes, every time Thea has a seizure, I feel like the fucking world is crumbling. And yes, I've thought a million times that Ethan is to blame, but I'm not allowed to get upset, I won't let myself, because I got what I wanted. Thea is here and Ethan is gone."

"Are you still seeing Grace?" Rose asked quietly.

"Mom." Anne's voice came down hard and Rose understood the subject was closed. She wanted to explain to her daughter that putting stock in the universe was all good and well, but when it really came down to life and death, getting what you want or wasting away, it was individual action that mattered.

ANNE

Anne sat, knees jangling against her fingers, across from Dr. Haddad, one of the most prominent child neurologists in the country. Dr. Haddad was the best, she heard again and again, but the doctor had a waitlist, a long waitlist. So here she was, a year later, at Boston Children's Hospital, sitting across from Dr. Haddad, waiting to hear the results from Thea's first brain surgery.

She'd changed her mind about accepting Thea's epilepsy and the advice of her local doctor, after Thea's epilepsy medication stopped working. Thea's seizures started occurring with more frequency, sometimes two or three times a day. Their local doctor, Dr. Novak, a thin, wiry man with a mustache, talked for a few minutes about finding the right dosage of medicine, how it could take a while but that they still wanted to focus on treating with medicine and diet rather than surgery. Brain surgery, Dr. Novak said, would be a last recourse due to the "potentially severe side effects, like paralysis or loss of speech."

Two weeks ago, in her first face-to-face meeting with Dr. Haddad, the doctor had looked up from Thea's file and said the words Anne had been hoping to hear since she started researching curative surgery eighteen months ago: "Based on her video EEGs and imaging studies, I think Thea may be a good candidate for brain surgery. What we want to do, ultimately, is a resection. The first step, though, is to cut through your daughter's skull and put several grids on the brain with about two hundred wires connected to the grids. The grids will give us the most accurate EEG reading possible and could point us to a very specific focus, which is then hopefully resectable."

Now, they had the results from the grid-mapping surgery—a surgery that had lasted around four hours and left Thea groggy and with throbbing head pain. Anne focused her attention on Dr. Haddad and asked slowly, "So what did the grids show?"

Dr. Haddad looked up and smiled. She turned a scan toward Anne and pointed to a tiny white blur. "Do you see this? That looks to be the focal point. It looks like they're starting in the right side of her brain, right here, and occurring on the left side of her body. From her records, I'm seeing that her previous doctors believed she suffered from a rapidly generalized epilepsy, seizures that do not clearly have one focal point but may occur in multiple areas of the brain—that seems to be because her seizures were presenting as grand mal when she was younger, yes?"

Anne wanted to cry with relief and throw her arms around her. Dr. Haddad was actually telling her something *real* about Thea's seizures. She decided that sobbing would not be an appropriate response to Dr. Haddad's question, so instead she said, "Yes." She knew what grand mal meant because of her hours of Internet research. Grand mal seizures are the seizures portrayed in movies and TV shows—the total loss of consciousness and body control, vibrating and jerking on the ground, foaming at the mouth. "So"—Anne's heart pounded in her ears and tears pricked her eyes—"they'll be able to go in and remove the focal point? And she'll be cured?"

Dr. Haddad smiled. "That would be the ideal scenario, yes." She shuffled the papers into a neat stack. "Today is Wednesday. I'll need to assemble the team—"

"Wait," Anne interrupted, uncrossing her legs and leaning forward. "We're doing the resection? You really think you can cut out the focal point?"

Dr. Haddad smiled again. "Yes, I do. The results from the grid mapping look good. I'll need to talk to the surgeon who will be performing Thea's brain surgery, get the anesthesiologist up here . . . Let me think for a moment. Time-wise, as far as assembling the team and scheduling surgery, I think we're looking at . . ." Dr. Haddad counted silently in her head. Anne mentally assessed her client load over the next few months. She'd already canceled all her appointments twice for three-week chunks. She focused back on Dr. Haddad as the doctor said, "I'd like to aim for Monday."

"Monday? You mean this Monday?"

Anne knew something was wrong when the surgical assistant sped into the waiting room an hour into Thea's surgery. The surgery, Anne was told, would take three to four hours, and then Thea would be under observation for several days. The surgical assistant, Dr. Au, should have been in the operating room, with Dr. Everett, the surgeon, measuring and cutting and doing whatever else they had to do to stop Thea's seizures, not walking briskly toward Anne with a barely concealed look of panic on her face. Anne stood and moved toward her. "What? What?" she said, her voice coming out fast but seemingly calm. "What is it?"

Dr. Au tugged her face mask off her mouth and nose. Anne waited, searching the doctor's face, icy blood sinking out of her head down into her toes. She felt preternaturally calm. She recognized this type of icy cool calm, when her brain and body slowed to a crawl as she braced herself for devastation. Time slowed as they stood, face-to-face, and everything other than Dr. Au's face blurred. Finally, Dr. Au opened her mouth. "Ms. Thompson, look at your cell phone." *What the hell?* The urgency in the doctor's voice stopped Anne from asking questions, and she simply reached into her purse and brought out her phone. There were five missed phone calls. She looked back to Dr. Au.

"Dr. Everett needs to speak with you."

Anne did not say a word. She would not speak until Dr. Everett told her what had happened. It struck her suddenly that something had gone terribly wrong—Thea was gone—and this woman, this stranger, knew before she did. The truth was just in front of her, just out of her grasp. She had been sitting in the waiting room, having thoughts about a scratchy chair and ice chips while Thea slipped away. She hit the missed call with shaking hands and brought the phone to her ear. Blood thudded through her skull. Half a ring sounded before Dr. Everett picked up.

"We ran into a bit of a problem, Ms. Thompson, and before we proceed with the surgery any further, I need to have a frank discussion with you. It looks like—"

"She's alive?" The room came into sharp focus.

"Oh yes. Yes, she's doing fine, but we had to stop the surgery, or rather, we're still in the middle of the surgery. This is atypical, but I thought it best to bring you up to speed before we proceed."

Dr. Everett paused, and Anne realized she was panting into the phone. "She's doing fine," he repeated, his voice impatient but not unkind; his tone relayed that he had been through this before and time was of the essence. She gulped down a lump. The room was vibrating. No, not the room, her own body. "Ms. Thompson, are you good for me to continue? I need to get back in there with your daughter, so I'd like to keep this as short as possible." Even though he must have been only a hundred feet away, his voice came through the phone tinny.

"Yes. I'm good. I'm listening. Go ahead."

"Unfortunately, the resection is not as straightforward as we had hoped. We believe that the focus of Thea's epilepsy may in fact be very near or even in a part of her brain that also controls motor functions."

She managed to say, "That's not good."

"If we cut out the focal point, and I'm correct about the location, there's a large risk of paralysis. She may be permanently paralyzed on the left side of her body if we proceed with the resection. We need to make a decision now about whether to move forward or stop the surgery."

Her vision sharpened again, taking in the room. A large, flat-screen TV displaying the news to the scattered half dozen people in the waiting area. A nurse writing on a clipboard a few feet away. The long corridor that led to the operating rooms—Thea was somewhere down that hall, through the large swinging doors, her eyes closed, skull open, brain glistening under a spotlight. All of this came in and out of focus as Anne found her mouth moving and the words, "Stop. Stop the surgery," came out.

"Yes. I agree." Before Anne could say anything else, he surged ahead. "We're stopping the surgery. I have to get back in there. Dr. Haddad will follow up with you soon, all right?" He didn't wait for an answer. Her cell phone flashed "call ended" as Anne looked at the phone numbly.

When Thea woke up from surgery and Anne had to tell her that they didn't get it, that the surgery had failed, she felt her insides squeeze and burst open as tears ran silently down her daughter's face. "Rest, love, it's ok, it's ok. Just rest," she said, keeping her voice smooth, not allowing herself to make any more hollow promises.

Thea was released from the hospital five days later. She slept for the entire four-hour drive home. Anne glanced in the rearview mirror and watched her daughter's chest rising and falling, glanced at the white gauze wrapping Thea's head. They pulled into the parking lot of their apartment building and she switched off the engine. She sat for a few minutes in the car, listening to Thea's soft snores.

Dr. Haddad had explained after the surgery that she wasn't willing to go any further with Thea's brain surgery. "Unless you would consider an awake craniotomy, which quite frankly might be our best option. Or our only option."

"An awake . . . what?" Anne had said, trying to keep her shit together, to hide the exhaustion and disappointment in her face and voice.

"She would be woken up during the brain surgery. Dr. Everett would give her commands, ask her to move her hand or say a word, while he touched certain parts of her brain. That way we can be absolutely sure that he's not removing a part of her brain that controls motor functions. She is young . . . but it's been done. I know it sounds crazy"—Dr. Haddad leaned forward and held Anne's eyes—"but an awake craniotomy, in Thea's case, is something we should seriously think about. If you want to move forward with surgery."

A few days later, Thea was discharged, and Anne was no closer to making a decision on what to do next . . . if anything. Before they left the hospital, she told Dr. Haddad that she would be in touch soon.

We're home, she texted Rose.

Any more thoughts on the awake surgery? Rose replied right away. Is there maybe another doctor you could talk to? She saw that her mother was still typing and clicked her home screen dark.

THE CABIN

ROSE

Rose watched her daughter's body for movement across the room. The fire threw flickers of light on Anne's crumpled form, lighting up her hair and parts of her back every few seconds. Rose held her breath and waited. The fire had brought some pink back into Thea's cheeks, but the temperature in the cabin must have been around freezing because when Rose let her breath out, it formed a thick cloud and hung in the air. Anne was still, deadly still, and Rose felt a chasm opening in her chest. She looked from Anne to Thea and then allowed herself, for a moment, to look directly at the gun. The man had a glock 19, 9 millimeter, 16 bullets, if fully loaded and topped off, or less depending on how many he'd already used. Rose knew this because it was the same gun that Sam had used, near the end of their lessons, when they were more competitors than teacher and student. Sam had started out so wary of Rose's request, and he never flat-out acknowledged that what they did was right, but by the end of their six months together in the woods, Rose could tell he was enjoying himself. It was almost ten years ago, but, sitting in the cabin, Rose remembered the exact weight of the glock 19, a bit heavier than her glock 26—she'd had to adjust for the increased pressure required on the trigger—but she'd been surprised when they'd switched and she'd been able to hit the target at fifty feet with all fifteen rounds. Of course, that was in broad daylight. She squinted through the dark. She could see outlines but not features, enough to aim at, though, she thought. Rose considered three substantial problems. The first was that her hands were tied. She'd been careful to keep bending her fingers and twisting her wrists every few minutes, but the shoelace had cut into her skin, rubbing a circle around each wrist, like a bracelet made of raw flesh. She had feeling in her fingers but it was harder to tell how strong her wrists and forearms were at this point because she had almost no leverage to move them. If she was lucky, she could still hold the gun steady but she wouldn't know until it was in her hands.

Which brought her to problem number two. How would she get it? The man paced around the front door of the cabin, to the right of Anne's body, clutching the gun close to his body. Rose tried to convince herself that she was imagining it, but she could swear that he was readying himself, psyching himself up. He muttered under his breath and closed his eyes, his facial expressions changing from anger to a distorted smile. If it came down to it, she would tackle him, which might at least dislodge the gun from his hand and send it to a dark part of the cabin. Of course, then it would be a matter of her or Anne—she glanced at her daughter's motionless body again—getting to the gun before the man did. And then if, against the odds, she possessed it:

Problem number three. Rose hadn't touched a gun in ten years. Not since the night with Ethan. The next day Rose and Sam thought it was a spectacular day to take their small speedboat out on the lake.

A little known fact: the deepest point of Lake Champlain is right smack between Charlotte, Vermont, and Essex, New York. They brought a picnic lunch, plenty of sunscreen, and a small black object to dispose of. This was the problem that concerned her the least as she was quite certain that, given the opportunity, her body would take over—Sam was right, her muscles remembered.

Rose sorted through these problems, one by one, and kept her eyes glued on Anne. At the same time that she saw her daughter move, ever so slightly, she also felt the man in her peripheral vision head toward Thea.

"Mom." The desperation in her granddaughter's voice caused the chasm that had been building in Rose's chest to crack wide open. She was on her feet and moving toward Thea and the man when she heard her daughter, close, whisper, "Mom, don't." Rose looked at Anne, who had righted herself against the wall, to the left of the front door. Anne's face was twisted in agony and it was impossible to tell if the root of the pain was physical or emotional.

The man pulled Thea to a stand and gripped her upper arm. Thea's eyes raced wildly around the cabin, landing on Rose first and then Anne. "Mimi," Thea whispered, "Mom, help me."

Rose moved toward Thea on instinct and heard Anne's voice, louder this time, command sharply, "Mom, NO."

Rose looked at Anne frantically as the man pulled Thea to the middle of the room. Thea twisted her body away from the man, but he gripped her shoulder harder and pulled; Thea's feet dragged on the floor like a rag doll. The man stopped abruptly. The gun dangled from his right hand.

"I won't kill her," he said, looking from Rose to Anne. "Stay where you are and I won't kill her. Either of you move, though." He didn't finish the sentence. Spittle hung from his lower lip. He pushed Thea to the floor and Rose heard her granddaughter scream. Rose started to take a step forward and, again, Anne commanded her to stop. Rose looked to Anne wildly but Anne was focused on Thea and the man. Her face was calm and she took measured breaths.

"Thea," Anne said over her daughter's cries. "Don't fight it."

Rose watched as her granddaughter left her body. Thea's eyes rolled back slightly into her skull and her head nodded forward and then to the side in small jerks. Her arms stiffened at her sides and her legs gave out. Rose froze; this could not be happening.

THEA

"It's time, baby." Thea's mom took her hand and squeezed. Her mom's hands were smooth with tiny creases, like a baby elephant's back. The pre-op room looked less like a hospital and more like a hotel room, with a green couch and a full-length mirror hanging on the door. They had been in the hospital for seventeen days so far. This was their second long-term stay in the past couple years. Thea had heard her mom talking to Mimi late last night, in a strained whisper from the reclining chair across the room from her bed, while her mom thought she was sleeping. "She's done, Mom. We're both done. She's not smiling, she's barely speaking. If surgery doesn't work this time, I'm not bringing her back. It's just too much. It's too much for a ten-year-old," her mom's voice had cracked, and then the room was silent for a while. Thea had almost fallen asleep, thought her mom had hung up, when her mom's voice drifted through the air again. "I know. I know. You're right. Yes, thank you, you're right, ok, I'll keep you updated tomorrow."

Now, Thea felt her mother's warm palm against hers and squeezed back. This would be her third brain surgery and her second attempt at resection. The first resection, almost three years ago, didn't work— her mom explained to her afterward that when the surgeon got a look at her brain, it didn't look like he thought it would and he decided to stop. Thea noticed that her mother no longer promised that they were going to find a cure for her seizures. She had heard the doctor's ambiguous responses to her mother's questions, heard them change their diagnoses and treatment plans multiple times. Thea was tired of the medicine that made her feel sluggish all the time, tired of being in and out of the hospital, tired of the EEGs and the blood tests and (these were the worst) the MRIs. But she also felt like her and her mom were on a mission and they couldn't give up yet. She trusted her mother completely, and even when she cried because she was just so tired all the time, she had an underlying and unwavering faith in . . . she didn't know what exactly, she just knew it was all going to be ok.

"I'm ready, Mom." Thea looked up at her mom and smiled. The surgery was important to her mom and, it had been explained to her dozens of times, important so that Thea could "live a normal life" when she was a grown-up. Right now, though, she didn't care about living a normal life, she couldn't imagine a normal life. She was too tired to care about anything other than trying to ease her mom's mind; she knew she had to be brave and let her mom know she wasn't afraid, even though, of course, she was. *Imagine you're in a movie,* she told herself, *and this is the big scene right before the end.* That made it easier because she could pretend she was playing a role and that the whole plotline was already mapped out. She didn't have to be afraid; the happy ending was already written. The surgeon would cut into her brain, take out the seizure part, and she'd wake up and get to run the whole length of a basketball court and watch entire movies and not have to hold her breath every time she walked down a staircase (after that one time when she seized at the top of the stairs and her left leg gave out and her mom caught her right before she fell).

"Dr. Haddad believes that the focal point of your seizures is in a nonessential area of your brain, but that it's very, very close to an essential part of the brain. She thinks they'll be able to go in and get it this time. And she's the best—she's the smartest and the best, so we're in really good hands." Her mom was whispering, though there was no one else in the room, but it did seem like a room one should whisper in, so Thea responded in a whisper as well, "How long will I be awake? It won't hurt, right?"

"It won't hurt at all. You won't feel anything. You'll be awake for about an hour but it will only feel like a few minutes. The whole surgery will take a few hours. You'll go to sleep and then you'll wake up and the doctor will ask you to move your left arm and leg—and then you'll go back to sleep and then—"

"I'll be cured."

"Exactly. You'll be cured. And I'll be right by your side." Her mom laced her fingers through Thea's just as there was a soft knock on the door. The door opened before her mom could say anything and Dr. Haddad slipped into the room, carrying a manila folder.

"Hello, hello." Dr. Haddad's voice was bright and warm. "Thea, how are you feeling?"

"I feel ok. How are you, Dr. Huda?"

Dr. Haddad laughed her nice, throaty laugh. Thea liked Dr. Haddad. She didn't seem like a doctor, more like a favorite teacher or aunt. She had told Thea to call her Dr. Huda during their first appointment. Dr. Huda Haddad. *It has a nice ring to it, don't you think?*

"Ok, guys." Dr. Haddad looked from Thea to her mom. "Let's go to the operating room, shall we?"

Her mom's face came into focus slowly. "Thea. Hi. Shh. Shh, don't try to speak. You've been asleep for a bit. Take your time waking up, ok?"

Thea's eyes fluttered open and closed. She licked her lips and coated her mouth with a thin layer of saliva. "Ice."

Her mom put an ice chip in her mouth and she sucked its coolness down into her throat. "Did they get the seizures?" There was a deep pounding inside her head. She opened her eyes again and saw her mom's face. "Mom, are you crying because it didn't work?" she whispered.

"No, baby, no, the surgery went as well as it could have gone. Dr. Everett and Dr. Haddad both said you did amazing—better than any adult they've ever seen. They think they got it, love. Dr. Haddad and Dr. Everett both believe the surgery will be curative. No more seizures, Thea." Her mom's voice cracked like she was trying not to cry, and Thea didn't understand why she was sad if the surgery worked.

"That's happy, Mom," Thea said, her eyes closing.

Her mom laughed. "Yes, that's happy, you're right. Go back to sleep and I'll tell you more when you wake up, ok? I'm so, so proud of you."

Thea smiled and closed her eyes. As she drifted back to sleep, she remembered that morning, a few hours before the surgery. She was in Dr. Haddad's office with her mom, waiting for Dr. Haddad to come in and talk to them about the awake craniotomy. She felt the seizure coming before it started in her body. The air felt staticky and then her mom was pressing lightly on her arms and side. She heard her mom whispering in her ear, telling her it was ok, and then, the words she always said, over and over: "Don't fight it."

THE CABIN

ANNE

It had been two years since Anne had seen Thea seize. She watched as Thea's body transformed: her eyes rolled to the side, her left arm jerked into a crook and vibrated, her leg went limp, and she slid to the floor. This looked like a seizure from when she was five or six years old—the ones that the doctors thought were grand mals. For a millisecond Anne was mesmerized by her daughter's body and how realistic the movements were—if Anne didn't know the surgery was curative, she would have believed her daughter was really seizing. And then she snapped her head up. The man was frozen, too, his eyes ran over Thea's body wildly, unsure how to proceed. One hand still held the neck of her coat, but he had stopped pulling. Anne watched as the other hand, the gun hand, dropped from the side of her daughter's head. *NOW!* screamed the voice inside Anne's head. She felt for the rock in her pocket and at the same time pulled herself from her knees onto her feet. Her chest was on fire. If she thought about the second snap that had just occurred within her rib cage, she was afraid she would collapse, so she concentrated on the rock between her fingertips. The shape was nothing like a softball—it was pointed and narrow at the end, widening into a flat line at the base—but she pulled her arm back anyway, like she did in high school, the same fluid motion, left foot forward (barely an inch because of the shoelace that bound her ankles), right hand behind her head. The man didn't see her do it until it was too late; his eyes were still on Thea shaking on the ground. He must have seen the motion of her arm out of his peripheral vision because right as he turned his head, the rock made contact with his gun hand. It hit exactly where she was aiming—his knuckles—his hand automatically opened and the gun flew out, skittering across the floor. She didn't have time to celebrate this small victory, to track the movements of the gun—she had begun shuffling toward the man and Thea as soon as the rock left her hand and now she was there. Her chest and stomach screamed at her to stop but she ignored their voices and lunged at the man. For a brief second she was reminded of two hours ago, when their bodies made contact over the snow. This time Anne had much less momentum, but it was enough to knock the man, already destabilized by Thea's seizure and the hit to his hand, off his feet. She was on top of him, but she knew that for everything that had gone right in the past thirty seconds, he would overtake her soon, and so she yelled "Run!" to Thea as she brought her closed fist down on his cheek. She ripped into him with her fists and it felt good to connect with his eye, nose, ear, before he jerked her off and threw her against the ground. The man mounted her and put his hands around her throat; she knew that he would easily kill her. She rolled her eyes to the side and saw the dark flash of her daughter's coat by the front door, just as the man released her throat and his fist connected with her nose. "Run, Thea," she said one more time, though Thea probably couldn't hear her, no one could hear her, because his hands were back around her neck, squeezing hard now, and the air was leaving her body, but it was ok because Thea was running. Something in her throat crushed and then all she saw was darkness even though her eyes were open, but nothing hurt anymore; she had left her body and she wished she could tell them, Mom and Thee, that it didn't hurt. And then she was back in her body, back in the pain, gasping for air. The man was gone. Far away, she heard the cabin door slam; he was going after Thea. She tried to lift herself from the floor to her hands and knees but she collapsed. Blood dripped down, the room came in and out of focus, so she was not quite sure if there was someone really crawling past her, until her mother said, "It's ok, Anne, I got it." Anne couldn't speak because her throat was burning, so she couldn't ask Rose what, what did she have? The last thing that she saw, before it went dark, was the gun, hanging from her mother's hand.

THEA

When Thea heard her mother's words, the same ones she had heard thousands of times before, her muscles responded almost immediately. The left side of her body slumped and convulsed, her head moved in jerking motions, her eyes lost focus. For a moment, she wondered if she was having a real seizure. She un-balled her left hand and flexed her fingers. No, she was in control; the realization gave her energy and the movements grew stronger. She felt the man loosen his grip on her shoulder and then everything happened quickly. She heard a yelp, like a wounded animal, and the man was a blur, careering backward.

"Run!" Her mom's voice, close, but when she scraped herself off the floor, she didn't see anyone, just the front door. She turned her head back as she limped toward the door and saw her mom on top of the man, thrashing, her face and body contorted. For a moment, Thea was stunned—she had never seen this person before, raw with anger and hatred, in the form of her mother, and it scared her, almost as much as the man—she pivoted her eyes to take in the rest of the cabin and saw her Mimi on her hands and knees on the floor, not moving. Thea hesitated by the front door; she had to help Mimi and her mom. The man was on top of her mom now and Thea screamed as his fist came down hard. She heard her mother's voice again, this time desperate, "Run, Thea," and so she turned and kept moving away from her family.

Thea pushed out of the cabin and a blast of cold air hit her square in the face, causing her eyes to water. She wanted to shrink from the cold but she steered her head into the wind instead, like a bull. She heard her mom in her ear on repeat, *Run, run, run*, and she forced herself forward, down the steps, and into the clearing. The air whipped her body, and she saw tiny snowflakes scatter and melt into the ground. It was dark, but not so dark that she couldn't see a couple of feet in front of her. Her head, specifically her temples, still pulsed with a sharp pain, and she didn't dare to turn her head quickly for fear of becoming dizzy, so she kept her eyes down and watched her boots striding one in front of the other. She heard something over the wind and realized she was croaking out the word "Mommy," a word she hadn't used in years, and she clamped her mouth shut. A thud sounded behind her and she heard the word "Fuck" over the wind. She turned her head quickly; her vision blurred for a moment and then focused. The man stood outside the cabin, looking. Thea dug her boots into the hard earth and started to run, a quarter speed at first, testing out her legs, her lungs, her head, and then she gained speed as she trampled into the woods.

She threw herself through the woods, closing her eyes against sharp branches that lashed at her face, leaping over roots that appeared only a moment before in the half-dark, and in her head she concentrated on the voice, *Run, Thea, run*.

THE MAN

The man was excited. He hadn't expected the girl to convulse like that and he had forgotten about the rock. He sat on top of the mother and squeezed her neck, not hard enough to snap; he was so careful. He didn't want to do anything that might upset the girl. He got up slowly, scanning the floor for the gun. He didn't see it. The mother wouldn't be moving anytime soon and the grandmother was frozen in the corner of the cabin. He made his way to the front door. He had to get to the girl, that was all that mattered. He understood now that this was all for him. He had mistakenly thought that his redemption lay in that parking lot, in that single bullet, but, as he stood on the cabin porch searching for movement, the realization hit him: Everything that had unfolded since the parking lot, everything that was happening now, was to make up for all the times he had been thwarted, misunderstood, rejected. The girl would more than make up for all he had suffered. The backs of his eye sockets filled with the pressure of tears, and the most pleasant sensation flooded his body as he walked to the edge of the porch. The stairs were slick with falling snow and the heel of his boot slipped going down; he landed with a thud on his tailbone and yelled into the air. The fall jolted him back to what he had to do, and the warm feeling was replaced by purpose. He pulled himself up and stood for a moment on the bottom step, listening.

The girl had disappeared into the woods, the back of her long, dark coat the last thing he saw from the porch. He jogged across the clearing and stood at the edge of the woods for a moment, listening again. If the wind wasn't twisting through the trees, it would be dead silent and he would hear her thick steps clearly. As it was, he had to stand still for longer than he wanted to, ears straining to hear through the wind into the woods. Right as he was about to head blindly in, there it was, the snapping of a branch, ahead and to the left. *Smart girl*, he thought—admiration lifted his mouth into a smile—she was heading in the direction of the main path. The man broke into a run, and for the second time in his life, he stopped struggling inside his own body and mind.

His body moved clunkily over the ground, through the branches, and he fell, puncturing his hand on a rock, but even so, he felt strong and it was only a few minutes before he saw the girl; in the dark she looked like a shadow twisting through the trees. He pushed himself faster, he felt like he could run forever, like he was superhuman. He caught up to her and grabbed the back of her coat; she screamed as she careened to the ground. He pinned her down, holding her wrists tightly. She kicked up but she was weak and the blows felt good.

"Thea," he said, over her cries. "It's ok. It's me. It's me. Look at me." He held her face with his thumb and pointer finger. "Open your eyes. I'm not going to hurt you," he said. "I just want to talk to you. We're the same, me and you. I finally found you."

"No." The girl looked at him and as soon as she met his eyes, he saw that he was mistaken. She hated him. She was terrified. Just like the others.

"No. No. No." The words increased in volume and she jerked her head out of his fingers. Her body wriggled under him and she kicked again, a sharp kick with more force.

He picked her up, draped her over his arms, just like before, it couldn't have been more than a couple hours ago, except that this time she was screaming.

"It wasn't supposed to be like this." A pause. "I'm not going to hurt you," but even while the words were dripping from his mouth, he couldn't be sure what he was going to do. *I am calm. I feel nothing.* He turned into the woods and they walked back toward the cabin.

THE CABIN

ROSE

Rose shoved her shoulder into the front door of the cabin and pushed. The man had slammed it closed behind him and the door wouldn't budge. She pulled back and heaved into the door again, throwing all her weight behind her. "Arghhhh," she panted as it flew open and banged against the outside wall of the structure. Her wrists were still bound together tightly with the shoelace, and she held the gun awkwardly at her pelvis. "Thea!" she yelled into the night. She marched down the steps and walked briskly into the clearing. "Thea!" she boomed again. Rose squinted; she could barely see a thing. It was not quite pitch-black, but she was nearsighted without her glasses, a new development after turning sixty. She spun around looking for something sharp to rub against in order to free her hands. She didn't want to waste time, but it was crucial that she was able to hold the gun properly. She was bent over, eyes on the ground, when she heard the crunching of boots from inside the woods. The man emerged into the clearing, Thea in his arms; she aimed the gun awkwardly. The man stopped when he saw her.

"Put the gun down, Grandma," he said.

Her grip was off, due to the shoelace that dug into her wrists and kept her hands too close together, but what threw her confidence the most was what happened next. The man lowered his neck and brushed his cheek against her granddaughter's tenderly. "Don't shoot, don't make me do something I don't want to do," he said.

Rose took a step forward, the closer she could get the better.

"Keep moving and I will have to hurt her. I don't want to, but I will. Don't make me do this. I said I didn't want to hurt her." He was screaming now, face contorted. "Why are you making me do this?"

Rose steadied herself. Inched her feet the right distance apart. Looked at Thea's face, so close to the man's that they blurred together.

"Mimi," Thea sobbed, and Rose had to rip her eyes away.

The man started toward her, keeping his head down, cheek to cheek with Thea. He was coming at her at an angle. Rose saw tears flowing from his eyes down Thea's face. She dropped the gun to her side. "Ok. Ok. I won't shoot." The man and Thea were only two arm-lengths away now.

"I just wanted to see her. I just wanted to talk to her. To see if we're the same. No one has to get hurt." One arm-length. "I've waited so long—"

Rose pivoted and aimed. The sound of the gun, Thea's scream, and the two bodies collapsing to the ground happened all at the same time. Rose took in Thea's ashen face and the fact that her granddaughter's chest was rising and falling. She brought her hands down forcefully on the jagged end of a rock and pulled her hands up and down in a sawing motion. The shoelace finally snapped and she moved quickly to Thea. The ringing in her ears from the crack of the gun drowned out her granddaughter's sobs. She looked down at the man and couldn't help but note the tiny dark hole that oozed blood was exactly where she wanted it to be, straight into the man's temple. *Lucky shot*, she heard Sam's voice say in the same cadence he used near the end of their training—an undertone of laughter in his voice—and she would smile back without breaking her stance because they both knew it wasn't luck at all that Rose's bullets were landing in the center of her target, no matter how far away she was. "Lucky shot," she whispered.

"It's ok, it's ok," she said to Thea. She was already wrenching open the man's hand, placing the gun in his palm and wrapping his finger around the trigger. Rose shoved his hand up to his temple and then let it fall. She did it again and again, until she was satisfied that the resting spot and angle of his hand on the ground was acceptable, or at least possible. She wiped down the gun on her coat, making sure to scrub every single inch. "Ok, that's good," she said, feeling her granddaughter's eyes taking in her quick movements. She carried Thea to the cabin, back up the stairs, through the front door, and plunked her down beside Anne. Rose knelt next to her daughter for several seconds, catching her breath. "The man is dead. Can you hear me? I'm going to go get help." She turned to Thea, who hadn't moved a muscle. "Stay with your mother. I'll be back soon." She brought her mouth down to Anne's ear. "If you can hear me," she spoke slowly, as if to someone hard of hearing, "I am going to go get help. I need to get somewhere with service so I can call 911. So, just . . ." She thought for a second. "Well, just stay here." She gave Anne's arm a pat and then stood up. "It's going to be fine," she said to Thea, who still sat frozen, eyes wide, shivering on the floor. "Thea." She squeezed her granddaughter's shoulder. "Do you understand why I did what I did out there?"

Thea nodded. "The man. He shot himself."

Rose paused. "Yes. Good."

"Mimi, my ears." Thea shook her head to demonstrate something was wrong.

"That will go away. I promise." Rose stroked her granddaughter's hair. "I'll be back soon with help. Stay with your mom."

Rose walked out the door through the clearing, past the man's body and back into the woods. She leaned against a tree once she was a good distance away from the cabin. It was then that she let herself have the breakdown that she had been holding in since the man took them, and she screamed into the night. Once recomposed, she continued toward the main path. The wind had died down. As she made her way farther and farther away from the cabin, only the man's voice in her head cut through the silence of the night as she tried to decipher the meaning: *I've waited so long.*

ANNE

Anne woke up in a hospital bed—clear tubes and blurry overhead lights, a burning in her throat, and throbbing in her temple. Rose sat on a chair across the room, silently, hands woven together in her lap, and when their eyes connected, Rose immediately said, "Thea is next door. She's ok." Anne's body flooded with relief that turned to fear as she realized she couldn't remember anything past lunging at the man. They were all alive, Thea was alive, but she couldn't remember anything past attacking the man. She watched her mother's face intently for what she really wanted to know. *What did the man do to Thea? Tell me, please tell me.*

"You don't remember?" Rose looked at her intently. "He didn't . . . He didn't get to her." Rose answered the question etched on Anne's face. Rose started to speak again but a rap on the door interrupted her. A female nurse entered the hospital room, followed by a male police officer.

"Ms. Thompson." The nurse moved quickly but spoke slowly,

"Officer Searle has a few questions for you. I've told the officer already that you are on voice rest and aren't yet able to talk, but he'd like you to nod or shake your head in response to his questions. Do you feel up for that?"

Anne nodded once, not sure she really had a choice; her mind was on her daughter. She had to see Thea with her own eyes. Her daughter was alive, but how badly was she hurt? Where was the man? These questions spun through her head as the tall, thick policeman lumbered over. Before he reached Anne's bedside, he turned around. "Sorry, I need to question your daughter alone, Mrs. Thompson. Your statement has been a great help, there are just some specifics we need to corroborate. The crime scene really speaks for itself." He looked from Rose to Anne with an apologetic smile. "This is more of a formality." As the officer began rambling on about preliminary evidence and piecing together the events from the past twenty-four hours, Rose quietly slipped out the door, but not before catching her daughter's eye. She looked at Anne hard and then stepped into the hallway. Anne switched her gaze back to the officer, uneasy about what Rose's parting look had meant. He averted his eyes from hers as he asked questions that she couldn't answer due to her swollen throat. Despite Anne not being able to speak and despite leading with the assurance that this would be brief, the cop asked question after question, jotting down Anne's head nod or head shake on his small lined notepad. The first questions related to the circumstances that led to the nature walk. "You were hoping to have a nice quiet weekend in the White Mountains with your daughter and your mother, is that right?" *Head Nod* "Nothing seemed out of the ordinary until about twenty minutes into your walk when you made contact with the perpetrator?"

Head Nod Finally, Officer Searle looked up from his pad and met her eyes. "I'll try to be sensitive with these next questions. I know you've been through a lot and, contrary to what you may have heard about cops, we do try to be sensitive to trauma." He twisted his silver wedding band around his finger. "I just want you to know that you did exactly the right thing. In these situations . . . Well, they don't usually turn out the way yours did. And that's in large part to you thinking fast on your feet under an enormous amount of stress. I really can't commend you enough, Ms. Thompson." The officer's eyes were glistening, and for the first time since waking, Anne was very glad that her throat was on fire. Officer Searle misread her look of confusion for distress. "I'll get right to it, ok? No reason to hash it all out right now. Just need to get the basics." He clicked his pen once. "The man attacked you, and your daughter managed to escape the cabin, correct?" Officer Searle stared at her. *Head Nod* "Do you remember your mother being in the cabin with you?" She paused but only for a half a second before . . . *Head Nod* "And, did you hear the gunshot?" *Head Shake What the fuck?* She wracked her brain. She remembered lunging, thrashing on the ground, and then . . . nothing. Suddenly, a flash of the gun moving past her eyes entered her mind, but the memory didn't make sense. She remembered a feeling of surprise and then a blank nothingness. Who had been holding the gun? She held this moment in her mind, and just as the image sharpened, Officer Searle broke her concentration.

"I have one more question for you, Ms. Thompson. Does the name 'David Redmond' mean anything to you?"

Anne searched the officer's face. *David Redmond.* She knew she'd heard that name before, *Redmond*, but she couldn't think through the thick fog that was starting to *drip drip drip* into her brain from the IV in her arm. She closed her eyes tight, trying to make it click. Nothing. She opened her eyes, shook her head no.

"That's all I need for now, Ms. Thompson. Again, I can't stress enough how differently this situation could have turned out were it not for your quick thinking and bravery. And, of course, if the perpetrator hadn't turned the gun on himself at the end. That's not usually how this type of scenario plays out. You are all very, very lucky." Officer Searle nodded once and stood at the bedside awkwardly for a moment. Anne nodded back, and as she slipped into heavy sleep the name echoed on repeat in her head, like a song with only one lyric, *David David David.*

When Anne woke up, she couldn't tell if it was day or night. She was in an interior hospital room and she could feel the fluorescent lights penetrate the thin skin of her closed eyelids. Before she opened her eyes, she heard slow breathing, and for a moment, she knew that the man had come to finish what he started. Her eyes flew open and she tried to tense her muscles, in preparation of flight, before realizing that she had no control over her body.

"Anne," said a voice. "It's ok. It's just me."

Anne focused her eyes, adrenaline slowed by the soft tone of the voice, and saw a woman sitting across from her bed. She sat straight, her feet crossed at an angle in front of her, hiding the interior of a tan skirt that draped just past her knees. Her black hair was cropped short and neat.

"It's me. Diana." The woman stared at Anne for a moment, searching for a flick of recognition. "Diana Redmond. I spoke with the doctor and she said it would be ok—"

"Diana," Anne's voice barely came out and her throat burned. "Diana. You knew Ethan." A long pause and then: "David."

"Yes. We spoke years ago. Ten years ago to be exact."

TEN YEARS
BEFORE THE CABIN

DAVID

The boy heard everything. The whole conversation between his mother and the lady on the other end of the phone. At least his mother's side of the conversation—and he could guess what the woman, Anne, had said, based on his mother's replies. When his mom talked about their family, she said she only had one son, his brother, Edward; she didn't mention him, David, at all. He crept back to his bedroom when his mom started saying goodbye and crying again, mumbling "thank you" over and over. His bedroom door creaked open a few minutes later and he felt his mother's gaze on his cheek even though he kept his eyes closed. He waited thirty more minutes, until the house was completely silent, before creeping back to the study. The newspaper clipping was folded neatly four times in the very bottom drawer of the desk, under a stack of books. David read it and then read it again, trying to figure out what it meant. The man that the article was about, Mr. Ethan Mills, was a bad man. That much David understood. His mom and grandma liked to say that there were no bad people, only people who did bad things, but David, at the age of sixteen, knew they were wrong. There were people who did bad things and there were also bad people who did bad things. He knew this for certain. David scanned the article for the fourth time and concluded what he had already sensed on the other side of the study door, and what he had known all along: there *was* something wrong with him; it was in his blood. He wasn't actually a Redmond at all. His biological father was dead, according to the article, but there was another person out there who shared his DNA. He read that line again: "*. . . survived by his daughter, Thea Thompson.*" He tucked the clipping into his waistband and walked back to his bedroom. Thea Thompson, a toddler in Vermont. This girl, his sister, would someday understand what he felt. She would think the kinds of thoughts that kept him up at night. He'd always thought that he was alone, a freak of nature, tolerated by his father, pitied by his mother, but he'd been wrong. This girl was his light in the dark. She would be the one to set him free, and tonight was the night he would stop fighting who he was.

ANNE

Anne was silent as Diana spoke. Partly because her throat was swollen and raw; mostly because the woman across the room spoke without pausing, using her hands and face to tell her story, barely stopping to breathe, her voice wobbling and righting itself.

"I'm so sorry, Anne," Diana was saying, "I never thought David would . . . No, I'm sorry, that's not true. I prayed that he would never hurt anyone again, but I knew. Let me start at the beginning." She sucked in a breath. "I had an affair a few years after I got married. My husband, Rich, changed after we got married—he went from being sweet and kind to drinking every night, barely speaking to me. He was always working, never home. And then I met Ethan and he just swept me off my feet." Diana gave a sharp laugh. "Suburban housewife has an affair with a mysterious stranger to spice up her life. It sounds so cliché. Ethan was smart and interesting, and he adored me. I met him at a coffee shop in town and he said he was in New Jersey for business, that he traveled all the time for his job."

Anne watched Diana's face; she looked like she was inside a dream.

"For a few months, it was incredible. We'd meet a couple of times a month, sometimes more. I was going to leave Rich. I really loved Da—Ethan." Diana's face clouded for an instant. "And then when I told him I was pregnant, he became a different person immediately. I still remember his eyes . . . They went almost black. His whole body changed. He said he was happy, but there was nothing behind the words. No emotion." Tears streamed down the woman's cheeks. "And then he was gone. I couldn't get in touch with him. It was like he never existed." Diana wiped her eyes. "Anyway, Rich never knew that David wasn't his. I didn't even know for sure that the baby was Dav— Ethan's. Though I hoped he was." She looked at Anne and then the floor. "That's why I named him David." She looked down at her hands, plowed on. "When David turned three, he started to act out in a way . . . It wasn't normal. Our younger son, Edward, was always easy, right from the day he was born." She smiled sadly. "But that's when I realized how . . . different David was." Diana paused. "There's something I have to tell you. David came to our house, two days ago. I hadn't seen him since before he went to—since before he went away. I almost fainted when he walked in the door. He looked right at me and said, 'Mom, you should leave. Go out of town for a few days.' I tried asking why, but he just kept saying I should leave, for my own good. I didn't know, Anne, what he was going to do to you . . . and to Rich. I'm so sorry." Diana's words came out between sobs. "I'm so sorry. I tried to fix him. He wasn't all bad."

Diana snapped her head up at the machines' loud beeps as a nurse rushed into the room.

"Please step outside, ma'am," the nurse said, pulling out a syringe.

As Anne sank back into darkness, she heard the dull clicking of heels leaving the room.

THEA

Thea lay in her bed, looking at the ceiling. Her night-light, the one she got three months ago, cast shadows on the ceiling, and she dropped her hand down in front of the light to make the shadows move. They'd gotten better, the nights. She'd only called for her mom twice tonight since going to bed. The first week after the cabin, her mom slept in her room, on the couch, because she was waking up so much during the night. Thea hadn't told her mom, but she heard her mom's nightmares, too, and she saw the sheen of sweat on her mom's forehead in the mornings. But, like her mom promised, things were getting better; the terror was fading, though she still felt different, older, and she thought she probably always would be a little bit different now. The anxiety attacks were less frequent, but she felt a heaviness, a wariness that she'd never felt before.

There was good that had come out of the cabin, too, though. Like her mom telling her about her biological father. The first week back, when they were up all the time at night, they would whisper back and forth from the bed and the couch, and Thea told her mom about the

Google search. She just couldn't keep it in anymore; she had too much stuff now, and she needed to get rid of something. Her mom was quiet for a while and Thea thought she was mad, but then she said, more sad than mad, "Oh, Thea, I'm so sorry I didn't tell you the truth. I could say I was protecting you, but I think I was protecting myself more than anything." And then she talked for a long time. They talked again the next night and the night after that and then they started seeing a counselor together and somehow, just by having another presence in the room, Thea felt safe saying things she'd never said before. Her mom, too, had confessed to feeling like she'd failed Thea in a lot of ways—by choosing Ethan, by not being able to stop Thea's epilepsy for so long, by not knowing the right things to say about what happened with Ethan. Thea had stared at her mother, genuinely shocked, and said, "Mom, you're like the best mom in the world. I mean, I've been mad at you a lot and you annoy me a lot, but you're my best friend." Her mom had burst into tears at that and Thea had rolled her eyes at the therapist and then hugged her mom for a long time. Thea was angry and sad a lot still, but she could feel spaces in her reopening and, even though she felt more, it felt weirdly better than before, when she knew nothing.

She closed her eyes, thinking about what happened in the cabin, how they survived, but how it also took a little sliver of each one of them, and when she finally fell asleep, she dreamed about her brother, standing across the room, not saying a word, just standing there in the shadows, watching.

"So, Thea, I'm going to say this again, even though I know you strongly disagree. I think we should file a restraining order against—"

"Mom. No." Thea set her jaw in a line. Looked out the window, away from her mother. She saw her school come into view and her stomach clenched. It was her first day back since "the incident," as her principal referred to it in their numerous meetings leading up to this day. Her mom and the principal argued that, though school was almost out for the summer, Thea should spend the last couple of weeks getting acclimated and reconnecting with her peers. "I told you, Mr. Redmond is gone and he's not coming back. The police don't even know where he is." Thea had told the police about her Spanish teacher when they asked her if she knew anyone named David Redmond in the hospital.

"David? Do you mean Ted?" Thea stared at Officer Searle, a look of confusion plain on her face. "Why are you asking about my Spanish teacher?" The officer was just as confused as Thea in that moment. Officer Searle and his colleagues would have discovered him sooner or later, but at that early point, only an hour into the investigation, they had not yet dug into David Redmond's file, so they did not know yet that David Redmond had a little brother named Edward.

"Are you saying you knew the perpetrator? And that he was your Spanish teacher?" Officer Searle took notes as he talked.

"What?? Mr. Redmond is my Spanish teacher, not the man from the cabin." Thea's voice rose with anxiety. Officer Searle put down his pencil. "Hold on. You have a teacher by the name of Redmond as well?"

Thea explained that Ted Redmond was her substitute Spanish teacher, he'd started at her school just a couple of weeks after she started in her new school and he was by far her favorite teacher. "Everyone's favorite teacher, actually," Thea said with a small smile. "And he *definitely* has *nothing* to do with that . . . man." Thea shuddered.

But now Thea knew she'd been wrong. Ted did have something to do with the man; they were brothers, or at least half brothers. The police found that out pretty quickly—that David had been paroled only twenty-four hours before he killed his father and went after Thea, and that his only surviving family was his mother, Diana, and his brother, Edward. And Thea, herself, as it was. Thea found out from Officer Searle that Mr. Redmond disappeared . . . or left, would be the less suspicious way to put it.

"There is a distinct possibility that they were working together, Thea," Officer Searle told her at a follow-up meeting a couple of weeks after she'd been released from the hospital. "But we don't have the smoking gun we need to put out a warrant for arrest. We can't figure out how Edward and David were communicating. The last time Edward visited David was months before his parole and there are no calls between the two of them. Something isn't adding up. Is there anything you can tell us about your interactions with your Spanish teacher . . . anything that felt . . . off about him?"

"No, he was just a normal teacher," Thea said. There was no way she was going to admit to her massive crush on her dead brother's brother. And then hastily added, "He did tell me I could call him by his first name. But that's because we were friends."

Her mom and Officer Searle shared a glance. "A twenty-four-year-old man isn't friends with a twelve-year-old girl," Thea's mom said sharply. "Those sick bastards."

"Mom," Thea said now, bunching her backpack into her middle as they came to a stop in front of her school. "He left. He's gone, ok? And what are we going to do? Sue him for saying I can call him by his first name?"

"He was basically stalking you, Thee. Do you really think he just happened to take a job at your school? And even beyond that, even if he didn't grow up with the man who tried to kill us, from what you've told me, his behavior with you was totally inappropriate. You're twelve and he's—"

"First of all, I'm twelve and a half. And second of all, can you please stop being a therapist for one second?" She looked at her mom pointedly but smiled when she saw her mom's grimace.

Her mom sighed. Her eyes slid to the top of the windshield and rested on the flag being slapped back and forth in the wind. "Ok. I love you, Thea. We'll talk about this more later."

Thea sighed, too, a big, dramatic sigh that filled the car. She wrenched open the passenger door. "Ok."

As she trod up the stone walkway to the front door of her middle school, she stopped suddenly and ran back to where her mother had been idling a few seconds before, but the car was gone. She looked frantically around the parking lot, eyes stinging with tears, though she didn't know why she was almost crying and she rubbed her eyes roughly, embarrassed. She turned around again and started walking.

"Thea?" She heard her mom's voice over the wind, thin but there.

Thea turned. Her face broke into a smile that quickly shrank as a group of eighth graders pushed past her.

Her mom jogged toward her. "Hi, honey, I saw you in my rearview mirror and pulled over. What's up?"

She looked around, embarrassed for a different reason now—her mom was smack in the middle of everyone swarming into school. So she said in a low voice, "I just wanted to say that maybe we can watch *Pride and Prejudice* tonight after dinner."

"That sounds great, Thee. See you tonight. I love you." As Thea trailed the other kids to school, she heard her mom yell, "Have a great day!" She cringed, but a small smile stayed on her face as she slipped into the closing doors.

That afternoon, Thea slid into her desk in Spanish class, ignoring the whispers coming from the other kids. In her previous three classes, she'd had Livi twice and then Gretchen to insulate her from the murmurings, but this time, she was alone. She stared straight ahead at the chalkboard and the cursive that spelled out the new substitute's name: Señora Perez. She suddenly felt like crying again and focused hard on her textbook.

"Hey, Thea." Rachel's strong voice carried across the room and Thea's head whipped up, color already rising into her cheeks. "I'm really sorry about . . . what you went through. The incident or whatnot." Rachel's voice stumbled for a moment. "Seriously, that's so awful."

"Oh, yeah, thank you." Thea gave a small nod.

"You're really brave," Ronan added from beside her, and the rest of the class buzzed in agreement.

Thea breathed out, "Not really," but smiled slightly and lifted her eyes from her desk. While they waited for the teacher to arrive, Thea reached into the hollow opening of her desk, feeling around for the book that she'd left there. Her hand folded around the spine and she pulled it out and flipped to the dog-eared page near the end. She looked down at her desk. A thick square of folded papers had fallen from the book. She looked to her left and right cautiously before picking up the pages. She stuffed them in her jeans' back pocket before picking her book back up with trembling fingers.

A few minutes into class, she raised her hand. *"El baño, por favor?"*

In the bathroom stall, she closed the toilet lid and pulled the pages out of her back pocket before sitting down. She took a deep breath, stilled her hands, and started reading.

Dear Thea,

I hope you get this. I put it in a spot that I thought you'd be sure to look. I wish I could have stayed to explain in person, but . . . well, I didn't think that would be a good idea, for various reasons. I'm not sure how to start this so I just will. I grew up with an older brother named David. From an early age, I knew there was something very wrong with him, but I tried to convince myself that maybe that was just how older brothers acted: mean, violent, scary. He started hitting me when I was just a toddler, probably before that, though I don't remember. At one point, when I was nine and we went to a pool party, he almost killed me when he held me underwater and wrapped the pool thermometer around my neck. Luckily, an adult saw and dove in—everyone thought I'd just gotten tangled up and I was too frightened to come out against him. Now I know words like narcissist *and* psychopath, *but as a kid, I only knew that I was terrified of my brother. I noticed that my mother took special care of David and always seemed to either come to his defense or turn a blind eye to his behavior. My feelings about my mom are complicated, but I believe she tried her best. And then there was my dad . . . who just checked out completely—I think David was too much for him and so he turned to work and drinking. I'm not writing this for you to pity me, seriously, I want to explain that from a young age, I suspected there was something wrong with my brother, but I didn't know how wrong until David did what he did when he was sixteen.*

I heard him leave the house that night. It was the middle of the night. I felt in my bones that he was up to something bad, but I didn't stop him. I just wanted him to leave. I wanted him gone. I was fourteen at the time and not perfect myself, and I'll admit that I didn't care where he was going or what he was going to do as long as he stayed away. I could have woken up my parents. Or called the police. I could have done something and I didn't.

The next day, when we started to find out details of what David had done . . . well, I won't go into it but I remember throwing up in the kitchen sink.

A few months ago, I went to visit my brother in jail, for the first time since he was arrested. I just . . . I needed to know if he'd changed, if maybe being in prison had reformed him or simply growing up had made him better. But, of course, it hadn't. He was exactly as I remembered him—dark, manic, scary. And he went on and on about a young girl, his sister, he claimed. At first, I thought he was just delusional—this was the first I'd heard of Ethan Mills—but the more he talked, the more I thought he might be speaking about real things—the newspaper clipping, his biological father, and you, his sister, the only person who would ever understand him, his "light in the dark," as he said. He never said so explicitly, he's too smart for that, but I left that visit knowing that he was going to try to find you. And I knew that it was very possible he would be paroled at his next hearing, since he'd been sentenced to ten years with the possibility of parole and had already served close to nine.

I failed that first girl, Thea, and I made up my mind to try to protect you, whatever I had to do. I found you pretty easily thanks to social media and the internet. I knew that he had taken the first girl from her school and so I decided to try to get a job near your school and couldn't believe my luck when your school was hiring for a sixth-grade Spanish substitute teacher. Did you know that all you need is a bachelor's degree to get hired as a sub?

If you're wondering why I didn't tell the police, well, I did. I made a call the same afternoon of my prison visit and was told that the information would be "put in his file." But I knew that if David got out on parole, he would go straight for you and I thought the only way I could stop him was to try to physically be there.

I'm sorry, Thea, for everything. I didn't save you; you saved yourself. Not everything I told you was a lie—I did study in Colombia and I'm headed back there now as my partner lives in Bogotá. You're a bright, wonderful person and I hope you can, if not forgive me, then understand why I did what I did.

Your Friend,
Ted Redmond

Thea sat on the toilet for a few more minutes, thinking, then she carefully refolded the letter, put it in her back pocket, and walked back to Spanish class.

ROSE

Rose sat and waited anxiously for the couple to arrive. She drummed her fingers along the kitchen countertop. She'd gotten good at waiting anxiously. This type of waiting, though, was different from all the waiting she'd done in the past—first waiting to kill Ethan and then waiting to kill the man. Unsure if she was doing the right thing, unsure how it would turn out. She wasn't waiting to kill anyone this time. That in itself relieved some of the pressure. But then again, Rose postulated, when do you ever know how something will turn out? She certainly hadn't counted on Sam dying and being a workaholic widow at the age of sixty-four. She got up from the island stool she sat upon and stretched. She looked at the oven clock. The couple's arrival was due to an e-mail she'd sent six months ago, followed by more e-mails, phone calls, and finally plane ticket confirmations forwarded with the subject line "See you soon."

It had been six months since they escaped. Every week, Anne and Thea made the short drive from Burlington to Charlotte and the three of them met at a coffee shop. Thea always ordered a chocolate frappé,

Anne a latte, and Rose black coffee. They sat and talked, not always about Ethan and David, but when the men did come up, usually brought up by her granddaughter, Rose and Anne tried not to shrink away from the subject.

"I remember a voice from when I was a baby," Thea had said last week, pausing over her milkshake. "I thought I'd made it up. I used to play pretend when I was little, and there was always a scary man in my games. I can't remember what he looked like or what he said but I remember being scared of him."

Rose glanced at her daughter. Anne set down her cup. "I think those memories are from your overnights with your dad. You only had a few before he died."

"Yeah," Thea said. She took a gulp of milkshake. "I know it's weird, but sometimes I feel kind of bad for my brother."

"That's not weird, Thee," Anne responded. "I think David did try . . . but he couldn't help the way he was. Ultimately."

"Yeah," Thea said again, and Rose couldn't quite discern her granddaughter's expression as she went back to her straw.

"Mom," Anne said slowly. "Have you thought any more about Burlington?"

"Yeah, Mimi! Are you going to come live with us?" Thea grinned over the top of her milkshake.

Rose chuckled. "I have been thinking about it, you two. And I appreciate the offer, but you know I have my life in Charlotte and I can take care of myself."

"I know you have a life, Mom, and obviously you can take care of yourself . . . and then some." Anne smiled. "Just . . . think about it some more. Oh." Anne's face changed. "Oh, I have to take this call. Sorry, guys!"

"Is that—" Rose raised her eyesbrows and smiled encouragingly.

"Yes! Yes, it is. I'll be right back!" Anne jumped up from the table and Rose heard, "Hello? Lana! Hi, oh my god, it's been so long—" as Anne walked outside to the street.

"Please think about it, Mimi!" Thea stared at Mimi. "We'd have so much fun."

"I will," Rose had promised her granddaughter. And that's what she was doing now, when suddenly the air outside the house changed. There was a crunching sound of tires over gravel followed by the slamming of car doors. Everyone, Rose, her daughter, and her granddaughter, perked their heads up; Thea from the book she was reading on the couch and Anne from her laptop at the dining room table. Anne and Rose made eye contact and a silent message passed between them: *There's no turning back now.* Scraping sounds came from just outside the front door, suitcase wheels being dragged up Rose's front steps, and then the doorbell sounded.

"Guys, they're here," Thea said, her tone somewhere between excitement and distress.

They all moved toward the door. Rose got there first and opened the door; Anne and Thea hovered behind her, forming a trifecta.

"Oh!" The one syllable escaped Rose's mouth before she could reel it back in. She had meant to open with "Hello!" or "Welcome!" but the resemblance was so striking that she brought her hand to her mouth. "Oh my goodness," she said again. She hadn't seen it at their wedding, Anne and Ethan's, for obvious reasons, but she saw it now, the uncanny similarities between Tom's face and Thea's. His light blue eyes, almost gray; the perfectly rectangular forehead; the small, neat teeth and the way when he smiled, one side of his mouth lifted higher than the other.

"Well, hello!" Tom opened his arms and widened the stance of his feet, as if to stabilize himself.

"Tom! Tom, get out of the way, let me get to my granddaughter." Lynette shook her head and feigned annoyance, but already she was crying and laughing as she plowed past Tom into the house. "Rose! Anne!" She gave them both a firm hug as she made her way to Thea. Lynette enveloped Thea in a hug. Rose, a few hours ago, had worried that this initial visit would be fraught with tension and the awkwardness of something so big looming in between them, but now she felt only relief and release; she found that she also had tears running down her face. Lynette and Thea pulled away from their silent embrace and looked at each other, wiping tears out of their eyes and giggling. Anne ushered Tom into the entryway, insisting that he leave the suitcases on the porch for her and Rose to collect later.

After Rose took Lynette and Tom through the house, showing them the upstairs and where they would sleep, they all settled around the kitchen table. Lynette placed herself next to Thea and reached out every few minutes to squeeze her arm. Thea looked from Lynette to Tom as if they would disappear if she took her eyes off them. Rose brought a pot of coffee to the table and poured four cups and they passed around the cream. There was stirring and clinking. The silence was comfortable but anticipatory. Tom put his mug down and cleared his throat. "We're so sorry, Anne. We've been talking around this for years, Lynette and me. We didn't know about . . . about Ethan," his voice dipped on his son's name. Anne looked quickly at Thea, opened her mouth, "Thea, I don't think . . ." She closed her mouth, took a breath in through her nose before saying, "Thea, I think you're old enough to stay and have this conversation with us."

Tom continued, "He had problems as a child. And a teenager. I won't sit here and tell you he was an angel. He was expelled from high school twice. We should have gotten him help, but that wasn't something you did where we lived. A counselor, therapy . . . That might sound silly to you," Tom looked at Anne, "being a therapist and all. Quite frankly we were glad when he moved to New York." He put both hands around his coffee mug. "But—"

"We were just so happy when we met you," Lynette broke in. "We had no idea what to expect, but when we met you . . . We were just so happy," she repeated. "We thought about saying something. At the wedding. Not a warning . . . but trying to gauge what you knew about the difficulties he had as a boy, but—" Rose watched Lynette's cheeks fill with color and felt the blood rising to her own face as well.

"You wanted to believe the worst had passed and the best was yet to come," Rose said. It was not a question. "And you were protecting yourselves from an uncomfortable truth. I can understand that," Rose finished quietly.

"When Ethan died, we called and e-mailed and when we got no response . . . ," Lynette's voice trembled and Rose looked sharply to Anne. "We thought it was best for everyone if we just stayed out of your lives." Lynette's voice caught and she stopped speaking.

Anne sat still for a moment. "I was wrong to blame you. At that point in time, all I knew was that I couldn't trust anybody. I could barely even trust myself. I thought Thea would be safest if I shut you out, everyone out, really."

"We can certainly understand that, Anne. We could have pushed back, too, but we didn't because we wanted to respect your wishes. Or that's what we said to ourselves. But, truthfully, we didn't because we couldn't confront the truth about our son." Tom let out a breath. "So, where do we go from here?"

The air filled with a heavy silence. Rose thought of Diana. From what Anne had told her, Diana and her husband had each chosen to live in an alternate reality to cope with their son's issues. She pitied the woman; Rose knew that confronting certain realities could feel nearly impossible—hadn't they all, in one form or another, tried to erase Ethan from the past?

She cleared her throat, breaking the silence. "Would you like to see my garden?"

Lynette's face broke into a smile. "I would love that, Rose." She turned to Thea. "Want to come?"

The three of them walked out through the rear door into the backyard. Rose closed the door behind them and saw Anne throw her head back and laugh at something Tom had said.

"Oh, wow, WOW, this is beautiful," Lynette's *wow*s were drawn out and laced with a Midwestern accent. "And that smell. Cilantro! My favorite."

Thea froze beside Rose.

"Thea." Rose took in her granddaughter's stricken face. "What's wrong? What happened?"

"I've always loved the smell of cilantro." Her voice came out in an awestruck whisper. "Ever since I was a baby. My mom even told me that I used to eat it in handfuls."

Rose watched Lynette put her arm around Thea. She watched her granddaughter's mouth curve up in a shy smile as Thea's grandmother said, "We have a lot of catching up to do."

ACKNOWLEDGMENTS

Thank you, first, to my parents, Lisa and Charles Waite; my sister, Lynsey Waite; and my grandparents Barbara and Chuck Waite, as well as the rest of my family. The reason the above members get their names spelled out is because I forced them to read the manuscript in its early stages (if you want unbiased feedback, make sure to ask your parents, sister, and grandparents to read your first draft . . . just kidding).

Next, I'd like to thank my brilliant literary agent, Myrsini Stephanides, who read the next draft and told me to change everything, and my amazing editor, Maya Ziv, who read a further draft and told me to change it all again. All jokes aside, these two women helped to make this novel richer, deeper, and better, and I am immensely grateful to them both.

Other astute readers and feedback-givers I'd like to thank: Suzanne Kingsbury and the women of the Ghost Ranch retreat, Ashley Curless, Kayla Stewart, Grace Gray, Joey Unnold, Evynne Morin, Annie Unnold, Sara Searle, Kristin Patti, Whitney Rockwell, and Angela Krakowska.

ACKNOWLEDGMENTS

From the depths of my being, I must thank the women and men who shared with me their personal stories of having a baby in the NICU and/or a child with epilepsy: Marianne and Steve Hauck, Susan Wexler, Erin Crothers, Randi Weiss, and Pamela Mohr. And to Katie Hauck—you are a fierce goddess and I can't thank you enough. Any and all errors pertaining to Thea's epilepsy and NICU details are mine alone.

To Sarah Ketchum, who introduced me to Anand Rughani, and to Anand Rughani, a neurosurgeon at Maine Medical Center, who, as a complete and total favor to a near stranger, read my medical scenes and gave me critical feedback and adjustments. Again, any and all errors in these sections are mine alone.

Thank you to Kayla Stewart, my neighbor and friend who is also an ER nurse, for providing general medical advice and answering my frantic texts about how long Thea could be conceivably knocked unconscious without incurring brain damage.

To Bill Keith for spending three hours with me at the Windham Indoor Shooting Range (word to the wise: don't wear overalls to your first shooting lesson because the casings WILL fly down the front and sear your stomach and thighs before they drop out the hole at your knee) and reading my shooting/gun scenes. Your instruction was invaluable.

Finally, to my daughter, Vivienne Waite, who is four years old at the time of writing these acknowledgments and just told me I'm making too much noise with my typing (another word to the wise: don't try to make a deadline on a day that daycare is closed). I love you, Vivi; everything is for you (no matter how annoying I am, and I'm sure we're just getting started on that front).

ABOUT THE AUTHOR

JEN WAITE lives on the coast of Maine with her young daughter, Vivienne. She is currently working on her third book, a novel.